Money
Can Be
Murder

Connie Shelton

Books by Connie Shelton

THE CHARLIE PARKER MYSTERY SERIES

Deadly Gamble
Vacations Can Be Murder
Partnerships Can Be Murder
Small Towns Can Be Murder
Memories Can Be Murder
Honeymoons Can Be Murder
Reunions Can Be Murder
Competition Can Be Murder
Balloons Can Be Murder
Obsessions Can Be Murder

Gossip Can Be Murder
Stardom Can Be Murder
Phantoms Can Be Murder
Buried Secrets Can Be Murder
Legends Can Be Murder
Weddings Can Be Murder
Alibis Can Be Murder
Escapes Can Be Murder
Sweethearts Can Be Murder
Money Can Be Murder

Holidays Can Be Murder - a Christmas novella

THE SAMANTHA SWEET SERIES

Sweet Masterpiece
Sweet's Sweets
Sweet Holidays
Sweet Hearts
Bitter Sweet
Sweets Galore
Sweets, Begorra

Sweet Payback
Sweet Somethings
Sweets Forgotten
Spooky Sweet
Sticky Sweet
Sweet Magic
Deadly Sweet Dreams

The Ghost of Christmas Sweet
Spellbound Sweets - a Halloween novella
The Woodcarver's Secret

THE HEIST LADIES SERIES

Diamonds Aren't Forever
The Trophy Wife Exchange
Movie Mogul Mama
Show Me the Money

CHILDREN'S BOOKS

Daisy and Maisie and the Great Lizard Hunt
Daisy and Maisie and the Lost Kitten

Money
Can Be
Murder

Charlie Parker Mysteries, Book 20

Connie Shelton

Secret Staircase Books

Money Can Be Murder
Published by Secret Staircase Books, an imprint of
Columbine Publishing Group, LLC
PO Box 416, Angel Fire, NM 87710

Book layout and design by Secret Staircase Books
Cover images © Thomas Bullock, Martin Bergsma, Eti Swinford,
Ayutaka
First trade paperback edition: March, 2022

First e-book edition: March, 2022
* * *
Publisher's Cataloging-in-Publication Data
Shelton, Connie
Money Can Be Murder / by Connie Shelton.
p. cm.
ISBN 978-1649140784 (paperback)
ISBN 978-1649140791 (e-book)

1. Charlie Parker (Fictitious character)—Fiction. 2. New
Mexico—Fiction. 3. Embezzlement—Fiction. 4. Con artists—
Fiction. 5. Women sleuths—Fiction. I. Title

Charlie Parker Mystery Series : Book 20.
Shelton, Connie, Charlie Parker mysteries.

BISAC : FICTION / Mystery & Detective.
813/.54

Dedicated to Shirley Shaw, my longtime editor who helped me to improve my writing in so many ways and who left me with so many fond memories. We miss you, dear one.

Acknowledgements
Dan and Stephanie—each of you contributes and makes my writing life so much easier and so complete. I love you. I also owe a huge debt of gratitude to my beta readers who catch the many little things that my eye misses: Marcia, Sandra, Paula, Isobel, and Susan—you are the best! Deepest gratitude to all.

Chapter 1

Sometimes when things change, they change rapidly. My brother's family is, right now, a case in point. Ron's three boys have been rocking along on pretty much the same path since they were little. Yes, there was the acrimonious divorce and bouncing the kids back and forth between Ron and his ex, but ever since he married Victoria life has settled for them and everyone seemed to be on track. Then Jason, the middle kid, hit his teens and suddenly went off the rails.

All of this is a roundabout way of explaining why I'm serving coffee and blueberry muffins to my gram, Elsa, her caregiver Dottie, and Victoria at my kitchen table on a Monday morning and why the subject of the conversation is teenage boys.

"Ron's completely at a loss," Victoria said, carrying the basket of muffins to the table, "and Bernadette has basically shrugged her shoulders. Says she did the biggest share of the work when the kids were little, now Ron can just deal with it."

"Catch me up." Elsa took a muffin and reached for the butter dish. "I thought Jason was the quiet one, the kid who never gave any grief."

"He was. Now he's smarting off to his teachers, pulling pranks in class. His grades have taken a dive and he's hanging out with a group of boys we don't like the looks of. I think this goes beyond a few childish shenanigans. One of his closest friends just dropped out and I can see the gleam in Jason's eye."

"Ooh, that's not good. Too much time on his hands and no skills to get out in the working world. Have you tried counseling?" I asked, eyeing the coffee mugs to see if anyone needed a refill.

Victoria sighed. "It's not getting through to him."

"Send him to the Army," Dottie said. "It sure straightened up my nephew. That boy was eyeing them drug dealers that hang out downtown."

Vic clicked her tongue and pointed toward Dottie. "Smart woman. That's exactly Ron's thought. Of course, Jason can't enlist at fifteen, but we've got his application in at NMMI, the top military boarding school in the state."

I remembered back twenty years. "Ron's military service really helped him get his bearings. He matured a lot during those years."

"And I remember a kid from one of our church families," Elsa added. "This one was a handful—the same kind of stuff you're talking about. Three years at NMMI and he came home saying 'yes, ma'am' and 'no, sir' and standing up straight and minding his manners. That's a good school."

"It's not cheap," Victoria said. "We'll have to pinch some pennies, especially with the oldest heading off to college next year, but we can swing it. I'll look around for some bargain items to furnish his dorm room, basic bedding and a decent suitcase. They don't allow kids to have a lot of extras there."

"You can come down to the thrift shop," Elsa suggested. "Dottie and I are volunteering there a couple days a week. This afternoon, in fact. They've got all kinds of stuff like that, and some of it's in great shape."

A text message came from Ron before the ladies had finished off the rest of the muffins. He's in! Since Jason would be starting the term slightly behind the rest of the class, it would involve some scrambling to get everything ready. Ron and Victoria had one week to break the news to the kid, pack his things, and make the transfer between schools. And that's what sent us to the thrift shop that same afternoon.

Vic drove us in her vivid blue PT Cruiser, swearing that the little car had plenty of storage space for our purchases. "If I had all the room in your Jeep to fill, I would. This'll keep my shopping in check."

We headed up Lomas, east to San Mateo. It's one of those major arterial streets that was once residential (Albuquerque never was one of those cities that planned these things in advance), so a number of the older houses had their front yards stripped away as the street widened and those small buildings became businesses. I'd never been to Heavenly Treasures before, but I knew the general area so I watched the addresses.

The building was a flat-roofed bungalow, stuccoed adobe brown, with bright blue shutters added as attention grabbers. The sign above the front door depicted a treasure chest overflowing with jewelry and gold coins and other things probably nowhere to be found in a church-sponsored thrift shop. But it was eye-catching and had apparently attracted a good number of customers. The parking lot was jammed. A driveway ran beside the building and a brightly lettered sign said "Bring Donations to the Back" and featured an arrow showing the way.

Victoria waited while an elderly pickup truck backed out and she whipped the Cruiser into the vacant space.

We walked into what was probably the original living room of the home. A wooden counter with a cash register stood across from the front door and I spotted Elsa there, making change for a customer who seemed to be stocking up on pots and pans.

A glance around the space told me that several of the original interior walls had been taken out to create room for shelves, bookcases, and clothes racks. The walls were all painted bright white, showing off the merchandise in vivid contrast. We bypassed four racks of clothing on hangers, sorted by men's, women's, and children's. Bins of baby clothes were surrounded by highchairs, playpens, and infant car seats. Two women were browsing them and discussing the merits of one of the highchairs in Spanish. I saw Dottie nearby, carrying a high stack of throw pillows.

"Hey, you made it," she said, walking toward a table that was already overflowing. "Miss Elsa still working at the register?"

"She is."

"Good. I tell them don't let her be moving furniture or nothin' like that. But sometimes the manager get busy and he don't watch what she's up to."

I had to laugh. Even with a heart condition, Elsa doesn't seem to think anything of rearranging things in her house or hoeing the garden. Thank goodness Dottie was there to keep an eye on things.

"You need some sheets and blankets and stuff, right?" she asked.

At Victoria's nod, she tilted her head toward a side room to our right. "If you need a nightstand or little furniture like that, it's all in the annex out back. They got tons of stuff."

While Dottie started arranging the pillows to fit among the rest of the collection, we worked our way through the space toward the second room. As she'd told us, there were piles of bedding on tables and shelves, some of the items still in brand-new packaging. Victoria began searching out the sizes that would work for Jason. She wanted to keep browsing, so I took an armload from her and headed toward the sales counter where I could see Elsa chatting with a dark-haired woman who seemed a little puzzled.

I found a space to drop off the sheets and pillowcases, indicating to Elsa that Victoria was still shopping, and I stepped aside to browse the bookcases. It appeared the thrift shop was *the* place to shop for hardcover fiction, providing you didn't mind reading the hottest authors a few years after the buzz had died down. I perused two James Pattersons and a Michael Crichton I hadn't seen before. I was reading the flap copy on an old Patricia Highsmith novel when I became aware of urgent whispers near Elsa.

Her Hispanic customer had left.

"Missing, I tell you," she said, none too quietly, to a man behind the desk. He was probably in his early forties, soft around the middle, with a border of brown hair surrounding a shiny bald head. He wore a checked shirt and khaki slacks, and his gold-rimmed glasses had slipped down his nose.

"Mrs. Higgins, calm down." He kept his voice low and patted her arm.

"Mr. Stevens, I'm just reporting it now so there's no question later that I might have made a mistake in giving change. Just after noon a woman bought about eighty dollars' worth of merchandise and paid with a hundred-dollar bill. I gave her nineteen dollars and forty-some cents in change. The hundred dollar bill is nowhere in the till. I placed it under the coin tray and it's gone now."

I stepped over and gave the man a firm look. "What's the matter?"

He shook his head and put on an indulgent smile. "How may I help you? Are these linens yours?"

Elsa spoke up again. "This is my granddaughter, Charlie. Charlie, this is Benny Stevens, the manager here at Heavenly Treasures."

We each gave the other a polite tilt of the head. "Sounded like there was some disagreement over money?" I said.

Stevens clearly wanted the subject to vanish, but Gram spoke up again and explained what I'd already overheard. "There's money missing, and I don't want to be blamed."

"Perfectly understandable." I turned toward Stevens, staring pointedly enough that he knew he should respond.

Just as he was opening his mouth, another woman

walked up and stepped behind the desk.

"Our bookkeeper, Carole Myerson," Stevens said. The bookkeeper was a soft, pink older lady, probably in her mid-seventies. Certainly younger than Elsa. She wore a coordinated outfit of burgundy slacks and a striped sweater and she flashed me a winning smile. Reading glasses hung by a beaded chain around her neck.

"Now, what's the problem?" she asked, looking toward the other two.

"A hundred dollar bill is missing," Elsa stated, folding her arms across her chest.

"The one under the coin tray?" Carole asked. "It's not missing, dear. I cleared the drawer of larger bills this morning so I could do the bank deposit. In fact, I've brought quarters, dimes, and nickels so you'd have more change. See?" She held out a hand with four paper rolls of coins.

Elsa seemed only partially mollified but she stepped back in good grace and let Carole put the coin rolls into the drawer.

"There now, everything's all right," said Benny Stevens, looking relieved.

He and Carole gave big smiles to Elsa and stepped away from the desk. I watched them walk toward a door near the back marked Office. Victoria walked up just then, holding out a blanket and bedspread.

"There! I think this covers my responsibility toward the dorm room," she said, pulling out her wallet. "Elsa, does the shop accept credit cards?"

"We do. Charlie, there's more to the story about the—" She halted when a man with a framed picture in his hands walked up. "—you know."

While they transacted business, I grabbed two of the hardcover books that had interested me. It was the least I could do to support the shop, right?

Victoria gathered her purchases and the man in line behind her slapped a ten dollar bill on the counter for his picture and walked away in a bit of a hurry.

I glanced around and didn't see any other customers nearby. "So, what's the rest of the story, Gram?"

"Carole, the bookkeeper, she said she cleared the drawer this morning. Well, the large bill I took in came from a sale right after noon. Someone did take it. And ..."

Benny Stevens had emerged from the office and was heading our way again.

"There's a lot more. *Tell you later,*" Elsa whispered.

"Do you need us to hang around a while?" I asked, picking up half of Victoria's bags.

"No, no. That's fine. We'll talk at home. Dottie and I get off at four."

Victoria stopped on the way at a dollar store, saying she could at least send Jason off to school with a few goodies from the snack foods aisle. I opted to sit in the car.

Puzzling. If Elsa noted and reported stolen money from the till at the charity shop, it seemed the manager would be the first to show concern. Why hadn't he?

Chapter 2

By the time Victoria dropped me off at home, I was fairly antsy to get outside and stretch my muscles. So I clipped the leash on Freckles' collar and we headed toward our little neighborhood park. I tossed a tennis ball for her a dozen times—and yes, the irony is not lost on me that she's the one stretching, while I'm the one standing around. For good measure, I briskly circled the park—which is only a couple of acres in size—twice before we headed home.

Dottie's car was pulling into Elsa's driveway when I rounded the corner, so Freckles and I jogged a little to catch up before they went inside.

"So, it's more than a hundred dollars," Elsa said, by way of greeting. It's amazing to me how she can pick up a conversation hours later, without missing a beat in the story. I want to be her when I'm ninety-something.

"Shall we go in? You've been on your feet all day," I suggested.

Dottie, looking over Elsa's head, mouthed *thank you*, which told me she hadn't had much luck in getting her elderly charge to slow down and take a break.

We went into Gram's kitchen and Dottie put on the kettle and got three mugs from an upper cabinet. Once we were settled with tea and a package of Oreos for good measure, I encouraged her to go on.

"Well. I've noticed missing money before this. And I heard one of the other volunteers questioning whether she had mislaid some money last week."

Over time, it could amount to quite a lot, I imagined. "Who all has access to the drawer?"

"Well, Benny the manager and Carole the bookkeeper, for sure. They are the only full-time employees. Everyone else volunteers. Most of the time there are one or two volunteers behind the desk. We get busy, you know, and it helps to have two of us. A lot of the customers don't speak English."

"We think a lot of them are undocumented, from across the border," Dottie added.

"Yes, most likely. They're struggling to make ends meet, even if they do find work somewhere, so the thrift shops are like a big department store to them." Gram picked up an Oreo. "So, it's helpful if at least one person at the sales counter speaks a little Spanish."

Most New Mexicans who've lived here a long time tend to pick up a few words and phrases but are far from fluent in the language. Still, I supposed Elsa's knowledge was probably enough to get by selling simple items and taking payments.

"Victoria used a credit card—do many of your customers do that?"

"Oh, no. I'd say the business is ninety percent cash. When people don't have much money, they generally don't have bank accounts. And a lot of our sales are just a dollar or two."

I nodded, thinking of the two books I'd purchased for a total of less than five dollars.

"So, you're handling cash …"

"And that's probably the other reason Mr. Stevens wants two of us behind the counter. The shop is run by our church—the proceeds support mission work and kids living in poverty—and most of the volunteers come from our congregation. But still. Some of the younger ones have been in trouble with the law and they're doing community service work."

Dottie piped up again. "But Mr. Benny, he keep most of them working in the back, unloading furniture and stuff like that. He don't really give them much access to the money."

Elsa brightened. "You know, you're right. I hadn't thought about that. It's usually the more responsible folks who work at the register."

I had a dozen questions and no clear idea where to start. Dottie again had an answer.

"You know, Charlie. They always want more help. Why don't you come in with us next time and say you could work a few days?"

"You could help me keep an eye on people," Gram added. "Maybe we'd spot the thief."

My mind zipped over the list of my own duties. My accounting work for Ron's RJP Investigations was all caught up. Drake's helicopter business had been a little slow recently, so it wouldn't take me long to do his invoices. Plus, I wouldn't be committing to a regular job at the charity shop. I could help out while keeping my eyes and ears open, find out if there was anything to Elsa's suspicions.

"Okay. When do you go back?"

Somehow, we never really know when we're about to open a really, really large can of worms.

Chapter 3

The next morning I dressed in jeans, trainers, and a sturdy cotton shirt that could take some wear and tear. With no idea what my duties might be, I needed to be ready for anything from shelving books to heavy lifting in the furniture department. Elsa and Dottie were ready to go a few minutes before nine, and I offered to drive.

Benny Stevens wasn't in yet, and Carole seemed a little surprised to see me tagging along. She dithered for a moment before calling over another volunteer and asking him to assign me something to do. She introduced him as Eugene Towner, a guy about my age, thin and pale, and unwilling to produce a smile.

Elsa evidently knew the man. "Eugene, how are you today? How's your mother? Still doing the honey business?"

He shrugged. "Yeah, I guess it's going okay."

He turned his back and I assumed I was to follow along. I gave Gram's shoulder a squeeze and whispered that I'd catch up with her later, then turned to see that Eugene was already halfway to the back of the room. I followed him out a back door and discovered there was a second building at the rear of the property, a garage-like structure with two large doors standing open. A woman and two men were chatting, apparently deciding which tasks to tackle first.

"Got you another helper," Eugene said to one of the men before abruptly turning and walking away.

"Um, hi. I'm Charlie."

All three smiled, showing lots of white teeth. "Well, we're always glad to get another set of hands," the woman said. "I'm Nancy. This is Mike and Todd."

Of them, Todd was the only one under forty.

"Just point me toward whatever needs doing," I said.

"Great," said Mike. "I like her already." He pointed toward some furniture pieces that must have just arrived. Two sofas, three non-matching armchairs, and a half-dozen coffee tables and end tables had been shoved into a corner barely inside the door.

Nancy stepped over beside me. "We find that the furniture sells better if it's arranged a little bit, sort of like it would be in a home. As long as we have space, we try to do that. You can also go into the main sales room and look around. Pick up a few throw pillows or a flower arrangement or anything that makes it look kind of homey."

"Sure. That sounds like fun."

"The fabrics may be dusty, so there's a shop-vac over there and boxes of latex gloves for handling the grubby stuff. Try to clean up the items as best you can. If the upholstery has stains, we have a little shampooer we can use on those. If something's broken, within reason, we have a few handymen who can reattach a table leg and that sort of thing. Hopefully, most of the donors obeyed the signs." She waved vaguely over her shoulder, where I noticed a large hand-painted sign warning that no ripped, torn, or soiled furniture would be accepted. I took it by her comment that not everyone's idea of 'gently used' was the same.

Nancy handed me a can of furniture polish and a couple of cloths. "Have fun. Get Todd to help you move anything heavy."

"Okay, here's our first," Mike said, turning toward the open door. He began directing a pickup truck to back up to a doorway at the other end of the building labeled Donations Here.

I watched in amazement as three other people emerged from the building and began lifting boxes, trash bags, lamps, and various other stuff that I would have labeled as junk. In under five minutes the piled-high truck was empty and the driver pulled away. An SUV took its place. Where would they put all this stuff?

"Um, Charlie?" Nancy was giving me a pointed look.

"Right. Sorry." I sprayed my dust cloth with furniture polish and went to work on a pair of end tables.

As I looked around, finding pieces that would look appealing together, I found myself really getting into it. Todd lent a hand with an especially large sofa, but I found that I could scoot most of the pieces on the concrete floor fairly easily. Within an hour I had three little 'living rooms' arranged, and I set about vacuuming and dusting them, as instructed. Standing back, I decided to follow Nancy's advice about the decorative touches so I went inside to see what I could borrow.

Dottie was folding T-shirts at one of the display tables. "I swear, they gotta look at every single one before they pick," she said.

I laughed. "I need a lamp and a few colorful pillows. Where can I find those?"

She directed me. I sent a smile toward Elsa who was behind the counter, helping a customer who had two small kids and overloaded arms. In the household goods area, I caught myself staring at throw pillows as critically as if I were choosing them for my own living room.

"Oh, come *on*," I finally said, picking up the three nearest me. The whole idea was to make the furniture displays a little more appealing, not to win some design award.

With the pillows tucked under my left arm and a slender table lamp in my right hand, I made my way back out to the other building. Nancy and Mike were going through the newly arrived items the donors had dropped off.

"Put this in my stack," Nancy said, holding up a painting of a realistic beach scene in a driftwood frame.

Mike took the piece and set it against the wall. I noticed a big-screen TV next to it. I set the lamp on an end table, tucking the cord out of sight, and placed the pillows on sofas and chairs. I stepped back to study the little tableau I'd created. Nancy looked up from the box of Christmas ornaments she was going through.

"It doesn't have to be perfect," she said with a chuckle. "You've done a great job."

"Thanks. Hey, I wondered—am I supposed to put prices on these? And how on earth do you figure out what to charge?"

"There are guidelines, loosely based on the items and

their condition. Don't worry about it. Mariah Blinker has a good feel for it. She'll come around later and put the tags on." She carried a glass Santa and placed it beside the painting she'd had Mike set aside. I noticed the ornament's box said it was Waterford.

"You really get some nice things here," I said. "Surprising people just give them away."

She gave a little shrug. "Sometimes there are estates. Someone dies, a person who collected things. Their heirs don't know what to do with it all, so they just box it up."

Standing closer, I recognized the artist's name on the seascape. "This donation must have been one of those—I mean, these look like some valuable things."

"Could be. I just set aside the painting for myself because it will go really well in my sunroom."

"So, we can do that? Buy things ourselves, before the customers even see them?"

"Oh, sure. Listen, how many of the customers in this shop are seriously looking for artwork? You've seen them—they're buying baby clothes and paperback books."

True. I hadn't spotted anyone who would be in the market for a painting that would most likely be worth at least a thousand dollars.

I heard a vehicle door and saw Mike getting out of a gray pickup truck. He walked in through the open garage door, picked up the big-screen TV, and carried it to the backseat of the truck. He draped a blanket over the set and closed the door before backing the truck against the wall at the rear of the property. Well, maybe he'd already been inside and paid for it. I turned back to the furniture on the other side of the room and resumed my dusting and arranging.

A little later I had a decent little display of several

'rooms' full of furniture.

"You can take a lunch break anytime you like," Nancy said. "It's really informal around here."

She and Mike had continued to offload donations from people who brought them by carloads or boxes full. Todd popped in from time to time and carried items to the main building. And an older lady—Mariah Blinker, I assumed—had come out, wandering through the intake center, jotting prices on bright orange tags and sticking them with astounding speed on the merchandise. It looked like Nancy was right—Mariah really did have a feel for what everything was worth in thrift shop terms.

"I'll go check on my friends," I told Nancy. "Elsa might be due for a break about now."

I walked back into the main building, found a restroom, and washed the accumulated grime off my hands. I should have used the gloves. Elsa was still behind the sales desk (she'd found a stool to perch on, I noticed), and Dottie was dusting some cute little parfait glasses on a shelf that held a variety of kitchen wares. I posed the question about taking a lunch break.

"Dottie and I only work until two today," Elsa told me, "so we usually just work straight through and eat something once we're home."

"Can I bring you some crackers or anything? Or I could take a spell here so you can stretch your legs or rest a little."

She gave me her indulgent grandma-smile. "I'm fine. You can check with Dottie."

One look at industrious Dottie told me she wasn't exactly lagging in energy, so I headed back to the intake building to ask what I could do next.

"Let's set these new bags over there," Nancy said. "We

usually sort the clothing into piles of men's, women's, and kids. The volunteers inside will group them by sizes as they hang or fold them."

The first bag I opened contained dressy women's wear—sequined tops, gauzy dresses, some pretty classy shoes. I began laying them across a worktable to prevent them from becoming damaged. Nancy had a bag of baby clothes, which she quickly went through, tossing out anything stained or torn, dropping the rest onto a growing mound of pastel fabric.

I held up one pair of shoes and took a look at the label. "Wow, I'm no fashionista but even I know this brand. Can't believe someone would give them away."

Mariah had been sticking prices on the Christmas ornaments I'd noticed earlier. "Take them," she said. "They haven't been priced yet."

"You mean—"

"Sure. Everyone does it. We volunteer our time, but we can get a little something for our efforts here, right?"

I thought of the TV set going into Mike's truck and the painting and Waterford that Nancy had put in her stack, a stack that had vanished while I was inside the other building. Were they really stealing the donations? Of course, I had no proof. They might have set the items aside and then gone in to pay for them.

Mariah was looking at me. I sputtered a little and came out with, "Oh no, these aren't my size." I set the shoes down.

"My granddaughter wears a six," she said, eyeing them. But I didn't see her move to pick them up.

I brought up the subject with Elsa and Dottie as we drove home that afternoon. "Did one of the volunteers,

Mike, come up to the register and pay for a big-screen TV today?"

Elsa shook her head.

"Or Nancy—did she pay for a painting or any Christmas ornaments?"

Again, a negative.

"I think they simply took them. And there was a pair of designer shoes I noticed. A woman named Mariah told me I should just take them. This is a charity shop. It doesn't seem right."

"I've never worked in the intake area," Elsa said. "All I know is to look at the price sticker on the item, add them up, and put the money in the till."

Dottie piped up. "I was back there for a couple days. Didn't think about it, but now you mention it. One of the other volunteers that day did put some stuff in her car."

I turned on Central and headed westward toward home. "Mariah was encouraging me to take the shoes. They were expensive ones, hardly worn, and after I turned them down I didn't see them again."

"That's terrible," Dottie said.

"Mariah made the point that the volunteers don't get paid anything for all their hard work. She seemed to think an item here and there was fair compensation."

If the items were an occasional book or a wine glass, maybe. But I'd seen well over a thousand dollars' worth of merchandise walk out the door in one morning. Was the thrift shop a money-maker for the church or for the people working there? Nancy's point that the shop's regular patrons wouldn't buy that sort of thing anyway, didn't set well with me. If the shop was there to support charity, the donors expected the money to go there.

"Shouldn't we report this to the manager?" Dottie suggested.

"But what if Benny already knows?" Elsa said. "He's not one to make a fuss, I guess. He didn't seem very concerned when I told him about the missing hundred dollar bill yesterday."

"True," I said, as I steered into our neighborhood. "And even if the people out back are taking home some items, it still doesn't explain how cash money goes missing."

Dottie looked over at me. "Sound to me like you gotta new mystery to solve, Miss Charlie."

Chapter 4

I called Ron after dinner that night, asking whether anything at the office needed my attention right now. "I might continue to volunteer at Heavenly Treasures for a few more days."

Drake looked up from his logbook, where he was filling in the hours he'd flown on a photoshoot this afternoon. I sent a smile in his direction, but my mind was already back on the thrift shop. What were the next steps I could take to figure out what was going on there?

"By the way," Ron was saying, "Vic and I are having a little going away party for Jason tomorrow evening. Barbecue. Our house. You guys are all invited."

"Tell him we'll bring potato salad," Drake said, somehow divining what the next question would be. "We've got a bag of potatoes that needs to be used."

Um, okay. It's not one of my specialties. Anyone who knows me is aware that I don't do much real cooking. It's gotta come out of a package or be something that is stuck into the oven and roasted for a prescribed amount of time if you expect me to make it. Drake, on the other hand, is a master in the kitchen so I will leave the intricacies of boiling, chopping, blending, and seasoning to him.

The three of us arrived at Ron and Victoria's home a little before six. Dottie would have come along, but this was her regular bowling night. She and Elsa had taken a day off from their volunteer duties, trimming back the dead vegetation in the garden. But Gram was still up for a party. Seriously, I don't know where she gets all this energy.

Drake carried the massive bowl of his special potato salad and set it on the kitchen island. A glance toward the backyard told me it was a good thing he'd made so much. Six teenage boys were gathered near the grill, where Ron was brushing sauce on two racks of ribs that reminded me of something out of The Flintstones.

"And that's not all," Victoria said, catching my stare. "There's a platter of burgers already cooked and waiting in the oven, and three packs of hot dogs are coming along. You can't believe how much those boys can eat."

Drake chuckled, obviously remembering his own teen years. Elsa merely looked puzzled. She hadn't raised children and didn't have a clue about boys. I'd been fifteen when she took me in, but as I recall I was in one of those girly snits where I swore I was dieting all the time. If I had to bet, Elsa would put away half of a burger and a tablespoon of potato salad tonight and then declare that she was stuffed.

"Help yourselves to something to drink. There are coolers of every kind of soft drink out on the patio, and

I've set up jugs of iced tea and lemonade out there too."
Victoria turned to stir something on the stove.

"So, did the new bedding meet with approval?" I asked,
once the others had walked out to the back yard.

She gave a shrug. "I suppose. It's been a rough week,
and Jason isn't exactly approving of anything right now."

"Giving you guys some grief?"

"I get it—he doesn't want to leave his friends, and of
course they're filling his head with all kinds of *stuff* about
how rough it's going to be, or how parents don't have the
right to make these choices for him. So, there's a lot of
belligerence, lot of stomping around."

I looked out through the sliding doors to the yard.
Jason had shot up in height this past year, becoming one
of the tallest among his friends. I recognized one of the
other boys as a kid he'd been friends with forever. Yes, it
would be hard to leave those buddies behind. But Ron had
told me some tales about other, less savory types his son
was chumming around with and I had to believe they were
doing the right thing.

Victoria got out a pair of tongs and began lifting
ears of corn out of a huge kettle on the stove. "We'll get
through this evening okay. We invited the older friends and
of course his brothers are supportive. Well, Ron sort of
laid down the law—they'd *better* be supportive." She gave
a little laugh and handed me the heaping platter of corn
while she began filling another.

"Anyway, the car is packed and we'll be on the road in
the morning."

I set the platter aside for a moment and gave her a
hug. "You're doing the right thing. Kids that age think they
know how to run their lives, but I remember how I was.

Without Gram and a fairly firm hand at times, I could have gone off in so many wrong directions. She made me do things I didn't want to—like staying in school and facing my grief about my parents—and I turned out okay for all that."

"Well, mainly, we just didn't want to see Jason follow the example of his one friend who simply decided he was bored with school and wanted to drop out. He's being raised by a single mom and she didn't have the nerve to stop him, I guess. He's been out of school two years now and is doing nothing with his life. He did get his GED, but there's no move toward a trade school or college, no job, and from what I can tell he's either playing computer games all day or hanging out at home. There's no drive or motivation to become an adult."

"Failure to launch."

"Exactly. And Ron will be damned if he'll let his son take that path." She gave a long sigh. "Anyway, we'll see if our idea works any better."

"It's about all you can do."

We picked up the two platters of corn and headed out the back door. Ron was cutting the slabs of ribs apart and Drake was carrying them to the already-laden picnic table. It looked like enough food to feed the army, but when I saw how much each of the boys loaded onto his plate, I realized there wouldn't be a lot of leftovers.

The kids headed for the far corner of the yard, settling cross-legged on the grass, while we old folks gathered around the table.

"So, I hear you've found a mystery for Charlie to work on," Victoria said to Elsa.

Gram's eyes brightened as she finished spreading mayo

on her burger bun and set the top in place. "We're going after a criminal mastermind!"

I had to smile. "Either that, or it's some greedy little soul with their fingers in the till."

Elsa went on in detail about the missing hundred dollar bill and her suspicions that it wasn't the first. "And Charlie witnessed some of the volunteers helping themselves to pretty valuable items."

"I don't actually know if that's illegal or not," I said. "Maybe there really is a policy in place that allows them to pick something in exchange for the time they give. I need to talk to the manager about that part of it."

Jason and one of his friends came back to the table for seconds—call me astounded—and I reminded Drake that we had a couple of little gifts out in the Jeep. Elsa had baked her world-class chocolate chip cookies, and I had found a backpack that I hoped would be cool enough for a fifteen-year-old. I'm discovering that the further past thirty I get, the less I can hang onto trends with kids.

"You do know that someone—the manager of the shop or maybe the church hierarchy—will have to press charges if you want to see your thief held accountable with the law," Ron told us, once the kids had moved on.

"True. I'll keep that in mind." I made a swiping motion at my chin, and he took a napkin to some barbecue sauce on his face.

Truthfully, I wasn't at all sure this whole investigation would actually go anywhere. But it couldn't hurt to check. At the very least, those who depended on the income from the charity shop should know about whatever we uncovered. The church leaders could then decide whether to press the matter or let it slide.

Chapter 5

We three ladies were on the schedule again for the following morning at Heavenly Treasures. Again, I volunteered to drive. Dottie shouldn't be using her own gas for this little adventure, and even though Elsa still had her old car, I had to admit I was a little nervous about her driving skills these days.

This time, instead of reporting to the back building, I decided to get Benny Stevens aside for a few minutes. Not that it wasn't interesting to sort through old junk and arrange furniture, but I really was here to look into the thefts. I went to the door marked Office and tapped. A mumbled voice came through, which I took as permission to enter.

The small room—no more than twelve feet square—had been divided down the middle by one of those fabric covered partitions so common in corporate cubicled offices. Carole Myerson sat in the one on the right, squinting at the screen on a really outdated desktop monitor. Her fingers pecked at the keyboard, but the gray-haired lady seemed to be struggling.

Benny Stevens' desk was on the left, and apparently he was the one who'd told me to enter. He stood and beckoned me toward a chair opposite his desk, sending me a friendly smile that held no hint of recognition, so I went back over Elsa's allegations from two days earlier. Benny shifted in his seat but didn't say anything.

I leaned forward. "If there's money missing, someone should look into it. At the very least you'll want to put systems in place to prevent it from happening again. I'm an accountant and also a partner in a private investigation firm so I'm pretty familiar with those things. Elsa has asked my help. She doesn't want to be suspected of doing anything wrong."

He fidgeted slightly. "I don't know quite how to ask this ... but how certain is Mrs. Higgins about this missing money? I ... well, she is quite far along in age ... maybe her memory is slipping and the money she's thinking about actually came in on a different day ..."

I could go into describing the precision-sharp memory of my elderly neighbor, but perhaps he'd actually handed me an opening. I simply nodded.

"So, maybe it would be a good idea for me, as an outsider, to conduct a review."

His eyes narrowed slightly.

"Strictly volunteer. My agency wouldn't charge you a dime. Personally, I'd like to know how well Elsa is doing in the, um, memory department. This would give me a chance to talk to others, see how things are done, maybe make some recommendations for you?"

"Well … that might work." There was still hesitation.

"All I would need to get started would be a list of the volunteers—everyone who has worked here in the past couple of weeks. Their contact details and a copy of the schedule would be very helpful too."

He turned to the computer on his own desk and clicked a couple of times. "I have a spreadsheet with the names and phone numbers. That's really all the personal information we ask. This—" he said, pointing to a chart on the wall, "—is the schedule. People tell me what days they're available and I pencil them in. Not sophisticated, but it works."

The chart was basically a calendar with big squares for the dates. "Could we photocopy this, and maybe last month as well?"

"Sure. Sure." He removed the pushpin and carried the calendar over to a copy machine jammed into the far corner of the room.

While it warmed up, I took a moment to stand and peer over the partition toward Carole Myerson. She quickly went back to her typing.

Nosy thing. I decided to get Benny somewhere else for my next set of questions. When he handed over the calendar pages and the single sheet printout of the names and numbers, I gave a nod toward the door.

"Could you get me started by showing me a few things out here?"

We walked out to the sales room, which was again bustling. Elsa and a young woman of about twenty stood behind the counter, and three customers were lined up to pay. Benny and I stepped aside to allow a young mother with a baby on her hip to pass by.

"Elsa told me there are normally two people working at the register. Is that always the case?" I kept my voice low.

"As you can see, it can get a little overwhelming for one person. Plus, some of our seniors ... well, they can become flustered."

"Makes sense. I assume it's also a measure toward keeping everyone honest." At his sputter, I held up a hand. "Not that anyone here is dishonest. I'm not saying that. But I've noticed that a big percentage of sales are done with cash. That's very unusual these days."

"I suppose it is. But it's what our clientele is accustomed to."

"What about at slower times, when there isn't a line waiting to pay? Is there ever only one person tending to the money?"

"Well, sure. People need a bathroom break, or sometimes a customer needs assistance with something elsewhere in the shop, getting an item from a high shelf, picking up a large item ..."

"So one of the cashiers might leave to assist ..."

"Yes, of course. We might operate a thrift shop, but it doesn't mean we can't be top notch in customer service."

I smiled at his corporate-sounding line.

"Are there certain volunteers who work at the register more frequently than others, or does everyone take a turn?"

His mouth twitched a little as he considered. "I'd say most of our volunteers tend to find their niche and stick with it. Elsa, for one is good at the register. She's old-school enough to know how to count out change, unlike so many younger people who need an electronic gadget to tell them what to do." He lowered his voice. "We've had two of the community-service kids who couldn't recognize and add up coins. American coins."

"Seriously?"

"I happened to be walking by when one of them was handed a plastic baggie full of miscellaneous coins to pay for a two-dollar item. The kid didn't know how many quarters, dimes, and nickels it would take. He asked the middle-aged person who was working with him to count it out."

Wow. I like to stay as tech savvy as the next person, but even I can see that society is taking a hit when kids don't know certain basic skills. Mental note—take some cash money over to Ron's house and work with his kids until they learn this stuff.

Stevens was continuing his previous thought. "Other workers like to be outside a bit more during their day, so they often gravitate to the back, the intake area where they can assist with unloading donations. Anyone who can lift furniture is especially needed out there."

"That brings up another question. I believe the volunteers aren't paid anything for their labors, but is it sort of an unwritten policy that they are allowed first choice of the donated items? That they can take an item here and there in exchange for their work?"

He gave a sigh and shifted a little from one foot to the other. "I know it happens. I'd be blind and deaf if I hadn't figured that out. But it's not sanctioned. People donate their items in the belief that the things will be sold and the money used toward our charitable work."

"They wouldn't be happy if word got out that some items, especially the more expensive things, were going home with someone who worked here."

"Precisely. Is there a reason you're asking?"

What was I supposed to say? Rat out those who'd been nice to me, the ones I'd worked alongside the other day? The ones I would need to talk to before this whole job was done? I looked Benny straight in the eye. "I'd suggest you keep someone you absolutely trust, a real play-by-the-rules type, working in the intake area. If it's happening, it's happening out there, before anyone else sees the juicy items and realizes something is missing."

He appeared to give it thoughtful consideration. "Good idea."

Maybe that suggestion alone would ingratiate me enough to get full cooperation.

Chapter 6

I held up my printout and excused myself, saying I ought to get on with the interviews. I had about thirty names on my list and had only met a half-dozen so far. I decided to start out back and work my way forward.

In the donation area, Nancy, Todd, and Mike were once again going through bags and boxes, carrying lamps and shelves and chairs to wherever they could find a bit of empty space to set them.

"Hi again," I said.

"Hey," Nancy responded. "Charlie, isn't it?"

"Yeah."

"If you want to clean up some more of the furniture today, the newer items are over there."

"Well, actually, Mr. Stevens has me on another task today. I'm updating the volunteer list, and he wants a list of who is working in which areas of the shop." I'd decided that coming right out with the 'money is missing' angle probably wasn't going to gain much cooperation.

"Why on earth would that matter?" She gave me a crosswise stare.

I shrugged. "You know, management." I stood where all three of them could see me, even though each was busy with a task. "So, do the three of you always work back here?"

"Sure. Usually," Mike replied. "Todd's back and forth between the two buildings a lot, right, Todd?"

"Yeah." The younger guy gave a little shrug. "When somebody buys a piece of furniture, I'm usually the one who helps 'em get it into their vehicle. Sometimes it's me and one or two other guys. You know, whatever's needed."

"Uh-huh. Can you give me those names? Just so I can jot them on my list."

He did, and I did.

"And Mariah … I don't see her around. You said she does most of the pricing?"

"True. And that's both inside and out here, so she's popping around all over the place," Mike said.

"Okay, good. Do any of you ever work at the sales counter inside?"

All three shook their heads. "Bor-ing," Todd said. "I gotta keep moving."

He did have a lot of restless energy, I noticed. Definitely the kind of person who couldn't sit still.

"Anyone else who regularly works out here with you?"

Nancy supplied two other names. Mike looked blank until she described them. "You know, the teenage girl with the pink hair and nose ring, and then there's the boy who always shows up in pressed trousers and a white shirt and freaks that he's going to get dirty."

"Yeah, yeah. Parole girl and mama's boy."

Nancy nudged him when he said it.

"Well—they're both short termers. She's working off her community service obligation and he … I don't know. I guess his parents want him to get out and experience volunteerism. I don't know."

I marked the names on my list. It didn't sound like either would have been assigned to work with the money.

"Thanks for the info." I stepped a little closer to the pair. "Listen, word in the office is that Mr. Stevens may be assigning someone to watch over the donation intakes a little more closely, make sure things really are making it to the showroom floor. In case I don't see Mariah inside, you might mention that to her."

Mike shuffled a little, and I wondered if a vision of that big-screen was going through his head. At any rate, I'd done what I could to help curtail the pilfering. Now, back to my main assignment, finding out about the missing cash.

Two vehicles had driven into the back lot and I hung around, listening in on the conversations between workers and customers. Todd lifted a fat, upholstered chair into the back of a pickup truck, while a pair of teens helped a pregnant young woman fit a crib and changing table into a car that seemed way too small to carry it all. Some twine helped hold the hatch closed, and she was soon on her way. After asking the teens their names and checking them off the list, I decided it was time to head inside.

I spotted Dottie and gravitated toward her familiar face. "I tell you, keepin' it lookin' neat in here is a full-time job," she said.

Today, she was dusting the books on the shelves. She supplied me with a couple of names, women who regularly worked at those same type of tasks.

"Do any of them alternate off and work the register?"

She shook her head. "Oh, there's one. Millie. I don't know her last name, but she's about Miss Elsa's age. She likes to organize the baby items, but she's at the sales desk a lot of the time."

I thanked Dottie and put a mark beside the only Millie on the list. I would need to talk with her at some point. I still had checkmarks by fewer than half the names. Benny Stevens had been less than informative when I asked specifically who handled the cash, but maybe I could put together a more comprehensive list by talking with Elsa and the bookkeeper, Carole.

Waiting for a lull in activity at the counter, I asked Elsa if she could use a break. Benny stood to one side, chatting with a man with short, sandy hair and wearing a clerical collar. He glanced at Elsa and gave a nod, so I assumed he would step in to help out if things got busy again.

"That was our minister," Elsa said as we approached the vending machines beside the back door. "He's the nicest young man."

"Does he ever volunteer here at the shop?"

"Oh, no. He's a busy man, what with hospital visitation, the youth ministry, and preparing two sermons a week. He and Benny are friends as well as having lots of deacon business, I'd imagine."

I fished into my jeans pocket for money and bought us a couple of sodas. We carried them to the outdoor picnic table where many of the workers took their lunch breaks. I showed her the list.

"Can you tell me which of these people work the sales counter?" I should have thought of starting with this, but it had seemed a good idea to eliminate those who definitely didn't.

Gram adjusted her glasses and studied the names. "Got a pen?"

I handed her mine and she made little dots beside three more names.

"Those are the ones I'm sure of, because I've worked with them more than once."

"Thanks. Now, here's the schedule Benny gave me. Can you tell me which days you are absolutely certain that money went missing?"

"Well, I'm only really sure of a couple. The day you and Victoria came in, when I told you about the hundred dollar bill."

I took the pen and made a tiny X on that date.

"And there was another time, about a week before that." She studied the dates and pointed to the previous Tuesday. "Had to be this one because, see, I was working that day."

"Good. This is a big help. I'll be able to sit down at home where it's a little quieter and go through all this, cross referencing everything."

We finished our sodas and I walked back inside with her. My next target was Carole Myerson, and I found the bookkeeper in her little cubby of an office. Benny's desk was empty and I wondered if he and the minister had gone out for lunch or something.

"Hi, Carole, got a minute?"

She looked up at me a little vaguely, the way I sometimes feel when I've had my mind deep into numbers and an actual person steps into the room and interrupts my train of thought.

"Um, of course. You're Charlie, right?"

I took the chair across the desk from her and posed some basic questions about how the flow of money was handled in the business.

"Pretty simple, really, compared to some of the corporate offices where I've worked." She settled back in her chair. "Sales come in all day. Usually in the late afternoon, I'll go and gather up the receipts—credit and debit charges and the cash—and bring everything in here to tally and write up a bank deposit. We don't issue any invoices so there's no accounts receivable. Once the deposit is ready to go, I'll either drop it at the night depository on my way home, or I'll put it in the safe—if you can call it that—here at the office and take it to the bank the next day."

"Does anyone else handle the cash, other than you?"

"Oh, yes. Well, the clerks out front. And then of course Benny sometimes does the deposit if I'm not working that day."

"So a deposit is done every day that the shop is open?"

"Not every single day. Sometimes we're not that busy and it hardly seems worth the effort. I'll hold it and combine the next day's receipts."

Something stuck in my head. "The safe ... what do you mean by 'if you can call it that'?"

She turned to the credenza behind her and bent to open a sliding door section. Behind it was a metal box with a combination dial on the front of it. I could see that it was one of those small devices designed to keep personal papers safe up to a certain temperature in case of fire. They were certainly not burglar proof. In fact, unless the thing were bolted through the cabinetry into the wall behind it, anyone who could lift twenty pounds could probably carry it out of here.

"I see what you mean. Looks like this is mainly to keep the money from being too easy to access and to protect it from fire."

Carole nodded. "You may have noticed that everything here is rather pieced together. There's no budget for office furniture or equipment, so the desks and our fabulous safe were things that came in as donations. The computers are ancient, but that's probably a moot point. I came up in the age of paper ledgers and handwritten entries, so generating monthly reports and P&Ls on this thing … well, it's a challenge. But I manage."

"You've worked here quite a long time?"

"Not really—about six months. I'm just repeating what I was told when I started. I guess I commented on the safe, to Benny, and that's the story I got."

"Okay. Back to the handling of the cash. Do you tally the day's receipts with a total from the cash register?"

She gave a sad nod. "Sometimes. That old thing is another freebie that came in as donated. It's on the fritz a lot, and some of the electronic functions really don't work well at all. Sometimes it just locks down and won't do a thing. Benny seems to have sort a magic touch with it, and he can usually get it working again. When it's being temperamental, I just tell the volunteers to use a notepad and calculator." She chuckled and pointed to her own gray hair. "I'm old-fashioned that way. Just figure out a solution and make it work."

"Have there been any days when you've noticed cash missing?"

She pondered that for a minute. "Not really. I know the older lady who's out there today said something was missing a few days ago … but really, it's so hard to tell. I'm not saying she's lying, but I didn't find anything to back up that idea."

Carole must have caught the way my expression hardened. Elsa may be old but she's still sharp and she never lies.

"Oh, she's a dear, dear lady. We've spoken many times. It's just that … Well, she is over ninety, and I mean …"

I forced myself to take her comments at face value and not get upset. "What about any of the others who work the register. Have you had any reason to doubt any of them?"

"Nearly all of them are members of the church, and I know Reverend Marshall thinks the world of them all."

"I'm sure." I was running out of questions for the moment. "Well, if you think of anything else, could you give me a call?" I handed her one of my RJP Investigations business cards, which she pocketed with hardly a glance.

I spent the next couple of hours tracking down the marked names on my list, those who had actually handled cash. Not one could remember a specific instance of money going missing. The older workers, including Millie, reminded me a lot of Elsa—retirees who were looking to fill their time with something worthwhile. A couple of younger ones, kids in their twenties who lived at home and had been strongly *encouraged* by their parents to find a purpose (I was *so* reminded of my nephew, Jason). Of this latter group, the level of distraction was palpable—eyes drifting toward cell phones, minds most likely on the opposite sex. I could see any of them misplacing cash, but most likely not masterminding a plot to steal it—none would qualify in a contest for brightest bulb in the chandelier.

It soon became apparent that the answers they gave were designed to be precisely what I wanted to hear. This was getting me nowhere.

Chapter 7

Iarrived home at a quarter of three, exhausted from talking all day. Elsa and Dottie, chipper as ever, had suggested we eat a late lunch or early dinner together. I begged off, needing some quiet time without voices in my head. Then my phone rang. It showed Ron's number.

"Hey, what's up?"

Victoria's voice responded. "We're on the road but wanted to give you a call."

"Everything okay?"

"A little glum, but it all went fine. We got here before noon, saw Jason to his room, had some lunch together. We offered to stay the night in a hotel and say goodbye in the morning, but the sergeant in charge said it's better to make a clean break and let the student start acclimating to his new routine." There was a short pause. "The feeling is sort of bummed right now—that's Ron—mixed with mild anxiety—that's me. Jason seemed fine. He'll adapt."

"Glad to hear it. Am I on speaker?"

"No."

"Tell my brother to let it go. I know he's not good at that, but it's what his kid needs right now."

She chuckled. "I will."

"Just think of it as practice for when Justin heads for college next year."

"It'll be way too quiet with only Joey at home for a while, won't it?"

"Probably, but then you two can begin to enjoy the life of real grown-ups, the kind who do what *they* want instead of what the kids want."

"I'm with you on that." She was still laughing when we ended the call.

On my way to the kitchen, I took three deep breaths, just to savor the quiet while Freckles was outside doing her business. Look at me, talking about what it's like not to have kids, when we treat our pup just like one.

I put on the tea kettle and pulled a little carton of yogurt from the fridge.

Settling at the dining table, I spread out the papers and notes I'd collected all morning. Comparing the calendar with the notes I'd made from interviews, I was hoping to spot a pattern where the same people were working on the days Elsa had noticed money was missing. Although I rearranged the bits and scraps of paper several times, I couldn't spot anything that made me go 'ah-ha!' so I got up and walked out to the garden to get a new perspective.

Besides the two full-time employees, there really were a limited number who handled the cash, so that was the good news. I didn't need to investigate everyone. Maybe a quick look into their personal lives would give more insight. Was there someone with a record of this sort of thing, someone who'd suddenly started spending more conspicuously, someone with financial woes?

Of course, another thought was to suggest that the shop put up a security camera near the sales counter and simply watch all the transactions. Two problems with that: I'd already been told they had no budget for equipment or services, and now that I'd interviewed most of them, they'd be on guard.

Still, knowing they were being watched—whether by me or by a camera—might make the thief quit. And that was something else I could watch for, whether any of the volunteers suddenly stopped coming in now that they'd been questioned. Their actions might point to the guilty party.

I decided to begin with the simplest method of learning about people's lives—social media. I began searching the major sites, including the ones the younger set like to use. It didn't take long to find several, primarily in the twenty-to-sixty age group. Even Reverend Marshall had a Facebook page where he posted lively descriptions of all the fun doings each week at the church. Hm. Who would've guessed?

Nancy Pomeroy was there, and I discovered the smiley woman who'd taken a valuable painting was married with at least three grandkids whose pictures filled most of her posts. I scrolled through her personal information and learned she was a native of Albuquerque, had attended UNM, and was now retired after a career in marketing. She made no mention of a church affiliation or volunteer work at the thrift shop.

Mike Weber, the big-screen TV fan, was a deacon in

the church. He'd posted about a bunch of friends getting together to watch football this coming weekend.

I didn't find Mariah Blinker anywhere online. She might be an expert at pricing used items in a thrift store, but she wasn't much for showing up on the internet.

Benny Stevens didn't show up on social media, but the church website listed him as a deacon, along with a picture of him and his lovely wife, Bonnie. Benny and Bonnie— cute. I looked for her on social, and she was all over the place. She tended to be a blabby little thing on Twitter, including one: **Big Yay! Our mortgage app came through!** To which several friends responded along the lines of: **Bet you're relieved**, along with lots of congratulatory messages.

Okay. I could see how first-time home owners would be thrilled to be getting their first house, but 'relieved' didn't seem to cover that. I made a little mark on my page to see if I could learn more about the Stevens' finances.

Carole Myerson didn't show up on any of my searches, which I supposed was not surprising. She wasn't as old as Elsa, but I'd still guess she was of the generation that didn't go in much for social media. She'd already admitted to me that she didn't care for the computer at all and would have been a lot more comfortable keeping the shop's records on written ledgers.

The name Eugene Towner was next on my list. I hadn't had the chance to really interview the taciturn guy who'd first shown me out to the back building and set me up with Nancy and Mike. From the schedule, it seemed he worked at the shop most days and I tried to remember his story. Mid-thirties and lived at home with his mother.

I'd overheard him talking with one of the other men as they carried some items from the intake area to the showrooms, and he seemed congenial enough with that guy. But when I'd greeted him the next day, he only offered a gruff *huh* and went on his way. I don't know if he thought I was flirting (seriously?) or if he just wasn't the chatty type. Anyway, there'd been zero rapport between us.

Social media searches for him led me to some groups where the conversation tended to consist of rants against whatever had appeared in the news that day—everything from gun control, to immigration, to the latest variation of the newest virus seemed to be fodder for rumor and vehement opinions. Some of the arguments were so blatantly out-there that I couldn't bring myself to read further. So, okay, Eugene was just one of those guys who doesn't fit the mainstream.

I looked up his mother, who reminded me of a neighbor who'd lived down the street when I was a kid, a sweet mannered lady who managed her kids' lives down to the minute but didn't have a clue what they were sneaking into when she wasn't around. Mrs. Towner's posts were all about the activities she and Eugene attended together, including their various church activities. I remembered someone saying Eugene worked at Heavenly Treasures because his mother had encouraged it. Could he be resentful enough to feel the church owed him something? Something like a few hundred extra bucks a week?

I put a mark beside his name as well. Tomorrow, Ron would be back in town and I'd ask if we could do deeper background checks into some of those on my list. I'd just begun a search of online directory information, looking for addresses for my suspects, when I heard a sound outside. Freckles came out of a solid sleep and bounded for the front door.

Drake was home.

Chapter 8

The Cadillac sat at the curb, waiting.

"Hey, baby. How was your day?" Rodney Day had seen his wife coming and walked around to open the passenger door. His old-fashioned gentlemanly manners were one thing that had appealed to her when they met, five years ago.

"Same old." Cee-Cee slid into the car and pulled off the wig, running her fingers through her short blonde hair to fluff it. Immediately, she found herself sitting up straighter. "Can't wait to get home and have a shower. Do we have time for a drink together before we're due at that party?"

"We do. And so what? No one's going to bat an eye when their largest donor and the best fundraiser they've ever had shows up a little late for dinner." He pulled into traffic and headed west.

"True," she said with a laugh. "A pledge to match up to a million in donations—that's probably more than the Theater Guild ever saw until we came along."

She looked across at her lover and partner. With his gray hair, worn longish and styled to perfection, and his handlebar mustache, he fit the role of a well-to-do gentleman behind the wheel of the classic car. She'd picked up the car a few years ago, loving the big fins and chrome accents. The fact that it was painted bright pink cinched the deal—she loved driving and being seen in Pinkie. She'd been at work when Rodney walked in one day and inquired about the car out in the parking lot.

"It's not for sale," she'd said.

"Perhaps you need a chauffeur." It was probably his British accent and the wink that convinced her to have dinner with him that night. A week later, she moved in with him.

Rodney Day was born Robert O'Flannery in a rough neighborhood in New York, where he learned, first and foremost, that he didn't want to remain little Robbie his whole life. He'd watched his da' drink himself to death at an early age, and his ma worked and scrounged to raise six kids. Not for him. At age twelve he stowed away on a freighter and ended up in London, where the streets were just as rough, but he quickly hired on to make food deliveries to the big hotels and there he spotted the men he wanted to become.

He got work at the poshest of the posh hotels, worked his way up from the loading dock to the kitchen and eventually to bellman. As he trolleyed suitcases up to the rooms, he listened to *everything*. Robbie had a knack for imitating accents and he was soon speaking the Queen's English as well as any highborn young lord—when it suited his purposes.

His listening skills told him when the guests would be out of their rooms, when someone had jewelry to store in the hotel safe, and what play they were attending in the theatre district. It took no creativity at all to figure out what time the muckety-mucks would return, and he also developed a knack for taking only one small item from any given guestroom.

Street talk during his New York days had taught him that when a place was ransacked, the police were called. But if one item went missing, the owner would normally chalk it up to forgetfulness. If the stolen item was reported at all, it was days later. By then, Robbie's network of crooks and fences would have converted the necklace or ring or tie pin to cash for him. Nice, untraceable cash.

Travelers who stayed in hotels were especially easy. Offering to deliver room service meals on behalf of the kitchen staff, he had access to the rooms. If a key was missing from a dresser top, the guest would simply request another at the desk downstairs. Sometimes he even checked up on his own work, listening in on a conversation the next day after he'd removed some lovely bauble from the lady's jewel box.

"Are you certain you brought the emeralds, darling?" a distracted husband would ask. "See, right there are your rubies. I'll bet you left the emeralds at home. We'll find them in your dresser when we get back."

The woman might send a poisonous look toward her husband, but she never gave the room service lad a second glance. The man would tip extra just to get the boy to leave so they could conduct their argument in private.

And Robbie would smile all the way down the elevator.

The 1950s were a delicious time—no high-speed trains, few trans-Atlantic flights, international phone calls were expensive, and the internet was not even a gleam in anyone's eye. To make himself personally less traceable, he'd even adopted a new name and biography. The surname Day was well known in European circles, and when Robbie called himself Rodney, he made it easy to assume he was a distant nephew. When it was convenient, he could revert back to his New York accent and claim he'd come from the American side of the Day family. No one questioned too closely, especially when he emulated the manners and phrases of those he'd observed.

"Where are you?" Cee-Cee asked now, from her side of the Cadillac.

"Ah, just reminiscing. Nothing important." He made the left turn into their neighborhood.

Two more turns on winding streets through an older part of the city and they came to the striking mid-century modern home that almost could have been an early Frank Lloyd Wright. The cream stucco, apple green trim, and many windows were reminiscent of the famed architect's Booth House, and it was in a country club neighborhood. Rare to find a rental in this area, the landlord had told them.

Rodney didn't care about any pedigree, they just needed a house that suited their purposes: to entertain lavishly enough to impress those from whom he planned to confiscate a bit of their spare wealth. That's all. And they talked him into skipping the credit check by paying a year in advance. That was six months ago. Their business in Albuquerque should be completed in plenty of time.

He pulled into the driveway, pressing the button at the precise moment so the garage door would be fully up and he could drive the Caddy inside without pausing. Cee-Cee waited until the door was down before she got out of the car. It was just a thing she had, not wanting to be seen in her 'day job' getup here in the neighborhood. Sort of the same reasoning why she didn't drive the classic pink car to work and park it alongside the ordinary vehicles of the others.

She preceded him through the connecting door to the kitchen and set her clunky purse on the counter.

"I only managed a couple hundred today," she told him as she pulled cash from the purse. "They've got some woman looking around, asking way too many questions."

"What, like an auditor?"

"I don't think so. She didn't sit with me at my desk or ask to see records. But I just about lost it when she handed me her card. Private investigator."

"Bloody hell." Rodney was in one of his British phases now. In other cities he'd adopted a French or German accent. He would use this one at all times until they finished their job here.

She set the cash on the counter and reached out to stroke his mustache. "I love it when you talk that way."

"I thought you disapproved of cursing."

"In that accent it really doesn't sound like a curse." She turned her back to him. "Unzip me?"

He lowered the zipper on the shirtwaist dress she'd worn to work, and she pushed it off her shoulders and let it drop to the floor, along with the built-in padding and unflattering bra that made up the outfit. His breath caught when she turned to face him.

Even at sixty-five, ten years his junior, Cee-Cee's body could pass for forty. She worked at it. The home gym had come with the house, and she barely ate a nibble or two at social functions. Sadly, Rodney couldn't exactly act upon his desires at a moment's notice anymore. And they had the theater fundraiser to attend.

"Make my usual dirty martini," she said. "I'll be out of the shower in ten."

Exactly twelve minutes later she emerged from the bedroom, dressed in a fitted floor-length purple gown laden in beadwork. Strappy sandals and a small evening bag completed the look. Her cap of blonde hair accentuated her high cheekbones and fine jawline. He never failed to be amazed at the transformation skillfully applied makeup and correct posture could bring about. Gone was the slump-shouldered look and the powdery foundation that would make any woman look worse than her age.

"New dress?"

"Yes, actually. I picked it up yesterday. You were there, in Dillard's."

He remembered waiting while she carried several expensive dresses into the changing room, then overheard her complaining to the fawning clerk how the attached anti-theft device was pulling the hem out of shape and causing the fit to be all wrong. He could only surmise that when they left twenty minutes later, the beaded gown had fallen into the bottom of her hobo bag, while fourteen dresses were left strewn about the dressing room for the clerk to sort through. Once the poor girl figured out one was missing, they'd been out of the mall and probably five blocks away.

"I love it on you," he said, handing Cee-Cee her drink.

"Thank you, kind sir." She took a sip and rolled her green eyes heavenward. "Remind me again who's going to be there tonight."

"I'll go over the whole thing in the car. Need to get into my tux now." He brushed a kiss against her cheek and headed toward his dressing room.

Chapter 9

I awoke at daylight to find Drake's arm across my waist and a little row of kisses trailing down my neck. It's one of our favorite ways to start the day because it means he doesn't have an early flight. I rolled over and returned the kisses and then, well, one thing led to another.

An hour later we were in the kitchen together, making toast and discussing plans for the day.

"I've got some movie producer coming in to scout locations around Santa Fe," he said. "Been thinking about what to show him, but he'll probably already have a wish list, and if he's anything like the last one, he'll want to see a dozen places that are all a hundred miles apart. And he'll have no clue how much fuel that uses or what he'll have to pay for the job." He gave me a wry smile.

"Just follow your standard practice. Estimate extra for

the hourly rate and bill his credit card *before* you take off. If there's credit left you can refund it."

"Right. Once burned, twice shy."

Important people tended to think their name alone would be enough to give them an open account with a lot of service providers, but we'd learned the hard way about extending credit. A couple of years ago, Drake relaxed his policy and took a mega star on a two-hour showoff flight for a woman. Afterward, the guy's credit card was declined, he claimed not to have another one with him, and said he'd mail a check. We still don't have our money for that one. Aviation businesses operate on a shoestring, and that twelve-hundred dollar loss really stung.

I sent him out the door with a lingering kiss before turning to get myself ready for the day. Ron would be back in the office and I was hoping to get his help with some background checks on my various suspects. I found a pair of clean jeans and a comfy red t-shirt, called Freckles to come along, and we headed to the office.

Surprisingly, Ron was already at his desk in his upstairs office at the converted Victorian house our private investigation business calls home.

"Hey, you doing all right?" I asked, peeking through his doorway before heading to my own office across the hall.

"Sure. Why wouldn't I?"

Because Victoria said you had a rough time letting go when you delivered your kid to boarding school yesterday? But I didn't say it. Instead, I went with, "Great, 'cause I could use some background checks on people from the charity shop."

He gave me a steady look.

"What? It's what you do all day—employment background checks."

"Yes, but those people have agreed to it. I assume you

don't have signed releases from these volunteers, letting you peep into their private lives?"

Oooh. I hadn't thought about that. And, realistically, I couldn't see much way of getting them to agree.

"Yeah, you're right. Bad idea. Guess I'd better just stick with interviews."

"Definitely."

I was about to ask if he could help me get addresses for the people on my list but decided that was something I could probably handle on my own. He already had a stack of messages on his desk to deal with.

There were a dozen names on my list and I had addresses for less than half of them, so I continued what I'd started yesterday afternoon. Online searches filled some of the gaps, and I even resorted to the most old-time source, a stack of old telephone directories we'd collected over the years. By mid-morning I had a decent list. I debated the best plan of attack and decided to go with convenience.

Sorting the list by neighborhoods, I would start closest to the office and work my way across town. The day was cool enough and Freckles seemed up for an adventure, so I beckoned her to come along out to my Jeep. We headed north on Rio Grande toward the small community of Corrales. While it's actually an incorporated village, Corrales feels like an extension of Albuquerque, although with a much more rural atmosphere. I had several friends who lived there when I was in high school, but that was a while back and the community has grown. I found myself using my navigator to locate Eugene Towner's home.

Two adobe pillars flanked a long driveway, and as I turned in I spotted a woman in front of an adobe house. She held a green watering can and stared toward the vehicle, obviously wondering who was showing up unannounced. I'd worked out my cover story, so I reached to the passenger seat and picked up my computer case.

"Mrs. Towner?" I asked as I got out of the Jeep. "Is this Eugene Towner's home?"

"Yes …" She eyed me warily, and I realized the computer case could be taken for a salesperson's briefcase.

I walked toward her, realizing she was very short, somewhat under five feet tall, with gray hair, cut severely short, and vivid blue eyes. She wore mid-calf capris with dirt stains at the knees, and her hands had clearly been working in the soil.

"I've been volunteering at Heavenly Treasures for a few days and I met Eugene there."

Her wrinkles softened somewhat.

"I'm not selling anything," I said with a chuckle. "I found this computer behind the sales desk at the shop and thought Eugene might have forgotten it there."

She set down the watering can and approached. "He has a computer, of course. But the case looks different. His is a Mac."

"Oh, then I'm sorry. This one's a Dell."

"It was awfully nice of you to drive all this way out here. Even if it was his, he could have brought it home next time he's in the shop."

"Well, I wasn't sure. I saw from the schedule that he wasn't working today, so …"

"He's not here right now," she said.

Did I detect a flicker of hope that I might be interested in Eugene personally? Yuck. I raised my left hand to rub the side of my face, making certain she saw my wedding ring.

"Oh, that's all right. Does he have another job on his days off from the thrift shop?"

"No, he doesn't seem to have found exactly the right thing as a career yet. I encourage him to take as many days at Heavenly Treasures as he can get. Can't have him sitting around in that 'man cave' of his all the time. But I can always find things for him to do around here. We have two acres, you know." She waved vaguely toward the back of the property where I spotted some wooden hives and a grove of trees laden with red apples.

It went along with what Elsa had told me about Eugene, that he was a thirty-seven year old who'd never left the nest. "That's too bad, about his not finding the right job opportunities. Must be hard to come up with spending money and whatever, especially since he probably has a girlfriend."

She bristled. "There have been girlfriends, of course there have. And Eugene has all he needs here, what with the monthly income from his late father's life insurance annuity. He does just fine."

I could see that it wouldn't do to come right out with any questions about whether he'd recently shown off any extra money. This mama bear wouldn't hear ill of her child, even when he was an unemployed middle-aged man.

Freckles rescued me with a whine. I looked back to see that she had her paws on the window frame and her head hanging out.

"Guess I'd better get going. Thanks, Mrs. Towner."

"Betty." She had visibly softened when she spotted my dog. A winsome spaniel face will do that to anyone.

"Thanks, Betty. And don't worry about mentioning the computer to Eugene. My mistake."

I found a wide spot in the driveway, turned around, and headed back to the road.

The next address on my list was for a Kylie Windom, one of the teens who'd had a hard time figuring out the difference between nickels and dimes. Still, it didn't mean the girl didn't know good and well what a hundred dollar bill was worth. I'd been told she was living in a halfway house on north 4th Street. According to the work schedule she had today off.

I headed up Alameda and made the turn onto 4th. The house sat too near the busy street, probably another of those that once had a front yard before the street was widened. There was no parking on the property, so I did a U-turn and pulled to the curb in front of it.

"Stay here and be good," I told Freckles, powering the windows up so she couldn't get through the space, while leaving her plenty of fresh air.

I rang the bell and used the lost-computer excuse again with the man who answered. "I thought Kylie might have left it at the thrift shop yesterday."

"She's in the den. You can ask her, but I wasn't aware she owned a computer."

I followed him into what looked like any average living room, if you shopped for your furniture at Goodwill. To be fair, it was probably what they could afford and their residents most likely weren't known for taking great care with such items.

I remembered Kylie when I saw her—pink hair, a nose ring, pretty face and good teeth. She would have a nice smile if she ever let one happen. She was slouched on a saggy plaid sofa, staring at a cell phone screen.

"Kylie," the man said in a voice loud enough to get

through whatever was playing on the girl's earbuds. "Look up for a second. This lady says this might be your computer?"

I held up the case. Kylie took a nano-second look and shook her head before going back to her screen.

The man shrugged and walked back the way we'd come. In the foyer-slash-dining area he paused and I took the opportunity to speak.

"I'm afraid this isn't the only reason I'm here," I said. "There's been some money missing from the thrift shop, and—"

He rolled his eyes and gave a small groan.

"We're not accusing any of the kids, but I have to ask. Has Kylie or any of the other kids who work at Heavenly Treasures recently started flashing any spare money around? Or buying things you're pretty sure they can't afford?"

He actually paused long enough to make it seem he was considering the question. "These kids ... if they had spare cash, I'd be the last person to see it. Kylie's not one of them but a lot of the kids here would take any cash they got, and it would go up their nose or into a handful of pills. We're not a drug rehab place—the really strung out ones go elsewhere—but I'd be foolishly naïve if I believed there's no contraband on the premises. So, if you're a cop ..."

I held up my free hand. "I'm not."

"Like I said, Kylie's never had drugs as a problem. She just came from a really bad home situation and needed a safe place. If she can finish school and get some kind of vocational training, she'll probably turn out okay. She's not stupid, but she hasn't been given great examples all her life, okay?"

"Thanks, I appreciate your candor. And I can see where

she can use some basic life skills that she's not getting through her phone."

"I hear you. I'm working on implementing phone-time limits. So far, I've got everyone putting their phones in a basket during meal times. It's progress, although not enough."

I reached into the purse hanging from my shoulder and pulled out my list of potential suspects. "Can you give me any insights into some of these other kids? I have this same address for these two." I pointed them out.

He studied the page and pointed at a name. "Trouble, this kid. I should have put him on a road crew or busting rocks in a quarry." He looked up and smiled at that comment. There are no quarries around here. "He shouldn't be in any environment where small items can walk off. I'll look at finding him some other work assignment. If he had access to your cash, just beware."

I noted the name, and he wasn't one who ever worked the register. Too bad. It might have solved my problem.

"This other girl, she's a lot like Kylie. I don't know that she *wouldn't* steal money … but she hasn't shown up with it around here."

I thanked him again and left one of my business cards, in case he thought of anything else.

Out in the Jeep I patted Freckles and sat there a minute, ticking off the names I'd just checked out. I could catch Paseo del Norte and take it to the far northeast heights, where the next logical home visit would be at Benny Stevens' place.

But it was nearly noon, and one slice of morning toast will only take a girl so far. I needed a Big Mac fix.

Chapter 10

Rodney dropped Cee-Cee off at the usual spot a block from her job, then headed toward the carwash. He'd promised to get the pink Caddy a nice detailing today and he knew just the place. It was only a mile or so away, and there was a young guy there who was enthralled with the old car. Rodney always got his money's worth when he went there, and he could grab a cup of coffee and read the newspapers while he waited.

Albuquerque didn't have a lot of newsstands—not like New York or London, most certainly—but he knew of one, and he stopped there to pick up the *Times* and the *Guardian* before dropping off the car. For one moment he wished with a pang that Cee-Cee could enjoy the life of leisure as much as he did. From his late twenties, Rodney Day had set himself up not to labor at a job. He worked—

oh, yes he did—but although his 'jobs' required meticulous planning, they were far more lucrative than anything with a salary attached.

He could savor the benefits of a gentlemen's club or a health spa, could linger over an expensive lunch or order the best wine with dinner. But Cee-Cee felt differently. She loved being in the midst of things, loved having a place to be each day and specific duties to perform. And she loved acting a role. She could have been an actress on stage or screen if she'd so chosen.

In fact, she'd once told him of playing a minor movie role when she was in her twenties. She was the girl who was supposed to scream when the rapist showed up at the window of her girlfriend's bedroom. It had taken two full days to get that scene down just right. Someone would miss standing on their mark or someone would speak too quickly. Sitting around the movie set while cameras and extras and makeup people fiddled about—well, it was all much too boring for Cee-Cee. She collected her union scale pay and decided she could earn more than that by simply using her wits out in the real world.

He spread the *Times* out on the coffee shop table, memories of the past blending with the present-day news on the page in front of him. Page one of the Arts section carried this headline: *Twenty Years Later, No Trace of Missing Picasso.*

Rodney chuckled. He didn't need to read the rehash of the details of what had been called one of the most daring art heists of the millennium. Silly, considering the new millennium was only a year old when it happened. He knew the details. He knew the parts the police didn't know. The article included a photo of the missing painting, one he knew every inch of, one he looked at each morning as he dressed, before he closed the secret panel over it again.

Of course, he had no way to reap the monetary reward from the heist. The painting was too well known. But there were always unscrupulous billionaires in the world who didn't care about a painting's provenance. They, like he, simply wanted to stare at it each day. And one of the reasons for his and Cee-Cee's fundraising work with the Theater Guild and others like it was to have access to exactly those types of people.

Perhaps today's reminder in the *Times* would bring out some discussion about the piece and that conversation could lead to another. When his ma used to say that patience was a virtue, he was fairly certain this wasn't what she had in mind. Nevertheless, he'd kept it in mind for twenty years now.

Someone had abandoned a copy of today's *Albuquerque Journal* at the next table, and Rodney picked it up before the wait staff could toss it away. The society pages had a piece on the Theater Guild's fundraiser, including the juicy bit that wealthy arts patrons Rodney and Cee-Cee Day had pledged to match donations, up to a million dollars, for the refurbishment of the theater property. The so-called article was little more than a PR piece to bring in added donations. So much the better, he thought with a smile.

There was, of course, no matching money. The donations were being held by Rodney himself, ostensibly to 'verify' them. He and Cee-Cee gave a little talk at each fundraising event, such as last night's, and reported the progress. Someone had suggested coming up with a poster of one of those thermometers with a rising red line to visually show how much they'd collected. How crude!

Cee-Cee developed a little computer graphic, which she filled in with metallic gold ink—a bit more each week—

and then had it printed on heavy card stock and placed next to each of the $1,000-per-dinner plates. The classy touch had been his idea; the computer skill was hers. They made a wonderful team.

He finished his Brazilian roast coffee and glanced at his Rolex. The car should be done by now. He abandoned the newspapers where they were. No one could say definitively that it was the man with the mane of white hair who'd been reading only articles about money and art. Then again, with his tailored suit, expensive gold watch, and three carat diamond pinky ring, who was to say those weren't his favorite subjects.

He strolled back to the carwash, admired the detail job on the Caddy, and tipped the young man handsomely. As always, the boy practically drooled over the extra attention. The lad would miss the strikingly handsome man in the big car, once they bailed out of this city. But that was too bad. They never remained in one place very long, and a million-dollar score was a good one, especially for an area as financially deprived as New Mexico.

With Cee-Cee otherwise occupied until mid-afternoon, Rodney considered his options. There was another fundraiser tomorrow night, this time at one of the wealthier country clubs on the east side of the city. He could go shopping—as she had—for another expensive dress for her. But Cee-Cee liked to choose her own clothes. And trying on a selection of the pricey gowns was part of the fun for her.

He opted, instead, to drive back to the house so he could admire his Picasso alone for a while, then take a dip in the pool and spend some time in the home sauna. Ah, the life of the leisure class!

Chapter 11

The home of Benny and Bonnie Stevens (yes, I still chuckled when I said it out loud) was in a nicer neighborhood than I'd expected. A new Toyota minivan with the dealer sticker still in place sat in the driveway. Maybe Bonnie was some kind of high-power attorney or something like that. But when I rang the bell on the two-story stucco and red tile home, the woman who answered was definitely not the maid. She wore a flowered sundress and blue sandals, and her highlighted hair looked freshly done.

"Bonnie? Hi, I'm Charlie Parker. I've been volunteering at Heavenly Treasures recently …"

"Oh, yes. My husband works there. Wonderful cause, the mission work." She stood aside and invited me in.

I knew in advance that my story about finding a

computer and wondering whether Benny was missing his wasn't going to work here. Any bit of logic would say that I could have simply put it in his office until his return the next day. I needed to go with something closer to the truth.

"I was hoping to get the chance to chat with Benny privately, you know, away from the shop, and since I just live …" I waved vaguely westward, as if my home were only a block or two from here, instead of nearly fifteen miles. "Anyway, is he home?"

"Well, no. He uses his afternoon away from the shop to do little personal things. Today, I believe it was a dental appointment."

"Oh. I hadn't thought to ask. It's probably lucky that I caught you here. Or do you work from home?"

Bonnie's already-perky smile brightened. "You could say that. Four kids and keeping up the house. Yes, home is definitely a full-time job."

We walked through a tiled entry into a large greatroom. Near a huge sectional sofa knelt a kid I guessed to be about four, who was focused on a coloring book on the coffee table. A dining table for six sat near the sliding glass doors that faced a well-manicured back yard. Bonnie stepped into the kitchen (all granite and stainless steel) and offered me iced tea. I accepted, thinking she might be talkative if I stayed a little while.

She poured tea from a glass pitcher, and I perched on a stool at the counter.

"You really have a beautiful home."

"Well, as I said, it's a full-time job." Her smile was starting to seem a little pasted-on. Did the woman have any other expression? "What was it you wanted to talk with Benny about? Maybe I could help. I'm quite involved with our church activities too."

In addition to being a mother of four who keeps a perfect house. And smiles all the time.

"Has he mentioned that there's been some money missing at Heavenly Treasures?"

"Oh. Why, no, he hasn't. Is it very much?"

"We're not really sure yet." I pulled out one of my business cards and slid it across the counter toward her. "A couple of the volunteers first noticed, and when they reported it to your husband, he asked me to check into it."

"Wow, a private investigator. That must be exciting work."

"Actually, I'm an accountant but my work has evolved into some investigations as well."

"Well, that must just be so fascinating! I took accounting classes in school. But of course that was before the kids, and my life just kind of filled up."

"My investigation is still just beginning. I've started with a list of the volunteers who have access to the cash. Basically, it's a matter of talking to each one, finding out whether they saw anything going on."

She nodded and took a long sip of her tea.

"As I understand it, other than the volunteers, the shop has only two regular employees—your husband and the bookkeeper … Carole Myerson, I think her name is?" I hoped the vague tone would bring out a little gossip, but that wasn't happening, so I had to come out and ask.

"Do you know Carole? I couldn't seem to come up with an address or anything much about her."

"I don't *know* her well. She started last spring, right before Easter, as I recall. I had taken a few of the children's old clothes and some brand new stuffed animals to the shop as a donation. I met Carole then. She seems awfully nice and Benny was really impressed at how well she took over the bookkeeping duties. Before she came along, I guess the record-keeping was kind of a hodgepodge of deposit slips and receipts. She set up profit and loss statements on the computer. I do know our church treasurer was most grateful."

"Have you ever been to her home? Socialized?"

"No. She's a very pleasant older lady, but it seems that she keeps her work and personal lives separate. Benny says she has talked some about her husband—apparently, he was a very successful stock broker and their investments have left them well off. I get the impression he plays golf a lot and she works at the shop to fill her hours."

Maybe the husband had a different last name, which could explain why I couldn't find Carole's.

"Is she a member of your church?"

"Oh, no. The shop is affiliated, because of the mission work, but the people there aren't necessarily church members. I'd guess maybe half are."

"Some of the people on my witness list seem to be doing community service and that type of thing."

"Yes, Benny has mentioned several really troubled kids who work for him." She gazed fondly toward the little one, still working away at his coloring book. "I'm so lucky to have been here to raise my kids and look out for their needs. Not all families have as good a situation as we do."

"That's very true. Do your older kids ever work at the shop?"

"They're all in school right now—our two middle schoolers were just accepted at Albuquerque Academy this term. And then, of course, they have tons of outside activities—sports, dance lessons ... you name it. I finally got the minivan this year, mainly to shuttle everyone around." She glanced back at the clock on her stove. "Oh my gosh, look at the time. I'll need to get going. A mother's work is never done ..."

My tea was nearly gone, and I'd pretty well run through my questions, so I slid off the stool and picked up my purse.

With quick movements, Bonnie set the tea glasses in the sink and called out to her son in her perky little sing-songy way. "*Ran*dy, let's get *go*ing."

The kid dropped his crayons in place and went along as Bonnie shepherded him toward the front door while grabbing her purse from the hall table. I found myself swept along as she efficiently got everyone out the front door in under a minute. Maybe she really was a supermom.

"Nice meeting you, Charlie," she called out as she headed toward the minivan and I walked to my Jeep at the curb.

I fiddled with my keys and let her back out of the driveway before I started up. Everything I'd just witnessed—the upscale home, new vehicle, her comments about the kids' activities and schooling—none of this could possibly be affordable on Benny's salary from a dinky thrift shop. As I found myself following the route of the minivan, a dozen thoughts ran through my head. Was the church subsidizing this family, maybe because of Benny's service? Were the couple deeply in debt?

As I watched Bonnie's vehicle make the turn at the entrance of the priciest private school in the city, I realized I needed to get a better idea of how much money the shop was missing.

Freckles was becoming restless and I had to admit I'd had enough for the day. We headed toward home.

Chapter 12

Much to her relief, I let Freckles out to the back yard right away. She raced around, did her business, and raced around some more. When the sound of voices came from next door, the dog ran through the break in the hedge toward Gram's house. I followed.

Elsa and Dottie were sitting at the patio table, talking about cutting some chrysanthemums to take indoors.

"Send Freckles home if she's bugging you," I said.

"Little Freckle-baby never a bother," Dottie said, sneaking the pooch a corner of the peanut butter cracker she was eating.

"How was everything at the shop today?" I asked, taking a seat.

"Mr. Stevens had the afternoon off, so it was kind of quiet," Elsa said.

"Yeah, but this morning—whew, that man got a burr under his saddle or somethin'," Dottie added.

"What happened?"

"He lit into a couple of the volunteers, somethin' fierce."

"About little things," Elsa said. "Nothing that doesn't happen every day—missing price tags, dust on the glassware. Silly things."

"Worried that I'm figuring out where the missing money went?"

Dottie shook her head a little. "You think it's him? I don't."

"I'm looking at everyone, but I have to say there's reason to give Benny a second glance." I briefly described his home and things the wife said. "They're living way beyond their visible means, unless there's an inheritance or portfolio no one has mentioned."

"Eugene Towner got it the worst," Elsa said, still on the topic. "Mr. Stevens started out by picking on the little stuff, but then it got personal. He said Eugene's mother enables him—I'm not sure what that means, exactly—but Eugene got really red in the face and was clenching his fists and everything."

"He even start pickin' on me, just a little. Jumped my case when I walked in with a box of new Christmas decorations. I give the man my fierce eye" —which she demonstrated now— "and he shut right up."

I could see why he would. Dottie's 'fierce eye' was a force to be reckoned with.

"It was nothing personal, Dottie. He nearly had that girl in tears, the one who was working at the counter with me." Elsa turned to me. "Her name's Bethany. She's friends with the pink-haired girl whose name I can never remember."

Kiley Windom. Anyway, I was definitely getting the picture that Benny Stevens had a bad morning. But was that related to my investigation, money pressures of his own, or something else entirely? Maybe he just hadn't had his coffee yet.

I stood up and patted my leg to get Freckles' attention as I turned toward the break in the hedge. Then I had a thought. "Are you ladies working at the shop again tomorrow?"

"We are," Elsa said.

"Do me a favor. I need to get a feel for how much cash passes through the place. For the next couple of days can you just keep a listing of that for me? I'll give you a little spiral notebook and you could write down the amount of every sale that's paid in cash."

Elsa rubbed her hands together and grinned. "A spy assignment. I like it."

I laughed. "Sure, just don't let anyone notice that you're doing it. Hm. I guess it really is sort of a spy assignment."

I was still grinning when I walked into my own kitchen.

"What's this all about?" said Drake.

I startled, my hand going to my heart. "I didn't know you were home."

"Quit the day a little early and left the aircraft for Paul's mechanic to do an oil change."

"Nice. Maybe we should make a plan this evening."

Since we'd started the morning with our favorite activity, I doubted sex was on the agenda again quite so soon. I suggested we call Ron and Victoria and meet them at Pedro's for some enchiladas and margaritas.

My brother's mood had definitely picked up since this

morning. It might have had something to do with the fact
that they walked into Pedro's childless.

"Joey has declared that a twelve-year-old can most
certainly stay home alone for an hour or two," Victoria told
us. "We agreed, on the condition that he have his phone on
him at all times and that he respond within thirty seconds
if we text."

Ron pulled out his own phone as he sat down across
from me and fired off a quick text. "I can almost make
the kid wish he'd come along. This will be like dinner table
conversation he can't get away from."

Victoria laid a hand on his. "Give him a little break,
honey. We have to show that we trust him on his own."

"No, we don't." His phone pinged with an incoming
response.

She rolled her eyes, and I looked toward the bar where
Pedro was blending our drinks. *Hurry!*

"And Justin?" I asked.

"Oh, he's off with friends. Now that he's driving, there's
not an evening at home for him. There's a girlfriend." Ron
looked none too happy about that.

"Let's talk about something other than the kids," I
suggested as the margaritas arrived.

Concha, Pedro's wife, stepped up and asked about our
food order, as if she needed to. I always have the green
chile chicken enchiladas and Ron goes for the beef burrito.
The others tend to follow suit—the girls having chicken,
the men opting for the burritos.

"How much longer do you think you'll be helping Elsa
at the thrift shop?" Ron asked, once we'd toasted to our
first night out, the four of us, in several months.

"Not sure." I dipped a tortilla chip into Concha's

homemade salsa. "I've talked to a lot of the volunteers. The shop manager seems to be living beyond his means, but I have no idea how much he could feasibly skim out of a little store like that one. I still haven't got much of a bead on the bookkeeper. Can't seem to come up with an online presence for her. She's in her early or mid-seventies, I'm guessing, but that doesn't put her out of the range for being active on social media. I wish I could get enough information to initiate a background check or credit report."

"Charlie ..."

"I know. You told me." Even though my little devious brain was still trying to work out a way around Ron's adherence to the rules.

"Maybe you could set up a concealed camera and catch someone in the act of taking cash from the drawer," Victoria suggested. "Hey, it helps a lot in convenience stores."

"I thought about that. I could poke around in the donated stuff out back. Wouldn't surprise me if someone has donated a usable camera."

"They aren't that expensive these days," Drake offered. "The fixed base operator at the airport has installed them all around the hangar now."

I decided I'd do a little shopping around. The camera was a good idea.

Our food arrived and I lost myself in the joy of green chile in my mouth and a fresh margarita to wash it down.

Chapter 13

Cee-Cee looked stunning again tonight, Rodney decided as she emerged from the Cadillac under the portico entrance at the Tanoan Country Club. This time she'd chosen an off-the-shoulder black knee-length dress, a diamond necklace that lay flat against her collarbones, and a shawl of some gauzy material with silver threads running through it.

Tonight's event was the kickoff to the annual holiday fundraiser for the local children's hospital. The president of the Theater Guild had been so impressed with Rodney and Cee-Cee's generosity toward that organization that he'd nominated Rodney as chair of the hospital committee as well.

Rodney practically salivated at the thought of how easily he could channel money from their banks into the special account he'd opened some years ago in Switzerland. This should be a snap. A very lucrative one.

He handed the Caddy's keys to a valet and took his wife's arm.

Half of the upstairs dining room had been closed off for the private function, and tuxedoed waiters passed among the glittering crowd with silver trays of tiny canapes. A good-looking, tall black man was talking with Jon Tanner from the Theater Guild, and the pair spotted Rodney and Cee-Cee and headed in their direction.

"Rodney, I'd like you to meet Phil Jackson," Jon said. "Doctor Jackson is chief administrator of Donner Children's Hospital and the man with whom you'll be working most closely on the holiday fund drive."

They shook hands and Rodney introduced Cee-Cee.

"Nice to meet you both. I'd love to introduce you to my wife too, but she had a surgery to perform this afternoon and it seems to have run long."

"Leandra Jackson is the top orthopedic surgeon at Donner. She's the reason kids with spinal deformities are now living normal lives and playing like every other kid."

Rodney swallowed hard and hoped no one would notice. Was it horrible of him to be planning ways to rip off funds from that kind of place? A scene from childhood flashed through his head, one of his younger brothers who might have lived beyond the age of seven if he'd had access to a hospital like Donner. Of course, New York had top-notch hospitals, but not ones his mother could afford. Rodney's vision clouded.

"Mr. Day? Are you all right?"

He blinked and remembered where he was. Who he was, now. "Yes, perfectly fine."

He looked around the room at the lavish décor,

heard the soft music from the grand piano in the corner, surveyed the crowd. In truth, the country club itself was more deserving of a big heist. He shook the thought away. He couldn't let his concentration lag.

"Let me introduce you around to the other board members," Phil Jackson was saying, taking Rodney's elbow.

Cee-Cee had wandered toward a group of women who were admiring the city view from the floor-to-ceiling windows on the western wall where the last of the evening light was dissolving into a fiery glow at the horizon.

"Dr. Jackson!" boomed a voice from across the room.

"Dennis, let me introduce Rodney Day, who might just be the answer to our prayers." Jackson turned to present Dennis Sanchez, the president of the hospital board. The men shook hands all around.

Rodney put on his most caring smile, the one he'd perfected years ago for this very type of moment.

Sanchez waved two others over, a woman in her sixties who wore a black pantsuit and a man who was probably thirty-five at the outside. Both were apparently members of the board. The woman told Rodney she'd heard of his fundraising work with the Theater Guild and was thrilled that he'd agreed to head up their own fund drive. The younger man said he was the board's treasurer and would be the one overseeing the financial reports and bank transfers.

"We're already set up for online donations via PayPal and Stripe. And the local PBS station has given us a two-hour window during one of the season's classic Christmas movies to broadcast our fund drive. Local newscaster Pippa Osuna has agreed to be the celebrity face of the effort. People love her, and I swear she could coax the socks off a homeless guy. She'll be wonderful in the position."

Electronic payments. Local celebrity. One of those upward counting tickers telling the whole state how much money was being raised. Rodney's alarm bells went off, but he kept his smile frozen in place.

"Of course all that takes place between Thanksgiving and Christmas." The treasurer continued talking as Rodney nodded and began planning an escape route.

Doctor Jackson was giving him a sideways glance and Rodney brought himself back to the moment. Too many of these people held important positions in common with several charitable causes. It's what rich people with extra time and money did. He couldn't let his discomfort over the hospital deal color their perception of him. He and Cee-Cee needed the other gigs too much to walk away now.

"Matching our donors' money, up to a million, is so generous of you," said the woman in the black suit. She turned to the treasurer guy and said, "We really must find a spot for Mr. Day to appear on the PBS special. You can make that happen, can't you, Ian?"

Ian. His little brother's name.

"You bet, Sally. With two million dollars we could do so much for the kids at Donner." He turned toward Rodney again. "You really have the face for it. And your accent—oh my gosh, I think the camera would love you."

"Say you'll do it, Mr. Day? Please?" Sally's wrinkles became a little frightening when her face turned to pleading.

But on camera? There was no way. Rodney and Cee-Cee had made it one of their cardinal rules never to appear in a photo, much less on video. Those things tended to work their way into the public domain and could be found by law enforcement from any place and at any time.

He felt his face turn stiff but he forced a smile and a nod. Not revealing what he was thinking was one of the tools of his trade.

The ting-ting-ting of a fork against a water glass attracted everyone's attention. "Dinner is served," announced an older gentleman Rodney hadn't met yet.

He breathed a sigh, excused himself, and found his way to his wife. He couldn't wait to get out of this room.

* * *

It took two hours to get away. People kept coming up and shaking his hand, congratulating them as a couple and thanking them for their service to their community. Rodney could barely eat a bite of the tenderloin and lobster, but at least he had the excuse of all the interruptions to disguise the fact that he really felt like throwing up.

"What are we going to do?" Cee-Cee asked. They were in Pinkie, heading west on I-40, and he had just gone through the conversations and his reservations.

"Let me think about it. I always figure out something. Meanwhile, if we hope to finish the Theater Guild job, I must play along with this hospital one as well."

Her face hardened in the light from the dashboard. "You're right. We've put in too much time. I didn't spend the summer in this climate that dries my skin to leather, just to give up that million dollar payday."

He chafed. A hard and fast rule, which he'd learned at the feet of some of the best cons in London, was to be ready to walk away at any moment. When something started to smell wrong, to feel like it was heading south, just get out. There'd always be another job. But not if you were in prison.

But the Theater Guild job was *so* close!

Pledges from the first gala, earlier this week, were already coming in. Big juicy checks. And he was putting them into the special account only he had access to, the moment they hit his hands. Of course, many of them were now in the form of credit card donations and electronic transfers. Which was another thing that had recently begun to eat away at him.

He remembered when money was cash, green stuff. And even big money would be handed over in the form of a check. Checks which were easy enough to forge, copy, or alter—skills he'd perfected in several languages in several countries.

He missed the good old days.

Chapter 14

The next day, Elsa and Dottie were back on the work schedule, and I tagged along again. We'd made our plan. Elsa would work the register all day and keep a discreet diary of the sales made in cash. I could substitute for her at the counter when she needed a break, and I would find little tasks that kept me nearby in order to help her keep an eye on what was going on.

Privately, I had to admit to being more than a little discouraged. What if Elsa had been mistaken about the hundred dollar bill she'd made such a fuss about? Maybe it had come in two or three days earlier, and had already been taken to the bank by the time she noticed it was missing. There were any number of scenarios. But if my gram was worried about being accused, then I had to dig in and find out the truth.

I felt I was on the right track with Benny Stevens. Everything I'd observed about his home life, and now the incidents Dottie and Elsa had told me where he got grumpy with the staff ... it seemed to point to his trying to conceal something.

Speaking of the devil, I spotted Stevens behind the counter with Elsa. I'd chosen to work among the clothing racks this morning. As in a retail store, the circular racks had little markers indicating where small, medium, large, and XL sizes could be found. But people would pull things out to look at them and then rehang them in the wrong slots. Men's shirts got mixed in with women's. It was a fairly easy spot for me to blend in, appear busy, and yet keep an eye on the rest of the shop. And if Benny started up with Elsa, giving her grief over any little thing at all, I was ready to pounce like a lioness.

A customer walked up to the counter and Benny became all smiles as the woman placed a small TV set on the desk. "And I'd like to get the stand this was displayed with," I overheard her saying. "A young man out back put my name on it." She handed over a price tag, and reached into her purse.

Elsa accepted her money and Benny offered to carry the television out to the customer's vehicle. While he was outside, I stepped over and whispered, "How's it going?"

"It's been a good morning," Elsa said. She pulled her little notebook from the pocket of her slacks and held it up.

A quick glance and some head-math told me nearly $2,000 had been received in cash already. "Wow, you really do move some things through here."

"A little more than a normal day, I'd say. A couple came in first thing to pay for a living room set they discovered yesterday." She slipped the notebook back into her pocket.

Benny came back through the front door, brushing dust off his hands. He stopped when he spotted me. Without so much as a glance to see who else might be nearby, he stepped in close. "You came to my house yesterday," he hissed through gritted teeth.

"Yes, I knew you had the afternoon off and thought we could speak privately, away from the store."

"What right did you have to do that? To talk with my wife and follow her after she left?"

I took a step back. The level of his anger was unsettling. "Bonnie invited me in. I only told her I wanted to talk with you."

"Okay, here I am. Let's have it then."

"Can we step into your office?" I turned in that direction.

We made it to the door before he turned on me again. "What are you doing here anyway? Has anyone officially asked you to snoop on us and ask questions of my volunteers? No, I think not." Gone was the guy who'd been so cooperative a few days ago.

I kept my voice low. "There's been an allegation that money has gone missing from the shop. One of the people dearest to me felt worried she would be accused of the theft. I've personally witnessed people taking items of value. Don't *you* want to know what's going on? You're the manager. Don't you answer to someone? If not a higher power …" I raised my eyes ceilingward "… then at least the deacons or treasurer, or somebody within the church?"

"Well, there aren't—" He stopped abruptly as an elderly man walked by, on his way to the adjacent restrooms.

Instead of finishing his thought, Benny turned on his

heel and walked into the office, pointedly closing me out.

I had intended to ask for access to the shop's profit and loss statements and the bank deposit receipts, but he clearly didn't intend to share information with me. Okay. Maybe this truly wasn't any of my business. But if money continued to disappear, I would simply find another way to get what I needed in order to prove it.

At the end of Elsa's shift, as we arrived home, she pulled out her little notebook. "Here you go. Grammy's spy network, at your service."

I laughed, loving the way she handled everything with humor. "I'll add this up and get the notebook back to you. We should continue to gather information for at least a few more days."

Sitting at the desk in our home office, I tallied the cash receipts on a calculator. More than three thousand dollars had come into the thrift shop, not counting credit or debit card transactions, in the few hours Elsa had been there. I ran the numbers twice, just to be sure. She'd even jotted the denominations of the bills, mostly fives, tens, or twenties. I could see why the hundred-dollar bill she'd received last week had been notable.

I wrote the total in the notebook and folded it closed, pondering what this meant. Granted, Elsa had told me this morning had been good for sales, with the one furniture purchase. But a quick calculation told me that if the shop brought in even two thousand a day, six days a week, that was close to fifty thousand dollars a month—more than a half million a year! I knew a few small retail shop owners who would kill for those kinds of numbers.

And the thrift shop had extremely low overhead—a donated building space, only two salaries and utilities to pay, and non-profit status on top of all that. The place was a little goldmine. A goldmine with practically no security in place.

We needed to make notes and gather information for a few more days and see how it compared, just to be certain I wasn't way off base in my estimates. Then, I needed to figure out what to do with this data. Who would I report it to?

Chapter 15

Rodney closed the refrigerator door, carrying two Michelobs by the bottle necks. He'd changed out of the suit he'd worn all day, opting now for a soft fleece tracksuit. His bare feet relished the cool hardwood floors after the restrictions of his stiff leather shoes.

"Cee-Cee? Honey, where are you?"

"In the study."

He passed the sleek dining table, through the living room and down the hall that led to the bedrooms. The owner had set up one of these as a study, and it suited his and Cee-Cee's needs perfectly.

"Brought you a cool refresher," he said, walking into the room. "What are you doing?"

She had pulled the drapes closed and stood at the desk, banded stacks of cash littering its surface. She was in the process of assembling and taping a cardboard box.

"Getting ready. You said we'd be clearing out soon."

He hadn't thought about this aspect of it, the cash. All of his attention had been focused on the cool mil he planned to siphon out of the Theater Guild donations.

That's what had taken up most of his afternoon. He'd planted the seed with two of the board members a few days ago, the idea that the bank where the Guild kept their checking account was charging exorbitant fees and had no decent financial instruments where they could park two million dollars and earn a good rate of return. He knew of a much better place, and all he needed were two signatures on the paperwork.

In reality he'd opened the account months ago, with himself as the legal owner. Getting the signatures was completely a bogus maneuver to make the board believe they knew why the donations were not accumulating in the account they knew about. Rodney assured them they could transfer money from the better, interest bearing account into the Guild's operating fund at a moment's notice when the refurbishment project began. And since that was not set to happen until well into the new year, at least six months from now, he and Cee-Cee would be long gone. By that time her expertise with computer transactions would have landed the million safely in their own account.

Her activity here at the desk suddenly clicked.

"My smart girl," he said, slipping an arm around her waist.

"I'm doing it a little differently this time. It makes me nervous to have all the money in the trunk of the car, and us driving across country like we'll be doing."

He eyed the box and noticed three others on the floor near the desk.

"Express Mail. As soon as we know what day we'll leave, I'll have the boxes shipped on ahead."

"Through the mail? Isn't that ris—"

"Baby, taking the cash in the first place was illegal. You think they'd come down any less hard because I sent it through the mail? Sure, there's a risk. Risk is the thing you and I thrive on, and it always has been." She flashed him the smile that had won him over, five years ago.

He still remembered the day he walked into that Houston pawn shop, hoping that—in the throes of another oil-bust period—he could walk out with some of the pricey jewelry those suddenly-broke millionaires were pawning in order to keep up the mortgages on their McMansions. And there she was, working behind the counter. She had a sparkle in her smile and a gleam in her eye, and he recognized a fellow con artist the moment the conversation started.

There was no way he was going to pull the gun out of his pocket, not against this classy lady. Instead, he asked her out for a drink after work. They saw each other every day after that and shared their life stories. She was impressed with the daring nature of his crimes—he'd walked right out of the most prestigious gallery in New York City with a Picasso rolled up inside his coat sleeve, keeping cool and calm as the alarm rang and three police cars roared up to the building. Completely unflappable, he'd given them the most cursory glance and strolled away.

Her adventures, he learned, were less grand in scale but no less impressive. Little Carole had been raised by her grandparents on her mother's side, taken in by the elderly Quakers when both her parents died in a theater collapse where the young pair had walk-on roles in Othello.

The Myers grandparents had very different ideas about parenting, and miserly ways. There was never money for ice cream or a pretty dress or a simple bottle of nail polish. During her junior year, Carole hopped a southbound bus and found herself in Charlotte, North Carolina.

She got a dream job in a laundromat where the owner paid her to sweep the floors, wipe down the washing machines, and give out quarters in exchange for dollar bills. They never did figure out why it seemed their business had dropped off by twenty percent that summer.

In those days, nearly any business had a high percentage of customers who paid in cash, and Carole could palm a twenty dollar bill just as easily as a single. In each new town she gave a slightly different variation of her name—Carole might be Carla or Cathy or Carolyn or Chris. Her last name could be Myers, but it could just as easily be Matthews or Marks or Malone or Manley—or Myerson.

She told Rodney during their first drink together that she simply loved making things up and changing to suit her whim. "For me, it's like getting a new hairstyle or buying a pair of red shoes. I pick a name that I know I won't have any trouble answering to."

She was very good with disguises, too, he learned. She had ways of appearing to gain or lose twenty pounds, even as far as making her face seem fuller or thinner. Wigs—she had a collection. Clothing styles—from ultra conservative to super hip. She had one persona where she emulated an older woman trying to dress and act half her age. People bought it every time.

They planned the Houston pawnshop job together, and two weeks later, a pile of cash and the best of the best jewelry had disappeared from the pawnbroker's safe. They were a thousand miles from Houston that same night. She wore a two-carat diamond from the heist, and he nicknamed her CC.

Robbie O'Flannery had a network of fences and forgers he'd put together from his days as a street kid in New York, all the way through his life as Rodney Day in London and back to the States. Less than a month after skipping Houston, the jewelry had been stripped down, serial numbers ground off, and the gemstones and precious metals were all converted to cash. The pair were well off and carefree. And Carole Myerson became Carole Day, although Rodney's pet nickname for her, Cee-Cee, was his alone to use.

Life in Cleveland became boring, so they hit the art scene in Chicago, then it was on to New York for a while. They always rented a showplace home in a pricey neighborhood, ingratiated themselves with the locals who had philanthropical intent, stayed a year or less, and then left—richer and ecstatic, albeit sometimes with the law on their heels.

They'd spent some time in Phoenix, but the area was so huge and spread out it was hard to find the right jobs to focus on. Albuquerque seemed a more manageable size of a city, the in-crowd smaller, the potential marks more well defined. And there was money in this area—Santa Fe fairly reeked of it. Hence the Theater Guild connection.

What would come next? Plans, in their line of work, were usually best left to the last minute, but now it seemed the Rockies and perhaps the Pacific Northwest were calling to them.

Now, he looked on, sipping his beer, as she packed the neatly banded money into the boxes.

Chapter 16

I carried a heavy table lamp to the sales counter for a customer. The thing must have been made of concrete, and the petite older woman seemed grateful for my assistance since she had two garments draped over one arm and a large teddy bear in her other hand. Benny Stevens stepped out of the office just then, not making eye contact with me but telling Elsa that he was leaving for an hour or so. He didn't glance back as he walked out the front door and got into his car.

Elsa nodded and proceeded to calculate the total of the woman's purchases. I saw her jot a quick note in her little book when the lady pulled out cash to pay.

"I'll help you get the lamp out to your car," I offered. "Do you have someone at home to carry it inside for you?"

"Oh yes, my neighbor is a big burly man and he's so

much help to me." She sent a sweet smile toward Elsa and Kiley and picked up the shopping bag containing her other items.

Outside, I removed the lampshade and set it carefully on the backseat of her Hyundai sedan, then I wedged the heavy lamp base into a spot where it couldn't roll around. She thanked me and reached into her coin purse. I realized she wanted to tip me so I quickly thanked her for visiting the shop and turned to go inside. At the door I nearly bumped into Carole Myerson.

"Oh, sorry," she said, skirting around me and heading toward the street where an older model Cadillac waited.

I stared in fascination at the classic car for a moment. Carole got into the passenger seat and the car pulled away. There was too much glare on the windows for me to clearly see the driver, but I assumed this was the husband she'd bragged about. I guess vintage autos were another of his interests, along with golf and playing the stock market.

Back inside, I walked over to Elsa as soon as she finished helping her current customer.

"Was Carole leaving for the day?" I asked.

"No. She said something about going to the bank and ... what else?"

Kiley piped up. "Meeting her husband for lunch."

"Thanks." I realized this was one of the first times since I'd been working here that both Benny and Carole were gone at the same time. I wondered if she'd locked the office when she left. My heart raced a little as I realized what I was about to do.

I scanned the room, spotting three of the volunteers. Everyone seemed busy with their tasks. Elsa and Kiley, the only ones with a clear view of the office door, had their attention on a new customer. I walked purposefully toward the office door and tried the knob. It turned in my hand, and I slipped inside, closing it behind me.

Most likely, both Carole and Benny would be gone an hour or more. But what if one of them had forgotten something and came back? I needed to hurry. Carole had left the duplicate copy of the bank deposit slip on her desk. I picked it up and memorized the two important numbers—the cash amount and the total of the whole deposit, including checks and credit card receipts. If this represented the income from yesterday, the cash was only about half the amount Elsa had recorded.

I replaced the deposit slip exactly where I'd found it, slid open the lower desk drawer, and looked through the tabs on the hanging file folders. The bookkeeper seemed to be very organized; all her files were the very same type I kept in my own desk. There was one labeled Bank Deposits. I picked it up and flipped through the slips inside. Consistently, the cash was a very similar amount each day. Without proof to the contrary, that was about all the information I was going to get here. I closed the drawer and moved to Benny's desk.

I'd been unable to find out much of anything about Carole Myerson online, but surely the store manager would have employee records. While volunteering at a place like this didn't necessitate a paper trail, a regular employee was different. When Carole applied for the job, she would have needed to give an address, social security number, and all the other paperwork that goes along with holding a job and collecting a paycheck.

A slender folder in his drawer seemed to hold the answer. There was an employment application for each of them. Disappointingly, Carole's address was only listed as a post office box. She'd checked her marital status as married, but only gave her husband's first name. So, if he had a different surname I still didn't have it. And a PO box address wasn't going to do me any good. Then something caught my eye. The zip code for the postal box was the same as my own.

Hm. That meant her mailbox was in the same neighborhood where I live. I know that post office. I've been going there my whole life. Maybe I could do something with that information. I'd need to give it some thought.

Voices—close by—caught my attention. I had no business in the office without Benny or Carole. I needed to invent a quick story or get myself out of here. I heard the restroom door open and close.

Pulling my camera out of my back pocket I snapped a quick picture of the employment application and then stuck the file back in the drawer. Back at Carole's desk I did the same with the slip showing today's deposit.

Phone back in pocket, I slipped to the door and opened it a tiny crack. The woman who'd gone into the restroom came out and walked past the office door without glancing in my direction. I waited five beats and walked out, bold as you please, as if I'd been in there on business. Which, I suppose, I had.

At the sales desk, there seemed to be a lull and I volunteered to take Kiley's place if she wanted a short break. She accepted with a smile and was already looking at her phone screen before she got to the alcove where the vending machines sat.

"I saw where you went," Elsa commented under her breath.

"Did anyone else notice?"

"I don't think so." Her eyes lit up. "So did you find anything juicy?"

"Maybe. I need to go over it again and also to look at your notes from both yesterday and today."

She held up the little notebook.

"Keep writing down the cash transactions for the rest of today. I'll borrow that when we get home this afternoon." I paused while she accepted a five dollar bill in payment for a book and watched the customer leave. "I have one question, and it's an important one."

"Sure."

"Who carries the cash from the register here to the office? Do you take it to them, or does either Benny or Carole come get it and take it in the office?" I couldn't very well start pointing fingers until I had a chain of custody for the money.

It would be simple enough for Benny to come out here and pick up the day's receipts, then pocket a random fistful of the cash on the way to the office, well before Carole ever saw any of it. Or, I supposed, it would be easy for either of them to implicate Elsa or another volunteer if they were the ones with their hands on a wad of money that no one had yet counted.

Elsa was giving it some thought. "Mostly, I'd say it's Benny. He stops by the desk right before I leave most days. It's early afternoon then, and Carole likes to write up the deposit and get it to the bank before they close."

"Does Carole ever pick it up herself?"

She nodded. "Sometimes."

"Do you or your helper ever carry it to the office?"

"No. We're usually too busy out here, plus we've been

told that we aren't supposed to take the money anywhere away from the register."

"Okay, thanks."

I glanced out the front window and saw a car pull to an abrupt stop. Benny was back from his meeting—quick one—and from his body language it appeared he was in a pissy mood. Again. He stomped into the shop, passed the desk, and closed the office door behind him with a *snick*. Would he notice that I'd been in there? I supposed we'd have the answer to that if he came storming back out.

Five minutes went by and all remained quiet. I thought about going in there and asking him straight out, but I simply didn't have enough evidence yet. Elsa's little notebook would help, but I needed more.

"If no one needs me here, I'm going to run a little errand," I told Elsa, once Kiley had returned to her post.

There was a good electronics store a few blocks away and I headed there. The clerk was a guy who looked about fifteen, with red hair and more pimples than freckles. Had I somehow slipped over that line where everyone was looking younger and younger? I'm not even close to forty yet—okay, closer than I'd like to be, but still.

"Hi," I said. "I need to purchase a nanny cam."

"Good idea," he answered with a smile. "Can't be too careful about who you're leaving with your little ones."

I didn't bother to correct him on the purpose for the hidden camera. "I don't know much about them."

"Okay, then, let's take a look at the basics," he said, leading me toward a shelf filled with boxes that depicted gadgets that looked like tiny one-eyed robots. "First off, is there an electrical outlet near the spot where you're gonna put it?"

No clue. "Um …"

"Better go wireless then. Batteries will cost you more, but you have the flexibility of moving it around the house."

"Good idea."

"As for features, I'd definitely recommend it have pan-and-tilt or a wide field of view, and you want to be able to zoom in and out. Gotta go HD. That just goes without saying. Night vision's a plus, too. And you gotta be able to monitor it from an app on your phone."

I couldn't help but notice the most expensive camera on the shelf had all these features.

"It's a plus to have both local storage—the more capacity, the better—and you'll want cloud storage too. Can't have someone disable the camera or bust it up and you've got no cloud backup. The monthly fees for that can vary quite a bit …"

"So, point me to the one that's got most of those features and is still affordable."

He plucked a small unit from the middle of the shelf, and ten minutes later I walked out with the camera that would do the trick, having spent way more than I wanted to.

I asked myself once again why I was doing all this, why it mattered. This wasn't *my* charity, wasn't *my* church to support, and I had no particular emotional connection to the place. Other than Elsa and Dottie. Those two, I care about. And I knew Elsa couldn't just sit back and watch someone get away with a crime. So that's what it boiled down to—neither could I.

I drove back to Heavenly Treasures, pondering how I was actually going to get the camera in place without any of the twenty-some regulars or the numerous customers catching me setting it up.

Dottie and Elsa's shift was officially over by the time I got there, and both were itching to get home. One look around the state of the store told me there was no way I could sneak a camera in, conceal and test it, and casually walk away without someone figuring out what I was doing. And the only way this was going to catch the thief in the act was for *no one* to know they were being watched.

I would simply have to come back after hours and break in to do my dirty work.

Chapter 17

I herded my little group out to my Jeep for the ride home.
"We could stop for ice cream," Elsa suggested.

"I do love that double brownie delight," added Dottie.
"Say, what's in the bag?"

She was sitting in the front seat and I'd dropped the bag
from A&B Electronics into the footwell there. I explained
about the camera and how I hoped to catch someone
slipping a few bills, or a bunch of them, into their pockets.

"If it's not happening at the time the sale is made—
and that would have to be outside of your work hours,
Elsa—it must be on the way from the register to the office.
That's why I asked you who usually picked up the money."

"My money's on that Carole woman. Somethin' strange
about her," Dottie said

"I was looking around the sales area and front of the

store, trying to figure out where I could place the camera so it catches activity at the register and would pick up anyone who might stick something in their pockets as they walk toward the office or restroom."

Elsa pulled the little notebook from her purse and handed it up to the front seat. "Today felt to me like sort of a slow day, but we still took in more than $800 in cash during my shift. Hey, there's the ice cream place."

I made the last-minute turn, and I seconded Dottie's suggestion for the double brownie delight. We parked and all three piled out and went into the store, where the scents of vanilla, chocolate, and peppermint swirled into my nostrils and filled my senses with happiness.

Back out in the car with the cones of our choice, we licked at them in silence for a couple minutes. My mind, however, was still working on what I'd seen earlier inside the office.

"Today's bank deposit included about half the amount of cash you recorded yesterday, Elsa," I said, catching a drip that threatened to run down the side of my waffle cone. "And that's not taking into account however much was sold during the late afternoon and evening."

"So, no matter who is actually taking the money, only a fraction is making it into the shop's bank account." Elsa had chosen mint chocolate chip, which was also looking good to me.

"I don't see any choice but to set up the camera and find out who it is. I've decided to go back tonight after hours."

"I'm going too," Elsa declared, mumbling through a large bite of her cone.

"Oh, no you're not. If someone were to see me moving around in there and call the cops …"

"Then you'd look far less guilty if you had an elderly woman with you. One who's a church member."

I was shaking my head vigorously. "No, no, no."

"You need the person with the key. How else are you getting in there?"

"And, by the way, I'm goin' along. No way is Miss Elsa doin' this thing without old Dottie."

I had to admit I hadn't got quite as far as figuring out how I would actually get inside, but I've been known to get into places where I shouldn't be. There's always a way.

"Wait a minute—key? You have a key to the thrift shop?" I held my hand back toward Elsa. "Hand it over."

She clamped her lips together and shook her head, like a kid refusing to eat spinach. I looked over at Dottie, whose mouth was similarly tight, although there was a big smile tilting her lips upward.

"You two. You can't gang up on me like this. I'll go through your purse—I'll take your whole keyring."

"Won't do you any good," Elsa said with a smirk.

"Why not …?" I stuffed the last of my cone into my mouth and watched her in my rearview mirror.

"Because she don't actually *have* the key?" Dottie supplied.

"But I do know where it is. Benny hid one outside after he accidentally locked himself out one time. I heard him telling a friend of his he didn't want that embarrassment, ever again."

"Okay, so where's it hidden?" I knew the moment I asked the question that I was fighting a losing battle. She wasn't going to give up this secret—or her chance at being in on the adventure.

* * *

We resembled three chubby ninjas as we climbed out of my car, which I parked half a block away, around the corner. All dressed in black, Elsa's puff of white hair and Dottie's luminously white teeth were the only things that showed up in the dark. I handed Gram a spare knitted cap I'd brought along, and told Dottie not to smile so much.

"Nothing will go wrong, but if we should get separated get yourselves back to the Jeep. I'm leaving it unlocked."

"Is that a good idea? This isn't the greatest neighborhood."

Gram had a point. "Okay, I'm locking the car. But the idea is the same. Get back here so we all go home together."

"Little dramatic, don' you think?"

"Let's hurry up and get in there," Elsa said. "I gotta pee."

Really? You didn't think to go before leaving home? But I didn't say it. I aimed my phone's flashlight at the sidewalk. Heaven forbid someone trip on uneven concrete and we end up in a way worse place—the hospital.

There was enough ambient light from the street lamps that it wasn't too difficult to make our way back to San Mateo, and Heavenly Treasures was only three doors to the south. Elsa pointed the way around the north side of the building, away from the driveway and halogen light that shone on it.

"He put the key under a fake rock by the back door," she said.

I aimed my light and spotted one of those Hide-A-Key devices made to look like a rock. Sure enough, two keys were inside. The first one I tried fit the back door, and just like that we were in.

Two very tiny night lights provided the only illumination at the back of the store, and we slowly edged through the cluttered space filled with tables of merchandise, racks of clothing, and the odd small furniture item (I know, because my knee found one little end table). Once we walked into the front room, there was light from the streetlights and another, brighter lamp at the sales desk.

Elsa seemed in a rush, and I remembered her bathroom request. "Yes, go, but don't switch on the light until you've closed the door behind you."

I had no idea how much light could be seen from the street, and I wondered how often, or if, the police patrolled these businesses. I sent out a little prayer that if they did it would be later, like middle of the night. Heavenly Treasures was open until six p.m. and it was now approaching nine. Traffic out on the busy thoroughfare raced by without a pause, but I didn't want to take any chances.

Luckily, at home I'd studied the instructions for how to mount the camera and activate it. I just needed to figure out the ideal location. Dottie and I conferred on that and decided there was a good spot at the top of a shelf of trinkets near the register. From that perch, the camera could point downward toward the sales desk, and the wide angle would still pick up people walking toward the office and restroom.

I found a wooden chair, set it up in front of the shelf, and climbed up. I needed something in which to conceal the camera. There was a cute stuffed rabbit, but someone might decide to buy it, and there would go my spy gear. I could take an old book and hollow out the center, but that seemed like a lot of work and we were trying to hurry.

Dottie tapped my leg. "Think this'll work?" She handed me some crumpled material. "It's the dust cloth I used today. Jus' set the camera, dump this on top of it so only the lens peek out. Nobody gonna buy no dirty old rag."

She had a point.

"What if Benny notices it, thinks it looks sloppy. He could pull it down to put in the laundry."

She made a *pfft* sound. "You ever seen Benny clean up anything around here?"

It was getting near my bedtime and I didn't have the energy to think of all the reasons that might not work. If I thought too hard, I'd come with a dozen ways in which this whole idea was dumb.

"Where's Elsa? She's been in there a long time," I said. "Can you go check on her while I get this thing set up?"

I got the device in place, set the dust cloth on it, and stepped off the chair. The rag was rumpled enough not to look important, flat enough to not show up well, except maybe to somebody six and a half feet tall. And that was not Benny Stevens.

With the wooden chair back in place on the other side of the room, no one would have a reason to poke around on top of the shelving unit.

Elsa and Dottie returned just as I was opening the nanny cam app on my phone. I'd already synced it to the camera, now I just needed to check and see how the picture was coming through.

"I wish I could see how well this is going to work in daylight," I told them.

With the room in darkness, all I could see were three gray blobs moving about. At least the angle looked decent. The lights from the street outside showed the outline of the sales desk and cash register. I could barely make out the shapes of the office and restroom doors against the white-painted surrounding wall, but hopefully that was enough. I hoped I wouldn't regret passing up the night vision option.

We three were on the work schedule again tomorrow, so I could check my setup and if something wasn't quite right, I supposed I could always pretend to be cleaning the top of the shelf and rearrange things slightly. Simple!

Maybe.

Chapter 18

The study was beginning to look like a postal service annex, Rodney thought as he pushed past the stacks of boxes. He missed leaning back in his chair with his feet up on the desk, having a scotch and a cigar.

Cee-Cee bustled down the hall, spotted him, and came to a halt in the doorway. She seemed agitated.

"You're home early, darling. Errands completed?"

His British accent softened her expression, and she walked into the study.

"Yes, my salon appointment went fine. I kind of like the girl I found here. She knows exactly how to get my hair the right length, and she's an expert with the color." She ran her fingers through the feathery blonde cap on her head.

"I sense something more. May I make you a drink?"

She nodded. He pushed a carton aside and reached for the gin decanter on the bar cart.

"I had an unsettling experience at the post office," she said, taking the G&T he handed her. "That woman who's been snooping around the thrift shop. She was there. I was standing in line and she was at the window. She asked about the post office box number, the address I gave on the application for Heavenly Treasures."

He froze in place.

"What else did she say?"

"I didn't hear much at all, just the number. She's on to something. I can feel it."

"Did she see you?"

"No. Well, I'm fairly certain she didn't. I'd been standing in line, so her back was toward me. I ducked out of the line and pretended to be busy addressing an envelope at one of those little stations full of forms and such. She finished her business at the window and left."

"Were you wearing your—"

"No, I was dressed exactly like this." She pointed her free hand toward her jeans and tunic top. "She's never seen me in anything other than my frumpy outfits."

Rodney smiled. He wanted to assure Cee-Cee that she never looked frumpy at all, but this was not the time.

"What about the car?"

"It was in the post office parking lot, of course, but she's never seen me coming or going from the thrift shop in the Cadillac." She became pensive and then took a long swig of her drink.

"You can quit the charity shop job any time, you know," he said gently. "Don't take unnecessary chances." More than one of their con artists friends had gone to prison because they didn't let go and leave quickly enough.

"How much longer do we need to stay here, in Albuquerque?" She set her empty glass on the desk.

"Donations are still rolling in. In fact, I'm supposed to give a keynote speech to the Rotary Club dinner tonight. Supporting the theater isn't quite their normal project, but I think I can make the case and gather some decent checks."

"We've definitely decided to pass on the children's hospital plan, right?"

He nodded. "Several reasons, not the least of which is that it would entail staying here through the holidays. Two more months, I believe, would be pushing our luck. The theater board has already begun asking for specific numbers, and they'll want to see an accounting of the money in the account very soon."

She visibly relaxed. "I can mock up some statements that will keep them pacified for a little while …"

"But the danger is in one of them knowing someone at the bank and asking to see the bank's actual records."

"Exactly."

"Cee-Cee, we need to be ready to move on short notice. Gather your most important items …"

They each had a short list of non-negotiable things: the bag of loose gemstones, enough cash to get them established in a new locale, a few handy bits of disguise, the Picasso—it amounted to a small duffle bag for each of them. Everything else could be abandoned.

"So, how soon?" she asked. She paced to the far end of the room and stared out into the back yard where the sycamore trees were beginning to turn yellow.

"A week, maybe less." He stepped up behind her and rubbed her shoulders. The muscles were taut as wire. "It will help you relax if you abandon the shop gig."

"It's just so damn … lucrative."

"Cee-Cee …"

"I know. One or two more days. I need to make sure I didn't leave any personal things behind."

"Darling, you can accomplish that in an hour. Check your desk, plead a stomach ailment, and get out."

"I'll think about it."

"Does anyone at that shop know where we live?"

She shook her head. "I don't see how. I never speak of our personal lives with any of them. Conversation revolves around the weather and whatever was on the news last night."

"Good."

But the question gave him reason to pause. There were others who did know where they lived and would be able to link the couple to some missing money. A *lot* of missing money. Unable to resist the temptation to show off their lifestyle, if only a little, they'd hosted a party of the top-level donors, board members, and a few celebrities connected with the Theater Guild. It was more than four weeks ago now, and those in that crowd had probably attended a dozen more posh events in the meantime. Would they remember the distinctive house in the older part of town, the original country club neighborhood? He couldn't rule it out.

If Cee-Cee was insistent on going back to that shabby thrift shop another time or two, he would spend his days scouring the rental house for any traces of them, any scrap of information that could tie into their past or future plans and allow the law to catch up with them.

As a final act, he could arrange for a cleaning team to

come in after they'd left the property. He would claim that one of them had contracted a bad viral infection and the place should be sanitized thoroughly. That should take care of any fingerprints or bits of their DNA that might be left behind.

At least he hoped so. He set his empty glass down and cleared his throat. "Well, we'd best get moving, dress ourselves up and put on our most winning faces for the new group of donors tonight."

Cee-Cee sighed and followed him to the bedroom.

Chapter 19

I sneaked into the bathroom at the shop and locked myself in one of the two stalls, pulling my phone from my pocket. The nanny cam app opened and, for the fourth time that day, I played the footage. There was Elsa at the register. Today's other cashier was Nancy Pomeroy, the woman I'd met on my first day, the one with an affinity for art. I'd noticed that on the chillier autumn mornings she was opting to work indoors more often.

I'd had my eye on her, but it didn't seem that she felt the same entitlement toward the cash as she had with the donated items out back. Plus, as far as I knew, these past two days were the first time she'd worked at the sales desk.

My guess at the camera angle had turned out right. The video showed both the pathway to the office and the desk transactions, and the electronics clerk's recommendation that I get the zoomable feature was paying off. I could home in and see the cash in their hands, right down to the denominations of the bills. It had turned out to be a very cool setup. The only problem was that I hadn't yet caught anyone snitching a single dollar.

So, was it money well spent or a total waste?

On the two days I'd been spying, Benny was the person who picked up the day's receipts and carried them into the office. Carole had taken yesterday afternoon off, and so far had not come in this morning. Until she filled out a new deposit slip with the current receipts, there wouldn't be anything to compare with.

Unless something revealed itself in the next couple of days, I could only assume that either Benny or Carole was pocketing the cash after it was taken behind the closed door of the office. I could look for another opportunity to get in and move the camera there. That could be risky. They were both very familiar with everything in that room. I would have to choose my moment wisely.

I let myself out of the bathroom stall and pocketed my phone again. Eugene Towner had replaced Nancy Pomeroy at the sales desk.

"Everything okay?" Gram asked when I walked up to the desk. "You were in there a long time."

Flashback to childhood when my mother monitored my digestion, almost daily. I ignored the question.

"Are Benny or Carole in the office now?" I asked.

"Benny is. Carole has the morning off," Eugene supplied.

"Thanks."

Perfect chance to talk with him alone. I decided to bring up the personal question about his own financial situation. Venturing there would either reveal something or get me kicked out. I tapped on the door and decided to take the benevolent tactic.

"Hey, Benny. Got a minute?"

As far as I could tell, he was doing nothing but staring at the wall. He nodded halfheartedly and I sat down in front of his desk.

"Some of us have been a little concerned," I began. "You seem awfully tense this week. Everything going okay?"

He gave me a steady stare.

"I don't mean to pry, and I would certainly understand if there were, um, some kind of concerns at home—kids, finances, anything like that." Something flickered across his face, but I couldn't exactly read it. "Or maybe it's just the shop. Things have been pretty busy lately. Have you asked for some time off or something? It might help."

"I can't afford that."

"But surely you're due some paid vacation …"

"Probably, but it's—" He spun his chair around, his back to me, and I wondered if I'd just opened the door to one of his recent tirades. But when he turned toward me, his expression was glum. "I could be in danger of losing this job. The thrift shop isn't as profitable as it used to be, and the church treasurer has brought it up more than once. I'm worried that the deacons will vote me out, cut back the shop hours, and just run the place entirely by volunteers."

"When did this downturn start to happen?"

He seemed surprised that I took him seriously and didn't just blow it off by suggesting that he could surely find another job elsewhere. Which, of course, is precisely what I probably would have said.

"The last few months … I can't say exactly when."

"Has there been a big drop, like all at once? Or has it been more gradual?"

"I'd have to go back through the treasurer's reports to be sure. I'd guess four or five months ... over the summer. I've had my hands full with scheduling and managing the people. Guess I haven't kept as close an eye on the income and expenses as I should have."

Maybe money management just was not his forte, judging by the personal lifestyle of the family. I'd definitely gotten the feeling that Bonnie didn't have a concern in the world and just bought whatever she and the kids needed. And maybe Benny couldn't add two and two to come up with four.

I studied his face for some sign that this whole story was a cover, a way to steer me clear of asking directly about the missing cash, but I couldn't tell. He seemed genuinely worried about losing the job. Maybe it paid more than I guessed.

"You do remember the day Elsa said a hundred dollar bill was missing?"

He thought about it as he removed his glasses. "Oh, yes. A week or more ago, that was."

"Right. What if that wasn't the first time? What if it's been going on for a few months now?"

Still no sign that he might be the guilty party. His bald head wasn't sweaty, and he sat there polishing his lenses with steady hands. So, maybe it truly was my other suspect, the mild-mannered, sweet old lady with the checkbook.

Benny was saying something I'd missed. "... don't want them to know."

I nodded, but my brain had switched over to Carole. If the shop's profitability had indeed dipped within a couple of months after she started working here, that seemed suspect. I thought about asking Benny if I could access Carole's computer and take a look at the accounting reports, but I didn't want to alert her too soon.

Plus, if she hadn't shared the P&Ls with her manager already, there was a strong possibility that she was doctoring the records anyway. I could wait.

"When will Carole be back to work?"

He turned to look at the schedule on the wall. "Hm. She should have been in this morning."

I thanked him for his candor and assured him I wouldn't be reporting anything he'd told me to the church authorities. It wouldn't serve my cause, or I should say Elsa's, if they sent people storming in here looking for a scapegoat. I wanted to know the truth and have a case all laid out before we brought them in.

Whether Benny Stevens would agree with my approach, or not, would depend on how well his story held up. I didn't like to think I'd just been played, but it was possible.

Chapter 20

The Rotary dinner last night had been a big success, especially Cee-Cee in a chic business suit that managed to accentuate her shape and reveal a hint of cleavage. As soon as she passed from table to table, after his keynote speech, the checks began rolling in. She had a way of leaning toward a man that made him want to part with some cash. Even the president of the local club seemed surprised at how much they'd raised for the theater.

Rodney lingered over his lunch after his wife left for her day job. She had already used some gadget on her phone to electronically deposit last night's checks, and she knew of some way to process the credit card transactions, although she cautioned him that those were much more traceable.

He felt as though he was keeping up a false image—a brave front, if you will—to appear more tech savvy than he really was. He could toss around some of the terminology but, truthfully, didn't have a feel for it. The new ways of doing things were beyond him and he hated it.

Would Cee-Cee leave him behind in her ability to keep up with the new ways of doing things? What if she actually left him, moved on? He dreaded that thought.

"I'm not ancient!" he shouted to the Picasso as he walked into the closet and stared at his prized possession.

He realized he'd never be able to get away with a painting like this, ever again. Museums and galleries had much more sophisticated security systems nowadays. It seemed the con games of today all involved knowing how to hack computer systems, to get into large corporations and banks and such. It was a young man's game now.

Back in the day, it was all about your story. Walking into a bank, talking to the manager, gaining trust and then taking advantage of it. Fitting in with the right social set, getting invited into their homes, learning enough about them to figure out the combinations to their safes. Hell, even walking brazenly into the master bedroom while a party was going on downstairs and walking out with a diamond necklace in the pocket of your tux. He'd done it more than a few times.

Walking into a man's study on the pretense of admiring his collection of photos of himself with important people (those types of guys *always* had some of those). A quick peek into a desk drawer, ripping a couple of checks from the middle of a checkbook. He puffed up a little—with a short sample of someone's handwriting and a copy of their signature, he was an excellent forger. He could operate that way. But so few people wrote checks anymore, or even simple notes. It was getting harder and harder to locate a checkbook in their homes.

And the crowd who flashed a lot of 'bling' as they called it, who spent money on ridiculous items like a diamond-encrusted highchair for their baby—they were young rap stars or sports figures. They weren't going to invite an old man like him to their parties.

He could work up a story, become someone's manager or agent, he supposed. When you read stories of those instant-success types, it always seemed like it was someone in their inner circle who ripped them off for millions. It took time to work your way into those positions. The backstory of a con man no longer depended on a news clipping from a paper somewhere or getting a couple of important people to introduce you around within their crowd—he would have to build a whole identity online, establish all those profiles and accounts and *friends*. He just didn't have the heart anymore to learn the jargon and pursue it. And those who might've helped him—his old-time buddies—they were all gone, either died or in prison or retired to a cabin in Montana or something.

His shoulders slumped and he stared at the Picasso.

"Well, old friend, it's time for us to move along again. Maybe a cabin in Montana wouldn't be so bad after all."

How long did they have before the Albuquerque gig would fold? A couple of days? A week, at the outside, he imagined. Time to get moving.

He lifted the framed painting down from the wall and carried it into his study. Very carefully, he began to pry out the pins that held it in the frame. Then came the staples which attached the canvas to the stretcher bars. From the bottom drawer of the desk, he fetched the metal tube in which the rolled-up painting had safely traveled around the world with him.

With the end caps in place, Rodney carried the tube out to the Cadillac in the garage. He raised the trunk lid and then the carpeted floor of the compartment. He'd constructed a little space where the tube fit exactly, where it couldn't roll around or get crushed by anything else.

He sighed as he placed the piece into its hiding spot. They were nearly ready to hit the road.

Back in the study, he disassembled the picture frame and stretcher. It wouldn't do to leave them behind, where the landlord or cleaner might question why an empty frame had been left. Those little details were the type of thing that tripped up too many great thieves. He would dump the pieces in various trash receptacles around the city.

His gaze fell on the stacks of boxes Cee-Cee had packed. She'd left instructions for sending them out and now it was up to him to start the process. He drummed his fingers on the desktop, planning his moves. He shouldn't drive around the city with the Picasso hidden in Pinkie's trunk. First, he'd better bring the painting back inside and find a spot to keep it in the house until they were actually ready to drive away.

That done, he returned to stare at the boxes once more.

Chapter 21

My talk with Benny Stevens had revealed a lot about his money worries, but I wasn't yet convinced about his innocence. Before I could report anything about the money theft, either to the church officials or the police, I needed more than speculation. The hidden camera hadn't picked up anything out in the sales area, but what went on behind the closed door of the office was still suspect.

In the guise to getting right back to work, I pulled my faithful old chair up to the display shelf, picked up the dust cloth, with the camera concealed in its folds, and carried it around the shop with me.

Dottie and I had worked out our maneuver. She would come up with something that demanded Benny's attention near the back of the shop. Once they were out of sight, I would slip into the office and find a spot for the camera.

I'd done a little visual recon when I was in there earlier and thought I had a good place for it, on top of a four-drawer file cabinet that sat in the corner nearest Carole's desk.

I needed to move fast. Benny had already told me he expected Carole to arrive for work at any minute. On that, I enlisted Elsa's help. She was to grab Carole—physically, if necessary—and ask for help with something at the register. It helped that Carole was the main person who seemed to know much about it.

It was 11:25 when the plan went into action. I watched Dottie as she led Benny into the second room. Her voice raised to draw attention, she seemed to have the situation in control. I caught Elsa's eye and then I ducked into the office, my extra-heavy dust cloth in hand. It took me less than a minute to set the camera in place, but then I had to look for some items to help conceal it. I settled on a couple of books and a black three-hole punch that didn't seem as if it was used very often. I stacked the items and rechecked my camera angle using my phone.

It would have helped to set the device higher, more than six feet above the floor, but there was simply nothing in the room to accommodate that without putting it out in plain sight. This would have to do.

I heard voices outside the door. Too close. I backed away from the file cabinet and began dusting the top of Carole's desk.

"What are you doing in here?" Benny asked.

"Just thought I'd clean up a little."

"I'm going to lunch," he announced, picking up a lightweight jacket that hung over the back of his chair. And with that, he was gone.

Since he hadn't ordered me out of the office, I used

the next few minutes to snoop while I dusted. Until I heard Carole's voice out front. Good old Elsa had done her part by detaining the woman. I made a show of dusting the woodwork on the office door as I exited, giving Elsa the all-clear to let the bookkeeper go.

I'd hoped to speak with Carole today, to see if I could pry anything out of her that would implicate Benny in the money theft. But it was too soon for that. I should let the camera run inside the office for at least a couple of days, and then maybe I'd have more ammunition. I gave her a smile and stepped aside so she could get to her desk.

"I gave her this morning's receipts," Elsa said under her breath.

"Good idea." If the thief actually was Carole, this would be her opportunity—alone in the office, fresh cash in hand.

I dropped the dusty cloth on the counter and walked into the bathroom. In the privacy of my favorite stall I looked at the camera app on my phone. There was Carole on the live feed. She placed the money Elsa had given her in the center of her desk, then put her purse in a drawer. She wasted a little time fiddling with her hair and then pulled a bottle of water from the tiny fridge on Benny's side of the room.

Finally, she settled onto her chair. I felt a little impatience, hoping no one would come into the bathroom and need this stall.

Carole took her sweet time, booting up her computer (no, I couldn't read anything on the screen) and pulling a pad of what appeared to be bank deposit slips from the desk's center drawer. She began counting the cash and writing numbers on the deposit slip. I didn't see her remove any of the bills or slip anything at all into a pocket or drawer.

Until she appeared to be nearly done with the task. As she reached for a paperclip to fasten the money and checks to the deposit slip, she very quickly slid the drawer open with her left hand and pulled some of the bills into the drawer. It was closed again in less than two seconds.

I had her! I slid through the options on the app and made sure I'd saved the short video clip.

Now, what to do with the information? Should I stomp in there and demand to look in the drawer, or would it be better to gather more evidence first, to record multiple incidents so there was a clear pattern and no doubt as to what she was doing?

A sound caught my attention. Back on the live camera feed now, I saw Benny Stevens enter the office. He wished Carole a good afternoon in a sarcastic tone and stalked over to his desk, pulling his jacket off. Then he looked at the top of the file cabinet.

"What the hell ..." He was staring directly into the camera. He reached for the books I'd set up there.

Uh-oh. Busted.

I saw him look toward Carole, who now had a puzzled expression on her face. He walked to the office door and flung it open, camera in hand.

"Mrs. Higgins! Please come in the office this minute."

I could not let this happen. I lurched out of the stall and came out of the bathroom at a run.

"It's not her doing," I panted, trying to keep my voice down.

He spun on me. I realized the entire shop had gone dead quiet and everyone in the place was staring at us.

"Can we take this outside?" I asked, starting toward the front door. Gram came out from behind the counter and followed me, leaving Benny with no choice but to come along.

"What is this device—a camera?" he demanded before the front door had even closed.

"Let's not share this news with everyone," I said, stepping along the sidewalk to a spot where I hoped we would not be the main attraction for the volunteers and customers.

We didn't get quite that far away. "What are you up to?" His face was livid, the top of his shiny head bright red.

Elsa pushed forward and stood between us. "We're just trying to find out—"

"*You* are, as of this minute, off the volunteer schedule. Forever."

I gently took her shoulders and moved her aside. "Why? For trying to find out how much money is missing and where it's going? Which, if you're as completely innocent as you tried to convince me, might just save your job and your reputation."

He settled down a little. "So … what. Planting a camera in my office is the way to do that?"

I lowered my voice even further, making him step closer. "I saw Carole shove some cash into her desk drawer, just a few minutes ago. Don't you think we should ask her about that?"

"Did it ever occur to you that we hold out a little money for office expenses and such? For the coffee fund?"

Well, no, that actually hadn't occurred to me.

I stammered slightly and was about to suggest we walk right back in there and ask Carole about it, but he'd already turned and stomped back inside.

Eugene Towner was standing at the door and Benny bumped against his shoulder. "What are you staring at? Get out of the way, you useless—"

Elsa and I exchanged a wide-eyed stare. Benny's reaction seemed way over the top. Through the front window I watched as he slammed my camera down on the sales desk and proceeded through the store, berating a couple more of the volunteers.

Psychologists say that all anger stems from fear, but Benny's rants recently seemed overkill for a guy who just didn't want to lose his job. W*hat* was he so afraid of?

Chapter 22

Rodney's cell phone was ringing—he could hear it in the garage—but at the moment he was far too busy to drop everything and run back to the study. Most likely, it was Dennis Sanchez from the Donner Hospital board of directors. The man had been most persistent about gaining Rodney's help, ever since he'd heard about the success of the Theater Guild's fundraiser. That was one of the downsides of working within a smaller city. All of these people knew each other and compared notes.

He finished securing the false bottom in the trunk of the Cadillac and turned to pick up the two Express Mail boxes he'd carried out with him. Into the trunk they went. He had his list of errands for the afternoon, and then he would pick up Cee-Cee from the thrift shop.

They'd carefully worked out their plan last night.

Mailing no more than four boxes a day—all from different post office branches within the city—it would take them three days to get all the cash on its way. Half of the boxes were addressed to the various branches of the post office in their first destination city; the others would be delivered two states away. General delivery, no questions asked.

The two of them would take turns picking up the packages. One person, collecting multiple Express Mail boxes at once, could potentially attract attention. It would take time to locate each office, to time the pickups a few hours apart, and to nonchalantly walk away. But the precise execution of the plan was crucial to their success. They knew this from previous jobs, and it didn't do to deviate from the proven formula.

He went back into the house to bring out two more boxes. Checking the door locks, picking up his cell phone and keys, he headed out for his errands. He drove out of the neighborhood and headed north on Rio Grande Boulevard. His first stop was across the river, a postal branch in the northeast heights.

* * *

Carole slipped her cell phone into the side pocket of her purse, which sat near her feet at the desk. Why hadn't Rodney answered? Perhaps he was driving. She hoped her voice message conveyed just enough of the mild panic she was beginning to feel. A camera! Who would have thought the snoopy young woman would do such a thing.

Benny had stormed out of the office ten minutes ago, leaving the door standing open. She watched as he confronted the old lady volunteer at the sales desk, then as the young snooper came charging out of the restroom to the old woman's defense. The three had walked out the front door, where Carole caught a glimpse of them in a rather heated discussion out on the sidewalk.

She'd eased the office door shut, folded the pilfered cash into two wads, and jammed them into the cups of her bra. With an eye on the door she'd called Rodney. And then he didn't pick up. Her heart was pounding, and she could not let her nervousness show when the others came back inside.

She pulled out a folder of invoices and turned on her computer. Her fingers jittered nervously over the keys. There was no way she could enter data accurately, but she could pretend to be busy. A glance at the clock told her it would be another two hours before Rodney came to pick her up, unless he checked his messages and heard the panic in her voice. She exhaled, releasing the pent-up breath. For now, all she could do was to appear calm and address any questions with her usual wide-eyed innocence.

Benny returned about five minutes later. It seemed much of his anger had dissipated, but she could tell he was still in a mood.

"What's this?" he asked, picking up a small decorative box from his desk.

She took a long breath before answering, taking her eyes reluctantly from her computer screen. "I don't know. Maybe one of the volunteers put it there."

They did that sometimes, asked the manager about an item they thought might be particularly valuable. Mariah Blinker knew how to price a lot of things, but even she didn't always seem to know what the value of an unusual item should be. Carole didn't remember anyone walking into the office since she'd arrived, but her mind hadn't exactly been on the movements of others today. The conversation with Rodney, and the plans for leaving the city, had dominated.

Benny sat at his desk and she returned to her work, sneaking a peek at her phone screen to see whether Rodney had responded. Maybe a text? If so, it would be the first time. She had to admit that her partner was still pretty much a newbie at using the cell phone. He made and received calls—that was about it.

She pocketed her phone and pretended she needed to use the restroom. But the snoopy one with the long auburn ponytail was at the sales desk, talking with the older woman. Somehow, those two were related. Carole wasn't certain, but she'd observed that they came and went at the same time, along with a black woman in her early sixties. The three seemed very chummy, and that was the reason, Carole guessed, that Charlie—yes, that was her name!—had leapt to the other woman's defense when Benny charged out there on a rant.

She closed the office door and walked softly toward the sales room, intent on getting out the back door without Charlie seeing her. That one had far too many questions, and she seemed sharp enough to connect the dots and figure it out, maybe even back to the places where Carole had previously worked.

Her pace picked up and she dashed between two tall shelving units, forgetting for a moment that she was supposed to be acting fifteen years older and slightly feeble. She immediately got back in character. Right now she needed a private place to speak with Rodney. She needed him to come pick her up. Now. Or she would need to get a taxi and have it pick her up a few blocks away. But her purse was still in the office, and it contained too many things that could connect her to the fundraiser con. She couldn't simply walk away, not at this moment.

She stepped out the back door, pausing to study the activity around her. Two of the volunteers were helping someone unload a bunch of boxes from the back of their SUV. A younger man—his name was Todd, if she remembered correctly—had one end of a sofa, which he was lifting toward the tailgate of a pickup truck. No one glanced in her direction.

She rounded the corner of the building and stood in a shaded spot, pulling her phone from the pocket of her slacks. Nothing from Rodney. She called him again.

"Cee-Cee, what a delightful surprise," he said. At least he knew how to read the caller ID on his phone's screen.

"You didn't get my earlier message?"

"Sorry. Must have forgot to check."

"Where are you—home?"

"No, darling. I'm at a post office in the Alameda area. Just going inside with two of your packages."

Great. He was at least twenty-five minutes away, *if* he started toward Heavenly Treasures right now.

"I need to get out of here. I'll explain when I see you."

There was a long pause at his end. "Is it vital that I come directly there, or shall I mail the packages first?"

Both were important, but she could stall a while longer, pull her wide-eyed 'I don't know what you're talking about' act. Surely no one would demand a strip search, even if they did have her on camera putting the money into the desk. At worst, they might ask that she empty her purse. In fact, it would be better if she continued to work at her desk as if nothing unusual had happened. She needed to calm down and stay in character.

"Never mind, honey. I'll be fine here. Just continue with the mail, and come pick me up at the regular time."

"If you're certain?"

"Yes. I'm sure." She put the phone away and walked calmly toward the back door, retracing her steps.

She'd no sooner walked into the front sales area than she heard an urgent shout: "Call 911!"

Chapter 23

In the aftermath, I tried to remember where everyone had been. But the shop was as busy as usual, and keeping tabs on all the workers and the customers was like herding kittens. All I knew was that Elsa and Kiley were working behind the sales counter. I'd just asked Dottie if she could use some help folding a huge bedspread that someone had left draped over a table. Those were the only ones I could definitively pinpoint.

Oh, and the body. Benny Stevens was dead at his desk. But I'm getting a little ahead of myself.

Mariah Blinker was standing in the office doorway, less composed than I'd ever seen her. She was apparently the person who'd shrieked that we needed to call 911 because something was wrong with Mr. Stevens. Everyone else seemed frozen in place so I pulled out my own phone and made the call.

Then I walked over to Mariah, taking her by the shoulders, trying to get her to calm down enough to look directly at me. After a few seconds of watching her wag her head back and forth, I let go of her and walked into the office.

Carole's chair was pushed up to her desk and there was no sign of her. Benny was slumped over his desk, one hand in the center drawer. I felt a little creeped out but edged over to him and touched the side of his neck. I couldn't feel a pulse, but then I'm not really the best at those kinds of things. His face looked sort of bluish and there was a rash spreading on his hands and arms.

An ambulance, a fire truck, and a police cruiser came rolling up to the front door about a minute later. I'd already snatched my hand away from Benny's neck and put a good safe distance between me and what was probably (no, I knew for sure) a dead guy.

The EMTs brushed past me as I scooted out of the office doorway. Dottie was trying to get Mariah calmed down. Elsa had planted herself near the door, beside the police officer, and was announcing to everyone in the building that they needed to stay calm and not to leave. The cop looked a little amused, since Elsa had to be his great-grandmother's age.

"What happened?" I turned to see that it was Nancy Pomeroy who had spoken.

I shrugged. If the volunteers out back had not already heard about Benny's outburst earlier, I wasn't going to be the one to tell them. He could have easily brought on a heart attack by the way he'd been acting.

Word spread quickly, and I saw a half-dozen of the

regular volunteers hovering near the back of the room, whispering among themselves. Carole Myerson stood slightly apart from the rest, and I briefly wondered what she'd been doing in that part of the building instead of being at her desk.

Mariah had detached herself from Dottie and edged into the office doorway, watching the EMTs at work. One of them asked her to step aside as he walked toward the exit and said a few words to the cop. Apparently, it wasn't good news. He walked out to the back of the ambulance and retrieved a gurney. I noticed that he tossed a square of folded black plastic on top. A body bag.

The cop went into action, speaking into his radio and then turning to the gathering. "Folks, I'm sorry to say that there's been a death. We'll need everyone to stay here a little while and help us out by answering some questions. The medical investigator is on the way and, hopefully, we'll be able to let everyone leave before too long."

He turned toward the firemen. After a brief confab, the fireman who'd driven their truck turned over the Closed sign, went outside, and walked around to the side of the building where the rolling gate allowed access to the back building and parking area. With that closed off, no one would be able to make a run for the back exit.

The fire truck left, a white SUV with the medical investigator's logo arrived and the driver, wearing a white coat and carrying a little medical kit, came in and followed the cop's pointing finger to the office. The two EMTs stood aside and let the man do his job.

Meanwhile, two more cars arrived and a pair of plainclothes cops came in. They were obviously more experienced at group questioning. They divided the small crowd and asked basic questions about who worked here and who was a customer. The customers got away with giving their contact details and then were allowed to check out and leave the premises.

Those who worked at the shop answered the basics—what area do you work in, when was the last time you saw Mr. Stevens, can you provide any additional information? Then contact info and dismissal with the proviso that they might be back in touch if any further questions arose. I have to confess that I awaited my turn at the questions with a whole lot of trepidation.

Here's why: I had seen and touched the body, and I'd bet more than a few bucks that it wasn't a simple heart attack or stroke that got Benny Stevens. I was one of the last to speak to him, and it wasn't exactly a friendly little chitchat. People would remember that. They would also remember that we'd gone outside, and the fact that people indoors couldn't overhear what was being said, they could put all kinds of words in my mouth, including threats. And, okay, I *had* kind of threatened Benny—just a little—because he was picking on my Gram.

So, should I just be upfront with the cops and tell them all this? Probably.

Should I admit that I'd kind of unofficially been investigating the fact that money had gone missing and Benny was my chief suspect? Maybe, maybe not.

My investigation had nothing to do with Benny's death, but would the police believe that?

My whole train of thought was interrupted when I overheard Mariah Blinker, speaking in a low tone with Elsa.

"I was a nurse's aide, you know, before I retired," she said. "Of course, it was in a family practice, but we studied the symptoms of all kinds of things. Personally, I think Mr. Stevens might have been poisoned. His skin tone looked really bad."

I edged over to the pair. "Is 'really bad' a medical opinion?"

Mariah pulled herself up to her full height and tried to stare me down.

"I'm just saying, Mariah, that it's not good to voice an opinion like that. There will surely be an autopsy."

But the damage had been done. Kiley, standing nearby, gasped loudly enough to get the attention of anyone within twenty feet. "Poison! Oh. My. God!"

The word spread like a wildfire through the crowd.

And all at once I thought of Bonnie Stevens. Would the police notify her officially before someone with a quick finger on their texting button got the news out first? That would be a horrible way to learn of your husband's death. But then I supposed there really was no good way to get that sort of news. The standard method where two cops show up at the front door surely isn't a whole lot better.

The poor woman. At least with Benny as a provider, she and the four kids had a comfortable lifestyle. What would she do now?

My train of thought was interrupted when one of the detectives approached.

"Ms. Parker?" He was probably in his late fifties, with that worn expression that hinted he might soon be considering retirement. The knees of his brown slacks were stretched out of shape, his houndstooth jacket tight across a burgeoning belly. Other than the fact that his hair was still thick, he reminded me a lot of Kent Taylor, the homicide detective I'd come to know on previous cases.

I nodded and sent him a smile. Cops often get a bad rep, but most are just trying to do their jobs.

"I understand you had a conversation with the deceased shortly before his passing?"

We stepped over to a quiet corner near the kitchen utensils, although the crowd in the shop had thinned considerably. "Yes, that's true."

"Can you tell me about that? What was the tone of the discussion?"

"I'm sure others have already told you it got pretty heated."

He nodded slightly, studying my face.

"Benny got upset with me because I'd planted a nanny cam in his office." I realized how that sounded. "Okay, it really goes back further than that."

I gave the five-minute recap of how I'd been brought in to investigate the missing cash, the fact that I'd not had much success in catching the thief and decided to hide a camera. "Since nothing had shown up near the register, I felt the theft had to be taking place inside the office. I placed the camera there, and had actually spotted the bookkeeper slipping money into her desk drawer. My finding exonerated Benny from the crime, but he wouldn't listen to my explanation and he didn't want to see the footage."

"And that's what the altercation was about?"

"Well, I don't know that it exactly reached the 'altercation' stage, but yeah—we had words."

"What was his objection, regarding the camera?"

"I suppose I should have told him I would be recording movements of those who handled the money, just kept him in the loop. He seemed angry about that."

The cop waited.

"Frankly, Benny Stevens was on my suspect list. He seemed to live beyond his means, and even admitted to me that he couldn't afford to lose his job here at the thrift shop. In recent days he had been in a foul temper. Other than me, he'd snapped at several people. I suspected money worries as the cause of that."

"But you didn't catch him taking money," the cop reminded.

"Can I show you the video I did get?" I reached for my phone only after he nodded.

He watched the brief part where Carole slid the money into her drawer. "Wait right here," he said, turning from me and heading into the office. He was back less than a minute later.

"There's no cash in that drawer of the bookkeeper's desk," he said. "I glanced into each of the others and didn't spot it there, either, but of course we'll be doing a thorough forensic search of the room and I'll keep an eye out for the money."

"A forensic search ... so it's possible Benny really was poisoned?"

"What makes you think that?"

Ugh, I hate the way cops turn every question into one of their own, without revealing a damn thing.

"Right after Mariah yelled that someone should call 911, I went into the office to get an idea what it was about. To see whether someone needed an ambulance, or what. Benny was slumped over the desk and I checked for a pulse."

He was scribbling furiously in his little notebook, and now I was certainly down as having touched the body.

"His skin had a bluish tint and there was some kind of rash on his hands and arms, which I hadn't noticed a few minutes before, when we were talking outside."

Still making notes, he asked, "Did anything else seem out of place?"

"Not really. I mean, the room wasn't trashed or anything. Frankly, I wasn't about to hang around with a dead body. I got out. Then the emergency team showed up."

Some bumping and shuffling noises caught our attention. The medical investigator was directing the EMTs to wheel their gurney outside. The black body bag on top was a sad reminder, and those people still in the room moved back respectfully.

The man in the white jacket motioned to my questioner and the two stepped into the office. I was not invited along but I tuned my hearing in that direction.

Unfortunately, they kept their voices low. I caught occasional words: forensic team, evidence, and ... pollen? Maybe the man was just mumbling. I glanced over at Elsa. With no more customers in the shop, things were very quiet at the desk. Kiley had apparently been cleared to leave. Elsa and Dottie were waiting on me to drive them home.

I sidled over to the desk and asked Elsa what had happened to the nanny cam.

"I stuck it under the counter," she said. "I hope Mr. Stevens didn't break it, the way he slammed it down."

"The police didn't ask about it?"

"Nope."

Interesting that the one who'd questioned me didn't pursue that aspect either. I supposed they were far more concerned with a dead guy who might have been poisoned than with the disappearance of a little cash from the till. I seemed to be the only one who'd worked out just how much money that might have amounted to.

Chapter 24

In the way that humans always do, whenever there's been an upsetting event, we need to gather and rehash the details. This is why Elsa, Dottie, and I declared an early happy hour when we got home. Okay, well, *happy* might not exactly be the right term. And we certainly didn't imbibe in the traditional sense. Elsa and Dottie had big glasses of sweet tea, while I opted for a cup of cocoa. No particular reason for that choice—I just felt like I wanted chocolate. We settled on the cushioned furniture under the gazebo in my backyard, little Freckles sprawled out asleep at my feet.

From the conversation in the car, once we'd been dismissed by the police, I knew there was plenty being discussed that I hadn't heard about. For instance, Nancy had mentioned that Benny Stevens had some kind of allergies—he'd once had a severe reaction right after a

Sunday School picnic. Dottie heard that he had a heart condition. Elsa said one of the teens—a kid who never failed to show up in complete goth attire—was certain a vampire had gotten to the manager.

Those who'd been targets of Benny's temper the past couple of days had been somewhat subdued, Elsa told me, especially Eugene Towner.

"That must feel pretty awful," Dottie said. "Somebody make you mad, you kinda wish 'em dead, but then they are dead and you feel guilty somehow."

Even I felt that way a little—I'd been ready to accuse Benny of stealing money, but I certainly didn't wish him dead. What if the poisoning rumors were true, and he'd taken something to end his own life?

I must have said it out loud because Elsa responded. "Honey, you didn't actually accuse him. If he took something bad, there was another reason behind it."

I could probably put my mind to it and think of a dozen ways a person could kill himself, but swallowing something so toxic that you died within minutes, facedown on your desk, would go near the bottom of the list. How about a nice cocktail of pills one takes at bedtime, cozied up with a pile of fluffy pillows and wearing your favorite jammies? Just go to sleep and never wake up. That would be a lot more appealing way to go.

What was I thinking? Sheesh. Maybe I should have opted for something stronger in my hot cocoa, something that would put a giggle in my thoughts instead of this darker edge. But we *were* talking about the death of someone we all knew.

"What about Bonnie?" I asked. "I assume someone from the church would have gone over to their house by now, close friends to be with her?"

"Oh, sure," Elsa said. "That was the other big topic of discussion this afternoon. The ladies already have a whole casserole schedule—who's bringing what, and which day each will take their turn. I've got green chile stew to make tomorrow. I figured that's always good for feeding a crowd."

True. You couldn't go wrong with green chile stew.

"I can drive you to their house to deliver it," I told Gram. I didn't mention that I wanted the chance to ease a few questions toward Bonnie and see what I might learn. Not that I expected to spot a bag of money in the bathroom or anything like that, but I still had questions about the job I'd been asked to do.

I sensed movement near the back door, and Freckles bounded out of a dead sleep to go racing toward Drake.

"So this is where everyone is," he said, walking out to join us.

"We're mourning," Elsa told him. "Our store manager died this afternoon."

"What? Seriously?"

I assured him it was true and that we all had to drown our sorrows in our own ways. He eyed the iced tea and my empty cocoa mug. "I can see that."

Freckles nudged up to him, depositing white hair on his flight suit. He tickled her behind the ears, looking up at me. "Would it help drown everyone's sorrows if I went out and picked up a pizza?"

"Charlie's right—you really are the best man in the whole world," Elsa said.

He took that as a yes vote on the pizza and got out his phone to place the order. I shuffled the group indoors after he left to pick up our food. We gathered plates and napkins and decided a movie would go along nicely. I left the choice up to Dottie as she browsed through our video collection.

While we all loaded our plates and settled in the living room, it occurred to me that I hadn't seen Carole at all after I discovered Benny's body. Surely she hadn't left— the police were making sure everyone stayed around for a while. Maybe she'd been one of those who was feeling a bit subdued and just didn't have a whole lot to say about what had happened.

I wondered what would happen next at Heavenly Treasures. Would the deacons decide to promote Carole or someone else to manager in Benny's place? Or would they, as Benny had feared, do away with the management position altogether and only rely on volunteers? He'd seemed to think those in charge might justify not keeping the paid position open.

And what if the downturn in income had led someone to get rid of the present manager in a more permanent way? An unsettling thought.

Chapter 25

Cee-Cee seemed shaken when she climbed into the Cadillac at the corner of Manzano and Haines, two blocks from the thrift shop.

"I hope I pulled off the police interview," she said after telling Rodney that Benny Stevens was dead. "I wasn't sure I should go back for my purse, but then figured it would look more suspicious if I left it behind."

"You did the right thing," he assured her.

"Can we leave tonight? Is the house cleared?"

"Almost. But now there's a new wrinkle."

She leaned back in her seat and closed her eyes. "What's that?"

"Baxter & Company." The mega corporation's pledge was nearly a quarter of the donation goal for the theater, and they'd already waited two weeks for the money to actually come through.

"They're not backing out, are they? Please say they aren't."

"No. Worse." He brought the car to a stop, waiting on a red light. "Their publicity department got the brilliant idea that their donation should be presented at a press conference. The CEO is known for his big-philanthropy gestures. He wants his smiling face on camera, handing over one of those gigantic pretend checks."

"Impossible. We don't have the time to wait around for them to set up something, and we certainly can't be seen on camera. Honey, you know our policy about that."

"I do, darling. But we don't have the real check yet. They promise to hand us an envelope just before the televised presentation. I've been thinking about it all afternoon, coming up with an answer so we still collect our money and get out of town quickly."

Traffic began to move, and he gave his wife a moment to digest what he'd said. Her green eyes were focused sharply ahead, her thinking mode.

"When I spoke with the publicist, I insisted that we do the presentation as quickly as possible."

"You're going to do it? I can't believe this, Rodney. We're playing with fire, you know."

"It's going to be tricky, love, yes. But I think I have a way." He outlined his plan during the ten minutes it took to arrive in their neighborhood.

But, best laid plans and all that. The shock came when he turned the Caddy onto their street and spotted two news vans in front of their house.

"Oh shit!" Carole slid down in the leather seat until her face was barely above the dashboard. "Hit the door opener! I can't let them see me like this."

As smoothly as if he'd planned it all along, Rodney pressed the button and steered Pinkie into the garage just as the door reached its peak.

"Now what?" Cee-Cee demanded.

"Calm down. They must be here at the request of Roy Baxter. I spotted him standing at our front door. Change out of your Carole Myerson outfit and doll yourself up. I'll meet them at the front door and stall for a few minutes."

"You have an interesting concept of the time it takes a gal to doll up." But at least she said it with a smile. He'd seen her make the switch between characters in under five minutes. She could handle it.

While his wife raced toward their bedroom, Rodney smoothed back his hair and straightened his shoulders before he opened the front door.

"Roy! Great to see you again. Sorry we weren't ready when you arrived."

"Not at all. My apologies that we've come a bit earlier than planned. It was the window of time when two of the stations could send someone and still get the story to their six p.m. newscast."

And were we not meant to meet at your offices? How did this lot happen to know about my house? But he didn't voice any of this. When a man arrived to hand you a quarter of a million dollars you accepted it, no matter when or where.

His smile never faltered. "Well then, we shall give Cee-Cee a moment to freshen up. She will make much better eye candy for the cameras than this crusty old chap."

Baxter, bless him, didn't miss a beat. "My assistant has the display check ..." he motioned to someone out near the curb. "And here is the real thing. I'm afraid I can't linger once we do the presentation. My jet is waiting and I'm due in Houston in less than two hours." He reached into his jacket's inner pocket and pulled out a long envelope with the Baxter & Company logo, handing it to Rodney who slipped it quickly into his own jacket.

Cee-Cee emerged onto the front porch just as the assistant stepped closer with the awkward three-foot-long cardboard rectangle. She wore a fitted green designer dress, her short blond hair covered by a wide summer hat, and her makeup flawless.

"If we're ready then?" Baxter asked.

At Cee-Cee's nod, he turned to face the news crews. With a wink to his wife, Rodney stepped off the porch and edged away from the hungry lenses.

"Ladies and gentlemen," Baxter began, "I have a short prepared statement, and then Mrs. Rodney Day will be accepting our donation check on behalf of the Theater Guild."

He proceeded to read two paragraphs' worth of hype about how much Baxter & Company enjoyed being of service to the arts and to the community. All the cameras and microphones were aimed in his direction as he talked about their many philanthropic causes. The reporters would, no doubt, condense everything he said into one or two sentences and let the video footage be worth the other thousand words.

Rodney sidled around the edge of the media group, keeping one eye on the positions of the two cameramen, while appearing to be intensely interested in everything that was happening up on the porch. Cee-Cee's Carole persona was completely gone, but this was television. The wide-brimmed hat would only go so far to hide her face. If anyone from the thrift shop happened to record the Baxter story and pause their reception of the show, they might take a very close look and figure it out.

And that could not happen. To prevent either the thrift shop folks or anyone from the Theater Guild or those they'd met from the Donner Hospital foundation from making the connection, he could not allow his wife to be recognized. There must be a mishap.

He stepped up behind the two cameramen who were practically shoulder to shoulder as they competed for the best angle and light. Edging his way, he stepped between them at the precise moment Baxter's assistant handed the cardboard mockup to the boss.

"… and it's with great pleasure that we present this check for $250,000 to—"

The crash shifted everyone's attention from the porch to the front sidewalk, where Rodney Day lay atop a pileup, and the two cameramen and all their gear sprawled awkwardly onto the lawn.

Cee-Cee screamed—nice touch! And the female reporters fumbled for what to say next.

"Did you get the shot?" seemed to be the prevailing worry.

Both of the camera guys shook their heads. One of the cameras lay on the sidewalk, bits of it shattered. The other might be intact, but it was lying a good ten feet from the photographer, whose skinned palms were of greater concern to him at the moment.

"Ohmygod, ohmygod, ohmygod," Cee-Cee repeated. She'd stepped out of the shadows and her hat was sitting askew on her head. "Rodney—are you okay?"

It was his cue to take his time in getting up and dusting off his pant legs.

"I'll be fine, darling. But I'm afraid I've royally messed up things, haven't I?"

She dithered for at least another two minutes, watching Roy Baxter closely. "I suppose we could set everything up and do it again?"

Baxter looked toward the news crews. "Do you have enough footage to piece it together? I'm afraid I really do have a plane to catch."

No one seemed to have a ready answer. Without putting the cameras back together and looking over what video might be salvageable, no one knew the answer.

"It's okay," said the reporter from channel seven. "We'll use what we can."

She gave Rodney one of those pitying looks reserved for those deemed too old and clumsy. Good. Let him be perceived that way.

Baxter and his assistant bustled away to one of the cars and were gone in under a minute. Cee-Cee turned to the reporter.

"If I could have a few minutes to fix my hair and makeup I'm sure we could ..."

"It's okay," the other reporter said. "You did fine. We'll manage."

In other words, the teachers' strike and the pileup on I-40 and a dozen other stories would top this one anyway. The news people packed themselves into their vans while Rodney and Cee-Cee watched from inside the house.

"Heh-heh, good show, honey." She kissed his cheek.

He pulled the real check from his jacket and handed it to her. "Do whatever magic you have and get this into the bank right away. I don't want Baxter to rethink his donation just because he didn't get the press coverage he wanted."

They walked into the study as soon as the news vans drove away. She pulled out her cell phone and set to work while he stood and surveyed the Express Mail boxes which still littered the top of his desk.

He needed a drink.

Chapter 26

Visiting the recently bereaved is tough. You never know what to say or what you might do to help. It gets even trickier when you hardly know the family, but Dottie needed a day off to tend to some other things so I agreed to drive Elsa and her gigantic pot of green chile stew over to the Stevens home.

Bonnie answered the door, dressed in navy blue pants and a coordinated elbow-length sweater. Her face seemed wan, but her hair was clean and her clothing neat. She graciously thanked us for coming, while Elsa explained how she made her stew and that it would keep in either the fridge or freezer. It was even better when rewarmed, as the flavors fully blended on the second day after the stew was made. I wondered whether Bonnie was absorbing any of that, but she seemed attentive.

We were walking toward the kitchen during all this, and I saw that the four children were gathered in the family room with a large jigsaw puzzle, and some kindly adult sat there with them, making suggestions. Two other women were chatting quietly in the kitchen, where an array of coffee and tea options were set up to be offered.

The house was even more spotless than the first time I'd been there, with no sign that a complete disruption to this family's life had just occurred. Maybe Bonnie was one of those women who, under extreme pressure, launches into cleaning mode. I know I do.

A wall phone rang and the kitchen women sent glances toward Bonnie. She shook her head and excused herself to Elsa, stepping over to pick it up. We couldn't very well blatantly eavesdrop, so Elsa set the stewpot on the range top and introduced herself to the other women. I browsed the basket of teabags, which one of the ladies took as an invitation to pick up the kettle and pour me a cup of hot water. I let her do it. The activity gave me a chance to keep one ear on Bonnie's conversation, which went something like this:

"Yes, I see." "But I don't understand—" "All right, thank you for calling." She had carried the phone around the corner into the laundry room, so I couldn't watch her expression during the short call. When she returned to replace the handset on its cradle, she seemed to be making an effort to compose herself before she gave an abrupt exhale and looked up with a wan smile on her face.

"Are you all right?" Elsa asked, approaching and setting a gentle hand on Bonnie's shoulder. She's so much better at this stuff than I am.

Bonnie nodded. "That was a police officer, or detective,

or someone. I'm not sure."

One of the kitchen ladies took the cue and carried a plate of cookies to the kids in the family room, distracting them.

"We were at the shop yesterday when the police came. What are they saying about all this?" I asked, keeping my voice low.

Bonnie glanced quickly around the room, as if the answer might be lurking behind the cookie jar or someplace. "The autopsy is done, and they're saying my Benny died from anaphylactic shock—a bee sting."

Must admit I did not see that coming.

Her eyes welled up. "He was allergic, highly so, and we were always very aware. It's one reason why we have no fruit trees and very few flowers in our yard. We can't—couldn't—take the risk of attracting bees. I just don't understand. Benny always had his EpiPen with him. One in his pocket and usually another in his desk or the car … I don't know how this could have happened." That's when the flood of tears started.

I pictured Benny the way I'd last seen him. One hand was inside his desk drawer. Had he been reaching for the lifesaving medical device at the time?

The other women, Bonnie's friends or relatives—I wasn't sure which—all gathered around her and a series of long, comforting hugs began. I stepped aside, my mind churning. I guess I couldn't get the previous day's conversations out of my mind, when people were tossing out the word *poison* and speculating wildly. I'd seen the body, and Benny didn't look so good. Could the autopsy results be wrong?

I edged my way out to the foyer and pulled out my

phone. A quick online search might tell me something. I was well into learning the symptoms of anaphylactic shock when the doorbell rang.

Since everyone else seemed distracted, I went to answer it. A man in razor-sharp khaki slacks, a white shirt unbuttoned at the collar, and a navy blazer stood there. He blinked twice and gave me a questioning look. "Is Bonnie …"

"I'm just here with some of the friends. Bonnie's in the kitchen." I stood aside.

"How's she doing?"

I shrugged. Who was I to say? I barely knew her.

He had one of those kindly faces, like a clergyman or a soft-sell car salesman. The family did have a new vehicle— maybe this was the salesman … Nah, I seriously doubted it.

He walked into the foyer, talking as I closed the door behind him. "Such a shock about Benny, such a shock. At least she and the kids will be comfortable. I'm glad I convinced them to go to the max with that new policy."

Insurance salesman. That was it.

"Do you and your husband have life insurance, Mrs. …" Observant. He'd noticed my wedding ring right away.

I didn't take the bait.

"It's very important, you know. We can never tell when tragedy might befall a loved one."

I nodded, with an appropriately somber attitude. "We might think about that. How large a policy did Benny have?"

The guy was going to poke into my life, I'd dig some info out of him.

He lowered his voice to a whisper. "I'm not at liberty

to say—you know, specific details about someone else's financial situation—but I'd imagine a similar policy in the range of a million dollars would suit your needs."

"Benny Stevens had a million dollar policy?" I kept my voice low but couldn't hide my astonishment. This was clearly a man who was worth more dead than alive.

And that put an even more interesting wrinkle on the situation. With money as a motive, people will go to drastic lengths. But Bonnie? Mild mannered, perfect wife and mom Bonnie? And the kids seemed too young to be the murder-plotting type, so … What more could be behind Benny Stevens' death?

The visitor had thrust a business card into my hand and set off toward the kitchen. It must have been getting a little crowded in there because Elsa came out, obviously looking for me.

"Ready to go?" I asked.

"Yep, all set." She held up a keyring with two keys on it. "I have a new job!"

"What!"

"Until the Reverend Marshall and the deacons figure out what to do, Bonnie said I should take Benny's keys and keep the thrift shop open."

"Gram … are you sure you want that responsibility? Every single day?" We had reached the front door, and I pulled my key fob from my purse.

"It won't be forever. And Dottie will help. I'd imagine the deacons will get someone else chosen pretty quickly. There are other volunteers who'd love to have the management job, since it comes with a paycheck."

More people with motives.

I unlocked my Jeep and saw Elsa into her seat, chiding

myself for this line of thinking. Not every death was a murder. The medical investigator apparently had no doubts when he called the bee sting an accidental death, and I had to admit the symptoms I'd spotted online did seem to match that verdict. I needed to drop the ideas about poison—now.

"So, do you need to go home first or do you want me to head for the shop?"

"Heavenly Treasures await me," she announced.

Oh boy.

Of course, there was no one at the shop when we arrived, fifteen minutes later. The staff had all been sent home yesterday and the Closed sign still showed in the front window.

"What do you think I should do first?" Gram asked.

You're the shop manager now. "I'll bet we can find records in the office, get numbers for the volunteers, and see who's available to work. That would be a good start."

It felt very strange to sit at Benny's desk and open the drawers, but I found the file marked Volunteers quickly enough. I handed it over to Gram and suggested she use the phone at the front desk to round up some crew. Meanwhile, this was the first time I'd legitimately been alone in this office, and I intended to snoop to my heart's content.

Out of habit I found myself straightening the small items at Benny's desk—a stapler had fallen to the floor, a dish of paperclips had tipped into the center drawer. He must have been in the midst of preparing next week's work schedule—the calendar form was half filled out. I pushed that aside. Elsa would create a new one.

What was I thinking? There was no way a woman in her

nineties should be taking over management of a business as demanding as this one. The church would take over, and someone they hired would create the work schedule.

I tossed the form into Benny's In basket and pulled out the desk drawer as far as it would come. Benny's hand had been in this drawer (yes, creepy), so what had he been reaching for? My guess was the EpiPen that would save his life. But it was not there.

None of the other drawers in the desk revealed any sign of it. What had Bonnie said? He always kept the pen in his pocket or his desk. I'd gotten the impression he had more than one of the devices. And yet, he couldn't put his hands on one at the crucial moment. What happened to them?

I spotted the dust cloth I'd used yesterday and used it to pick up a bit of yellowish dust from the bottom of the drawer, and then I set about straightening up the pens, notepads, postage stamps, and paperclips that had become a real hodgepodge. My mind kept whirling. The absence of the EpiPen was suspicious, but more so … when and where did Benny encounter a bee?

All my doubts returned. I'd laid my purse atop the file cabinet, so I reached for it and found the business card of the cop I'd talked to yesterday—Gary Broadman.

"Did you receive a copy of the autopsy report on Benny Stevens?" I asked, once I reminded him of who I was. I explained that I'd been asked by the shop's new manager to go through Mr. Stevens' desk (only semi-true, but Elsa would back me up). "Was an EpiPen found at the scene of the death?"

He was apparently shuffling through some pages. I could hear noises in the background. "No. We made note of that because it seemed unusual."

"I'm trying to figure out how Benny got a bee sting. He was working here in the office, which has one window but it's tightly latched. If he'd been out back in the open air and received the sting, could he have made it back inside and been sitting at his desk? Wouldn't he have collapsed outside?"

"I don't know … don't have a lot of experience with that kind of thing." More paper rustling. "Wait-wait, there's something in the comment section here. The OMI's report notes the presence of a dead bee near the victim's hand. It's obviously how they quickly knew what to test for and narrowed it down to a bee sting. Too bad the guy didn't have that pen thingy near enough to reach it. Could have saved his life."

There were probably a dozen more questions I should be asking, but at the moment I couldn't think of them. A dead bee in the drawer. It resonated through my head well after we ended the phone call. *How* on earth did a bee get into a desk drawer?

Not accidentally. Of that I could be fairly certain.

Elsa showed up in front of the desk just then, a question on her mind.

Chapter 27

Rodney sat at the breakfast bar, holding his head with both hands. Why had he taken the third scotch last night? He knew better. Yes, it felt as though things were closing in faster than he liked, but he prided himself on keeping a cool head and dealing with any setbacks the jobs threw his way. Look at how well he'd handled the news presentation yesterday afternoon—how he'd neatly forestalled and prevented the chance that either of their faces would appear on a newscast, and had still pocketed the quarter million dollar donation. Celebratory drinking needed to wait until they were safely out of the state, several hundred miles away.

The aspirin finally kicked in and a cup of M&S Extra Strong #3 tea set him on a path to action. He donned a sportscoat and called out to Cee-Cee. "Any word on the deposit yet, love?"

She bustled in from the study, two Express Mail boxes in her arms. "Just checked it. Hasn't cleared yet. Honey, it's only been eighteen hours. We need to give it a day."

He grumbled a little, inwardly, but it wasn't as if they didn't have tasks to keep them busy a while longer.

"How many more boxes?" he asked.

"Six. We can finish the drop-offs that got interrupted yesterday and, if necessary, we can always leave these at the local branch."

He gave her a sideways glance. "So close to home?"

"We won't be using the PO box address any more. In fact, we'll drop off the keys and close that one out."

"Must we? I mean, surely people leave in the dead of the night. Not everyone makes a personal appearance to close down their address."

She gave that a moment's thought. "You're right. Safer to skip. We can stick the keys in an envelope and mail them back."

"Or we simply disappear."

She gave him an indulgent smile and laid one hand gently against his cheek. They'd used false names and identities when opening the box, as well as in renting this house, so there really was no need to tie up loose ends. Last night he'd talked at great length about the lure of a remote cabin in Montana. And while she didn't believe he would ever turn into a mountain man hermit—the lure of city life and glittering events would pull him back—she could pander to the scotch-induced fantasy for now.

She changed the subject. "What about the rest of our personal things? How much are we taking?"

"We've a big car with plenty of space. Don't need to fit

it all in two carry-on bags, as we've done more than once." At least he was smiling now. "Take a look."

He opened the door to the laundry room, revealing several duffle bags and suitcases stacked on top of the washing machine. The metal tube containing his prized artwork lay on top.

"There's room for your fancy gowns, if you'd like," he said.

"I'll think about that. Sometimes it's more fun to go shopping for new ones. Depends on where we find ourselves and what we decide to do next."

Despite the million in the bank and more than a hundred thousand in cash going through the mail, neither of them would definitely say this was the final job. There was never a final job for a real con artist, not until they were caught or dead.

Chapter 28

Elsa cleared her throat, drawing my attention away from the contents of Benny's desk.

"Have you ever seen a bee inside this building?" I asked.

She gave it a moment's serious thought. "I'm not sure I've ever seen a bee in this part of town. So many busy streets, freeways, businesses. Now, out in my back yard, sure."

My thoughts exactly. There weren't many sources of pollen around here—not for at least three or four blocks in any direction. But then, maybe bees traveled widely and three or four blocks was nothing to them. Maybe the bee had been carried here in someone's vehicle and flew out when the door or trunk was opened to retrieve their donation. I'd have to go with that.

Elsa handed me a sheet of paper, the list of volunteer phone numbers. "I've reached the ones with a checkmark beside their name. Those with a little star say they can work this week."

That included nearly everyone, I noticed. Probably couldn't wait to get back together and learn the latest on what had happened.

"So, what do you think? We keep the shop closed for another day or two out of respect, and then open up again?" She was watching me, as if I were the authority.

"Do you know who was in charge of hiring Benny? Who was the final say on things?"

"Probably Reverend Marshall, but I can find out." She turned back toward the other room.

I realized that if workers were to come back as soon as tomorrow, then right now was my perfect opportunity to go through the bookkeeper's desk without fear of being caught. I left Benny's desk as it was and walked over to Carole's.

On my last visit here, I'd barely skimmed a couple of days' deposits, and I'd been looking only for discrepancies between the cash amounts Elsa had noted. Now, I might be able to discover if Benny's fears were true and exactly when the shop had begun losing money. I pulled out her chair and sat down, opening the drawer with the files in it and pulling out several folders.

Paging through the reports went fairly quickly. Each month's profit and loss statement was filed in reverse sequence, newest on top. The problem was, the latest report Carole had printed out was four months old. Hm. Just about the time Benny had begun to notice the dip in revenues. Odd, too, because the quarterly gross receipts tax report would have been due in July, and she would have needed the information from the P&L in order to fill out that report. I flipped through the files in the drawer once again and found one labeled Tax Reports.

But there was no second quarter report in it. An envelope from the Taxation and Revenue Department was buried partway into the pages, and when I read the notification, it was a reminder that there were penalties and interest for not filing the report, even if no payment was due.

Had Carole, the marvelous bookkeeper who said she had it all under control, been fudging her competence, to fool her manager? Or had she been stalling while skimming as much as she could possibly take? When I first spoke with her, she'd presented herself as having lots of experience but feeling a little befuddled by the computer. Those kinds of things eventually catch up.

I turned on her computer. I needed proof, and I would look pretty foolish if it turned out she really had entered all the income data but just failed to print the reports and add them to her files in the drawer. After all, she might plead, the printer had been on the fritz for months and she hadn't been able to get anyone to fix it.

But once I got into the accounting program, I discovered that no new entries had been made since early May. I seemed to remember Benny saying something about how, before they hired Carole, the banking was handled sometimes by himself and sometimes by the church treasurer who'd become overwhelmed with other duties. Hiring Carole had been the answer to several people's prayers.

Yeah, well, faith is only a good thing when it's placed with the right people. Blind faith, especially when it comes to money … I was reminded of the saying some former president had used—trust but verify. It appeared to me that Carole had been pulling the wool over everyone's eyes, bustling about and looking efficient while failing to perform her actual duties.

And worse. She'd been skimming money, underreporting the cash intake, and stalling to avoid being caught by either church or state. Or her immediate supervisor, Benny. I froze with my fingers hovering over the keyboard.

What if Benny *had* caught on, had believed what I told him about the cash going into her desk drawer, and confronted her? This was a lot of money.

A fresh urgency surged through me—Carole could be getting ready to vanish.

I rushed into the sales area where Elsa seemed to be concentrating on the list of volunteers. "I talked with Reverend Marshall," she said. "He suggested we reopen the shop the day after Benny's funeral. He says the service will be tomorrow."

"Okay, good. Listen, who's the church treasurer? I've run into some questions."

"Let's see … that's Althea Benton. I've known her for ages."

"I'd like to speak with her. Could you give her a call and ask if I could come by and see her?"

While Elsa did that and got the address for me, I went back to Carole's computer and brought up the latest accounting data that had been entered. Compared with the printed reports in the file, it looked as though I had everything. I gathered several file folders to show the treasurer.

"Althea says come on over," Elsa called from the other

room. "She's going to be home all day."

What about the bank records, I wondered. There was a small key in Carole's desk drawer and I discovered it fit the metal file cabinet. I found a large-sized checkbook with a handwritten register, a petty cash bag, and rubber-banded stacks of deposit slips and cancelled checks that dated back several years. Wow, they'd really been going old-school around here forever. Carole had even admitted that her accounting experience went back to the days of handwritten ledgers and that was where she felt most comfortable.

I packed everything into a banker's box, realizing that I didn't know whether Carole had an office key or not. If she truly was planning an escape, part of that plan could be to come back here and destroy any incriminating evidence. I'd feel much better if all this paperwork was safely in the hands of the church treasurer.

I set the box aside and took one more look around the office space. Seeing Benny's desk again brought back everything the cop had said about the autopsy report and my ideas about the dead bee. Even if I went with the theory that a bee had somehow arrived at the shop, it still didn't explain how the insect had got inside the building and into Benny Stevens' desk drawer. That part seemed beyond accidental, which meant someone managed to carry it into the office and ... then what?

And why? Had someone with access to this office found the ideal murder weapon—an unsuspecting bee?

Had I now found myself with *two* mysteries to solve?

Chapter 29

The woman who met us at the door was a version of Elsa, ten years younger. I was glad I'd brought the entire box of handwritten deposit slips and the full set of financial statements, even though they were outdated. Althea fluttered about, showing us into her living room—a collection of furnishings and fixtures straight out of the '80s. She offered tea or coffee, which we declined.

"I'm not sure what I can tell you about any of this," she said, staring at the profit and loss statement I'd deemed to be the most recent. "Carole was so efficient at Heavenly Treasures, and we were so grateful to have her. Previously, we'd had a succession of volunteers who just did their best, but I never felt I had proper reports to show the deacons."

"See, this is where I'm running into some problems," I told her. "The financials are at least four months behind, and when I tried putting the deposit slips in sequence and matching them to the entries in the check register, well, it seems quite a few of them are not here."

"And don't forget to tell her about the missing cash," Elsa prompted. She then proceeded to relay her own observations and the fact that we'd tracked specific cash sales for several days.

"Oh dear." Althea reached for a wrapped hard candy from a bowl on the end table near her chair. "I'm very much out of my depth with all this. The only reason I'm church treasurer is because my late husband Archie was an accountant. He handled the church finances brilliantly until he passed away, ten years ago now. I inherited the job and no one ever questioned. I can balance a checkbook. It's tithes and offerings that cover the expenses of our worship center. The thrift shop began eight years ago as an idea to help the less fortunate in the community. No one really ever saw it as a business."

Which perfectly explained why it was prime pickings for the likes of Carole Myerson. The trusting nature of people like Althea and Elsa made them easy marks. I thought of the younger people involved in running the church—the Reverend Marshall, deacons such as Eugene Towner, Benny Stevens, and Mike Weber. I supposed each had his own area of responsibility and everyone trusted that the hired bookkeeper was doing everything just fine.

Althea's job basically boiled down to presenting a report at each deacon's meeting, giving them the church's current bank balance and a listing of expenses that needed their approval. She received the bank statements for both the church and the thrift shop in the mail and passed along the shop's business to the bookkeeper. No one seemed comfortable with online banking or electronic payments.

"Did the deacons question why there had been no financial reports from the shop for the last few months?" I asked.

"Well, not really. I told them what Carole had told me. She was running a little behind because of some family difficulties—I got the impression there's a sister in Virginia or someplace like that ..." The ball of candy in the side of one cheek made her look like an off-balance squirrel.

"The church has a bigger project going on right now," Elsa said.

"Oh yes, the Sunday School annex." Althea's face lit up. "It's going to be so nice when it's finished. Going over the construction costs and dealing with the contractor has taken most of their attention, going on six months now."

It sounded like the perfect storm of inattention, meeting up with a crafty bookkeeper who knew exactly what to say in order to stall for time.

Time. How much did I have, to connect the dots in a way that would constitute enough proof for the law to take a look?

Althea's face drooped. She spat the rest of the candy ball into a tissue, her expression beginning to look a little sickly. "If it's true that money has gone missing from the shop, I wonder if the deacons can hold me responsible." She turned to Elsa. "Can they, do you think? I can't decide what to do."

"I had the same worry," Elsa said. "I was the one handling cash at the register every day. I got the feeling Mr. Stevens was eyeing me, once I brought up the missing hundred dollars."

Shifting the blame seemed to help Althea recover a little.

"Let's not worry about that just yet," I told them. "I'm

fairly certain all of this falls to Carole. It's just that we need to put together some proof."

Which it now looked like was going to fall squarely in *my* lap. I couldn't see Althea being able to think straight, much less organize any of this material into something the police could use. And if I went to that effort, would the church officials actually go so far as to press charges? I should speak with Reverend Marshall before I put a lot more effort into this, find out how seriously he was willing to take it.

As Elsa and I drove toward home with the box of paperwork in the back seat, I thought about all this, trying to envision how it would go when they pulled Carole in for questioning. The older woman with her pink complexion and matronly clothing, stodgy figure, and hint of a developing double chin—if she looked at the judge with the same guileless wide eyes that she'd used on her employer, no court would convict a sweet little old lady like that of being a criminal mastermind.

Okay, Charlie, get real. You don't have to prove she's some master crook, just that she's figured out a way to rip off thousands of dollars from a religious organization and the poor people they serve.

"Can we stop at the post office on the way home?" Elsa asked, breaking the loop of my thoughts. "I need some stamps to mail out my bills next week."

We were almost there, and I made the turn into the parking lot of our neighborhood branch office.

"I won't be a minute," she promised, opening the passenger side door.

Judging from the number of cars in the lot, she would be a lot longer than a minute, but I could wait. I pulled out my phone and tapped in the number I'd found earlier for

Reverend Marshall.

He answered on the first ring, and I briefly went over what I'd discovered so far at the thrift shop and how the visit had gone with Althea Benton.

"How much did you say is missing?" he asked.

"That's the thing—I really don't know for sure." I tossed out a figure that was probably too low. "I'd need to go back through the records from before the current bookkeeper started, and then compare the income at that time with what's been reported recently. Benny Stevens told me the shop's income had drastically slowed down. So much so that he was afraid he'd lose his job."

"That wouldn't have happened," Marshall said. "We need someone to be in charge, even if Heavenly Treasures doesn't show a profit. It's a community service as much as anything."

"So, my more basic question is whether you'd be willing to press charges, to follow this up with the law, if I do find that there has been outright theft. Or would your stance be to turn the other cheek, forgive and forget … something like that."

"There's a time for forgiveness and a time for accountability. If someone has stolen as much as you are suggesting they have, my vote is that person needs to be held accountable."

"Okay. Just making sure we're on the same page." We ended the call on that note.

I'd been keeping an eye on the front door, watching for Elsa, but so far no sign of her. A classy woman of sixty-ish held the door for a young mom with two kids. There was something vaguely familiar about her smile, but I couldn't place where I might have seen the Jamie

Lee Curtis short hair. She bypassed the mom and strode toward the opposite end of the parking lot, her posture erect, her jeans perfectly fitted, and the bright teal sweater surely cashmere.

It was when I saw her walk up to the driver's door of a vintage pink luxury car, complete with tail fins and plenty of chrome, that something clicked.

Chapter 30

That does it for the boxes I planned to mail," Cee-Cee said, dropping her designer bag on one of the barstools.

"Glass of wine, love?" Rodney held up a new bottle of her favorite French Bordeaux.

She nodded and kicked off her shoes.

"You're not concerned about sending all that cash through the mail?" He uncorked the bottle and poured.

"I've done it lots of times. You know, they are so worried about criminals laundering money by using money orders, but this is so much simpler. Do you know how often a package actually gets opened and inspected? Almost never."

He handed her a glass, one eyebrow raised.

"Plus, I've used false names and addresses on the

return labels. Even if someone tries to trace them back, it won't be to me. Or to you, darling." She raised her glass and clinked it to his. "Let's go out and enjoy the garden."

"I must say, I will miss this home," he said as they stepped out to the stone patio and surveyed the tall trees, lush lawn, and abundant flowerbeds. "It's been one of the nicer ones we've had over the years."

She agreed as she pulled out a chair at the wrought iron table and set her wine down.

"Oh, there's the phone. I'll just—" Rodney turned back toward the open back door.

"Expecting a call?"

"No, but it's no trouble to check." He lifted the handset from the kitchen phone, setting his wine glass on the countertop.

"I'm calling for Carole Myerson," said a female voice. "Is she there?"

Rodney's stomach did a little lurch. No one except the thrift shop had been given this number for his wife. And everyone who was associated with their other charitable projects knew her as Cee-Cee.

"Who's that you're asking for?" Buying himself an extra moment as the woman repeated the name. "No, sorry. You've dialed a wrong number."

He hung up before the caller could ask anything more, but his heart was thumping. Was it more than coincidence that someone who'd gotten this number would just happen to call as they were preparing their departure?

Back outside, she looked up at him as he walked out and closed the glass door. She'd laid her hand over the top of her wine glass and he tilted his head, questioning.

"Another of those bees we've been seeing. This one

wanted a taste of my wine." She laughed and said she didn't plan on sharing.

"Yes, there have been more than a few this summer ..."

"Who was on the phone?"

He debated. "No one. Wrong number."

She sipped her wine for another minute or two, and he could tell her mind was racing ahead. He had already accumulated a tidy stack of the items they would take. The Picasso and a duffle bag of cash would go into the hidden compartment in the trunk of the car. Larger luggage would be stacked on top, suitcases with their clothing and toiletries, baggage that would attract no attention in a routine traffic stop or overnight at a hotel.

"Rodney, I do have one other thing that's weighing a little on my mind."

She had his attention. Cee-Cee was not a worrier.

"The thrift shop. I have a feeling there's a loose end that could cause some trouble later."

"Shall we go there now?"

She gave that some thought. "No. Someone could still be around, the police or that nosey investigator, and I'd rather not face any questions. Let's enjoy our wine and a nice dinner. I'll think about this other matter."

"Don't forget, darling, you haven't yet packed your bag. If there's clothing to be left behind, make certain to check pockets and purses and such."

Her jaw tightened.

"I realize you know this, love. It's just a reminder."

She relaxed slightly.

"I've a nice chicken for our dinner. I'll just go pop it in the oven now."

Chapter 31

Where had I seen that car? I stared after it as the slender woman backed out of her parking space and headed toward the exit. Something told me to follow it, and I chafed with impatience that I couldn't very well just drive off and leave Gram stuck at the post office.

The pink Cadillac made a right turn out of the lot but I lost sight of it as it passed behind an adjacent building. I closed my eyes for a second, thinking back.

This very parking lot. I'd seen the car here before. But that wasn't, in itself, suspicious. It was a neighborhood post office. I saw the same cars here frequently. No, there was more. Recent. And the only place I'd spent a lot of time recently was the thrift shop. Did the pink car belong to a customer—not likely. A volunteer. But I'd become familiar with most of their vehicles too. No …

My passenger door rattled and Elsa climbed in. "Sorry, there was a line."

I yanked the gearshift before she'd hardly fastened her seatbelt. "Do you know anyone at Heavenly Treasures who drives an older model Cadillac, a bright pink one with fins?"

"Oh goodness, let me think."

I didn't have time for that. My tires chirped as the Jeep bounced out of the exit and made the right turn. The street stretched ahead, empty. There was a stop sign at every other block, and I cruised by all of them, scanning the side streets, left and right, for any sign of the pink car.

"I think I know the car you mean," Elsa said once she'd got her balance back. "I have seen one like that near the shop. But I don't remember who it was. Not someone who parks it there all the time. I would remember that. My uncle's second wife had a car like that, only I'm pretty sure hers was white."

I tuned out the reminisces and kept my eyes on the side streets. The car didn't have enough of a lead to be miles away. And this was a residential area. Chances were, the driver lived nearby if they used the same post office regularly.

"Carole Myerson, the bookkeeper!" Elsa's face broke into a grin when she said it. "She's always dropped off and picked up by her husband, and it's in a big pink car."

Yes. It was someone picking up someone else that I'd seen. But the woman I knew to be driving the car now looked nothing like Carole, and I could be pretty certain this was no one's husband either. Maybe there was another family member, a sister or a friend who occasionally drove the distinctive car.

"Did you bring that volunteer schedule home with

you?" I asked. "And is Carole Myerson's phone number on it, along with all the others?"

"Yes, and yes," Elsa said, rummaging in her purse.

I pulled to the curb and called. A man answered. British accent, which was kind of sexy, but his wasn't a friendly tone when he said he'd never heard of Carole and I had the wrong number. I rechecked the number from Elsa's list against what showed on my phone as my most recent call. It was a match.

So, Carole had either given a false number or it had been incorrectly written on the volunteer list. Either way, I had hit a dead end. We drove on home.

The day's conversations kept rattling around in my head as I searched for answers to Benny Stevens' death. The police had officially closed their investigation with the ruling that it was accidental, but I couldn't see anything accidental at all about a bee finding its way into the man's desk drawer at the very same time that his EpiPen had disappeared.

Still, the cop hadn't seemed concerned. "We've seen stranger things happen" didn't sit well with me, but that was his official stance.

And then there was the missing money. Coincidence? Lots of cash disappears *and* a man dies—that didn't fit the category of *strange* at all. I'd call it motive—well, somehow. I couldn't quite piece it together, and I couldn't get the pink Cadillac out of my mind.

By eight p.m. Drake had noticed how restless I was. "Shall we turn off the TV? This show doesn't seem to have your attention."

"No, it's fine. Keep watching. I'm just going to give Ron a call and see if he can track something for me."

Victoria answered and after the initial pleasantries, including my asking how Jason was adapting to his new school (just fine, thanks), she handed over the phone to Ron.

"I'm trying to track down a particular vehicle that I think is related to this case of missing money I've been investigating. Can you do that?"

"With some limitations. You know I only have access to certain info in the DMV database. What's the make, model, and year of the car?"

"Uh …" I've always taken somewhat of an interest in cars, but not so much that I'd know that level of detail on a car I'd seen only a couple of times at a distance. "I'll have to get back to you."

So, where does one go for details about something one knows very little about? The internet. I got online and searched 'Cadillacs with fins.' Okay, it's not much, and it did take me a little while to narrow it down, but I came up with the Eldorado Biarritz. I couldn't find anything stating that pink was a standard color, and I passed all that along to Ron when I called him back.

"Okay, I'll see what I can come up with tomorrow at the office. You do still work at our office, don't you?"

"Smarty."

Chapter 32

Cee-Cee had a difficult time settling down at the dinner table, and she hardly touched a bite of her chicken and roasted veggies.

"Darling, this isn't like you," Rodney finally said, after trying to keep up a conversation. "Tell me what's bothering you."

She picked up the dinner plates and carried them to the kitchen sink. "I have a terrible feeling I've forgotten something."

He chuckled. "We all do that, walking into a room and not remembering why we're there."

"No, this is more. I should have stayed at the thrift shop and gone completely through my desk."

"For personal items?"

"I'm more worried about the paperwork I left behind.

It's evidence. And I always try to wipe down all my work area, remove fingerprints, before my last departure. If they're really on to what I was doing there ... I don't know, honey. There are times I feel like I'm losing my touch."

"The authorities are far more concerned with the death of that manager chap."

She stopped in the middle of scraping the chicken bones into the trash. "Yes. And what if they tie—" She set a plate into the dishwasher. "What if they can tie me to that?"

He went still. "Can they?"

"I've told you about my past, Rod. I've never killed anyone."

"But there *was* the one woman who died ..."

"Which no one ever connected to me." She paced to the far end of the room and back.

The connection was sketchy, way back then, but eerily similar. Her supervisor at a convenience store had fallen off a ladder while changing lightbulbs, a task she'd performed many times without a mishap. But this time they'd been the only two in the store, and the supervisor had just accused Carole of dipping into the cash. Then, as now, she wondered how many others the supervisor had expressed her suspicions to. Then, too, she had packed up and left that midwestern city on a moment's notice.

Rodney pushed back from the table and walked toward her, placing his hands on her shoulders, looking into her eyes. "Would it make you feel better if we go and check, do a thorough little mop-up?"

She relaxed into his embrace. "Yes. It really would."

"Then we shall. Leave the dishes. Change into something appropriate and we'll go."

She looked up with a loving gaze. "You don't think I'm

getting too old for this life?"

"Not a bit. You're a far younger spring chicken than I am." Which didn't exactly answer her concern. Maybe they were both at the point where they would begin making errors. They needed to look out for each other.

Forty minutes later, he'd parked the car down the street from Heavenly Treasures and they walked back, checking for passing traffic before edging around to the side door where Benny had kept a hidden key. By the light of Rodney's small penlight, she opened the door and they made their way carefully through the maze of junk-filled tables and shelves.

"How could you possibly work amongst all this clutter?" he muttered, nicking his shin against a tricycle.

"I didn't. Thank goodness there were others willing to get their hands grubby." She led the way, keeping her small flashlight aimed at the floor and her eyes peeled toward the windows that faced the street. Traffic moved at a steady pace, and there were no pedestrians in sight.

Rodney stepped ahead and held the door to the office open. Cee-Cee paused and looked toward the manager's desk.

"Looks like they've at least tidied up his work area," she said, staring around the office. "Things were really crazy right after the EMTs were here."

"You didn't keep your own paperwork at his desk, did you? What about that large file cabinet?"

"No, everything I generated is right here." She unfolded the dark tote bag she'd brought along and stepped toward her own desk.

But when she pulled out the drawer and aimed her light into it, she froze in place. "Oh no, oh crap!"

He peered over her shoulder. The drawer contained two slender hanging file folders, nothing more.

"Everything's gone." Cee-Cee sounded like she was going to be sick. "Someone's been here. They went through everything."

Her eyes were frantic as she shone the light around the surfaces in the room. "And the other thing …"

The erratic moves with the flashlight were making him dizzy. He stepped over to the north-facing window and twisted the wand to close the mini blinds. They could risk the light for a few minutes, surely.

When he flipped on the overhead lights, his wife's pacing jolted to a stop. "Let's calm down and think rationally for a moment, shall we?" he said.

"You don't understand. What reason would they have for clearing out my desk?" There was an edge to her voice he'd never heard before, as if she might be about to cry. "The cops were all over this place yesterday, questioning everyone. What if something that somebody told them is what led them to taking all the financial records?"

"They were here to investigate what happened to Stevens, weren't they? That seems unrelated to the financial records in your desk."

"We can't take the chance. They could be going through everything right now, closing in on me."

He raised his wrist. "It's nearly ten o'clock. The police most likely aren't—"

She grabbed his arm. "We have to get out. Now. Tonight."

Chapter 33

The day of Benny Stevens' funeral arrived. Elsa and Dottie would attend. I made other excuses, largely because I hate funerals.

After a hearty breakfast, I saw my husband off to finish the job he'd started with that movie producer whose name I couldn't even remember. Then Freckles and I headed for our RJP Investigations office, about ten minutes from home. The poor dog had been feeling neglected after I'd abandoned her for my thrift shop gig, more than a week now.

By this morning, I'd lost some of my fervor about the pink Cadillac. Spotting the car twice at the post office could be purely coincidence, although if it was the same car that had picked up Carole Myerson from the thrift shop … I did need to pursue all leads on the missing cash.

And I had started Ron on the path of trying to find out more about it, so I would spend a little time here and see what he'd learned. Plus, it was probably high time I caught up on my own work.

I parked behind the converted Victorian and saw that both Ron and Sally, our part-time receptionist, were already here. I grabbed a mug of coffee in the kitchen and paused at Sally's desk for a quick catch-up. She ruffled the dog's ears and handed her a biscuit. Her hubby and kids were doing great, and there were no urgent office related messages for me, so I headed upstairs.

Ron was behind his desk, phone to his ear, as usual. He saw me and handed over a single sheet of paper, which I carried to my desk. At the top it said: MVD search results — Cadillac Eldorado Biarritz, 1959. There were only two entries.

One of the vehicles was registered to the Route 66 Historic Auto Museum. I knew of that place, although I'd never actually walked in and checked out the exhibits. One thing for sure—if the car was on display there, it was not being driven out and about town. Although I supposed that couldn't be stated definitively—I could give them a quick call and check.

The second 1959 Caddy was registered to a C.M. Day. The address was a post office box, which—eureka!—was at the branch office where I had spotted the car. Maybe this C.M. Day was the woman I'd seen driving it. And—the best luck I'd had so far—the registration included a street address. I was familiar with the street, which is only five or six blocks from my own.

I was ready to drop everything and head over there, but when I rushed toward my office door I nearly crashed into Ron.

"I may have a good lead on the thrift shop thief," I said.

"You're welcome."

"Yeah, thank you. I meant to say that."

"Just curious. Once you have all this evidence that someone's been stealing and you have the person in your hot little hands, are you sure the church is willing to press charges against them? They would need to do that, you know."

"I know. I talked with the minister."

"Just saying. You could find out they don't want the publicity or the scandal. They could choose to ignore it."

They might be so thrilled with me, they'd reserve me a place in heaven or something, if I were to recover a bunch of missing money that they never knew they had. I mean, the mission work and all that. But I didn't bring it up to Ron. He's such a skeptic.

Mainly, I just wanted to make sure Gram was completely in the clear, regarding the money. And I couldn't let go of the idea that the missing money could be connected somehow to Benny Stevens' death. Part of the reason I'd encouraged Elsa and Dottie to go to his funeral this morning was to have them keep an ear open for gossip about Bonnie and the big life insurance policy.

I pondered all the various implications as I called to Freckles, picked up my purse, and we headed out to the Jeep.

It's amazing how you can live in the same neighborhood your entire life and still find something new. I'd explored all over the place as a kid on my bike, but in recent years I'd fallen into the habit of using the same routes to come and go. Things change in subtle ways—trees get taller, landscaping is replanted, a house gets a new paint scheme, places that had toys all over the yard now do not.

So, when I located San Carlton Avenue and began watching the addresses, I was surprised to come upon a gorgeous home with clean lines and lots of windows. It must have been built in the 1950s—nearly everything in the neighborhood was completed in that era—but this one had been beautifully maintained, with fresh paint and neatly trimmed shrubbery.

I couldn't see movement at any of the windows, and the double-car garage door was closed, but I parked at the curb and walked up to ring the bell. No response, even when I rang again. I decided to walk around and see if the side gate was unlatched.

"They're not home." The woman's voice, coming from the driveway next door, startled me. "Packed up. Vacation maybe, but it was a strange time to leave."

I stepped over a little closer to the hedge that divided the two properties. The neighbor was probably in her seventies, with beautiful salt-and-pepper hair. She carried a shoulder bag and had car keys out.

I introduced myself and offered my business card. "What do you mean, a strange time to leave?"

She sighed. "I have terrible insomnia, up half the night, so I sit by my bedroom window and read." She nodded upward toward her second story. "About midnight there was a bunch of activity over here, lights on all over the house, the two of them putting stuff in the car."

"Had they talked about a vacation trip?"

She shook her head. "Weren't real neighborly, kept to themselves. We actually never had spoken other than to say hello or remark about the weather. Nice enough, but other than having some kind of party one time, they didn't socialize. Not with us neighbors anyway. I'd see them all dressed up and going out."

"A couple, right? The woman is slim and very fit looking?"

"Yeah. He's older, kind of … um, gentlemanly. Has a British accent."

"That sounds like the people I'm looking for. I wonder how I might get in touch."

"I can give you the landlord's name. He lived in the house for a while before he moved up to Sandia Heights. Told me the rental market was so good he'd just hang onto the place and rent it, see how that went." She was rummaging in her purse while she talked, coming up with a slip of paper and pen and scrawling a note.

"Talk to him," she said. "Could be, these people will be back in a day or so. Sorry I don't know more than that, and I really do need to get going to watch my grandkids. My daughter's in some kind of seminar this week."

I wished her luck. With no sleep the night before, she seemed a little weary to be dealing with young children.

As the neighbor drove away, I climbed into my Jeep and phoned the landlord's number she'd given me.

"Jerald Cordova," came the answer.

How much detail to cover on the phone? I realized I hadn't quite thought through my story here. "I'm interested in your rental property on San Carlton Avenue."

"On the way there now," he said. "I'm about ten minutes away. Can you meet me there?"

Okay, that was easy enough. I worked on my cover story, which was that I worked with Carole and she'd left early this morning and we needed something for the office.

It had enough little scraps of truth to ring true. I just wasn't sure if a landlord would let me inside on that info alone.

A late-model blue pickup truck arrived, right on time. The man who got out was about forty, with curly dark hair and a muscular build. As he began pulling hoses and buckets out of the truck, I thought he looked more like a pool guy than a landlord. He caught me staring at the conglomeration.

"I never trust my tenants to do pool maintenance. They'll remember to check the chemicals—sometimes. Mostly they just let it go and by then the pH is a mess and leaves have clogged the filters. Easier to drop by every week and do it myself." He hefted a long coiled hose over one shoulder and headed for the back yard. I tagged along.

"So what was it you wanted to ask me? You interested in leasing the place, 'cause the current tenants have already prepaid."

"Oh, no. I already have a home, not far away actually." I launched into the story about working with Carole. "It's her day off and I thought I'd drop by on my way to the shop and pick up a file she brought home with her yesterday. Now it looks like she's not home and the neighbor said she saw them packing and leaving last night."

His brow wrinkled as he uncoiled the hose and set up the vacuuming apparatus.

"It's just that this file has to do with the store's finances and it's something we really need. If they've left, it puts us in a real bind. I'd recognize the folder if you could just let me in the house."

This was so outside the realm of what a landlord should do, I fully expected him to deny the request flat-out. I sent him the most winning smile I could come up with.

He set the pool vacuum to work and dipped a chemical test strip. "Tell you what. You describe the folder to me and I'll go inside and look for it."

Well, it was something. I described, with great precision, one of the folders I'd taken from Carole's desk at Heavenly Treasures. He wouldn't find it here, but it might give me a way in the door while he looked.

He pulled out a ring of keys and let himself in the back French doors. I saw him walk through a dining room, into the kitchen, and disappear through a doorway. He was back less than a minute later.

"Their stuff is all gone." He seemed more than a little surprised.

"Um, yeah, I forgot to mention ... when the neighbor said they were packing ... she said it was a lot of stuff."

Jerald scratched his head and glanced back at the pool where everything seemed to be running okay on its own. "The Days rented the house furnished, but it looks like all their personal things are cleared out."

"Damn. I really, really hope she didn't take that office folder with her. I'm in a pickle for letting her bring it home."

He shrugged. "I suppose there's no harm in letting you go in, take a look around."

"Thanks. You've saved my life." Men love it when you say things like that. "Look, I don't want to disrupt your work. I know exactly what I'm looking for."

Which was not at all true.

Chapter 34

I can't believe we only made it to Santa Fe. One hour into our trip." Their escape, he meant.

Cee-Cee sat up in bed and rubbed his shoulders. "It's all right, honey. We've known for some time that your night vision isn't what it used to be. And I'm sorry I was getting too sleepy to help with the driving."

"It's those godawful headlights. When did they start putting those horridly bright ones on cars?" He stood up and adjusted his pajama top. "And why didn't I press on, get us downtown so we could stay at the La Fonda. Room service would help to make the whole experience less insulting."

"We'll find a nice little café somewhere. Why don't you go ahead and get your bath first. I'll brew some coffee in that tiny machine over there."

"Bring me a foam cup while I lounge in that plastic—or whatever it is—bathtub." He pulled the curtain aside and looked out to the parking lot, making sure the Cadillac was still there. They'd left far too many valuable items in it, and the knowledge interrupted his sleep repeatedly through the night.

At one time in his life this would have been an adventure, a lark as they raced out of a city just ahead of the law, a vehicle full of loot, hiding out in a small motel off the beaten path where the two of them would make love on a lumpy bed and giggle over their situation. But now all he could think about was the comfort of the lovely house they'd left behind, its clawfoot porcelain tub in the bathroom, upscale espresso machine in the kitchen, the kidney-shaped pool in the back yard. Was Rodney Day growing soft? He chided himself as he adjusted the water temperature in the bathtub.

Cee-Cee came into the room, setting a small cup of very ordinary coffee on the Formica vanity top, poking about in her travel kit. She pulled out her toothbrush and paste and began scrubbing at her teeth, staring fiercely into the mirror.

"Still stressing over those documents?" he asked

She nodded and spat out the toothpaste. "I suppose."

"Nothing to be done about it now. Someone took them, and we have no way of knowing who it was."

But she had a suspicion. He knew she'd been watching that private investigator for days ahead of time, and the young woman had been watching Cee-Cee—or Carole. And his poor wife had nearly bolted when the police showed up, even though their interest was in the sudden death of the shop's manager. Nothing to do with them.

Or was it? He'd never actually come out and asked Cee-Cee if she had anything to do with the arrival of a solitary bee in the office or the missing EpiPen that could have saved the man's life.

She closed the bathroom door behind her, leaving him to undress and have his first cup of coffee in the tub. Just like home. Except there was no home right now. They would have to follow the trail of their cash stash and put down roots somewhere new.

He settled into the steaming water and imagined where that might be. For now, somewhere in the American West, although he wouldn't mind it if they made their way to England again. He had loved being part of London society. Maybe it wasn't too late to recapture that lifestyle.

Rodney was out of the bath, standing at the mirror and trimming his mustache when Cee-Cee tapped at the door.

"Good news," she called out. "Our quarter million is safely in the bank."

His mood immediately lifted, and he could tell hers had too, just by the tone of her voice.

"I've already transferred it around to the other accounts."

He opened the door a crack and smiled at her. "That's the kind of news we wanted. Well done."

She blew him a kiss and walked away, her attention on her phone screen.

I'm so lucky, he thought, having a wife and partner who knows how these things work. "Find an excellent restaurant for breakfast," he called out. "No holds barred. We have all day to get to Denver."

Chapter 35

I didn't dare spend more than a few minutes inside the home. Jerald had been gracious enough, but I couldn't afford to have him thinking I was there to rip off the furnishings or anything. I walked through, getting the lay of the house, discovering there was a study. That's where I concentrated my efforts.

The desk didn't contain much—either the Days had cleared out their things really well or they'd never thoroughly settled in. I did find an empty file folder and half a pack of copy paper. I stuck a few sheets of the blank paper into the folder, the necessary prop I would use when I said goodbye to the landlord.

Next step was to find a window appropriate to my plan and twist the latch open. The guest bedroom had two windows that served this purpose nicely, and I pulled the drapes closed when I'd finished. Although I felt myself itching to delve into closets and drawers, for now I needed to stick with my story.

Jerald Cordova was measuring some kind of powdered chemical for the pool when I walked out the back door. I held up my file of papers and put a song in my voice. "Found it! Thanks so much!"

He gave a nod, seemingly happy to have helped me. Such a nice guy.

I walked around to the front of the house and got in my Jeep, started it, and drove to the end of the block. At the corner I parked where I could still see his truck, which was facing away from me. This should be ideal. I kept one eye on the truck while scrolling back through my emails. Nothing really new.

Ron had probably given up on me as a business partner, and Elsa and Dottie were at Benny Stevens' funeral this morning. I came to the document from Ron, with the name of the Cadillac's registered owner, C.M. Day. It would have been nice to take a peek in the garage and see if the vintage car was in there. It was always possible that the couple owned another vehicle and had abandoned the Caddy in the same way they'd left the house behind.

Movement near Cordova's truck caught my attention. He was loading the pool equipment into the back, a reverse of when he'd taken it out. Within a minute, he'd climbed inside and driven away. Now it was my turn.

I timed a wait of five minutes. By now he would be far enough away that he wouldn't come back. I left my Jeep parked where it was and walked back to the house. Didn't want to take the chance that the neighbor I'd spoken with would come home early and see it.

But the street was quiet, that midday lull when people

were either away at work, out to do their daily activities, or
whatever it was that stay-home people did in the mornings.
I carried the file folder with me. That type of thing can
make a fantastic disguise—I could be a census taker, an
insurance salesperson, or somebody handing out religious
pamphlets—just in case someone happened along and
questioned me.

Fortunately, no one did. With an eye peeled toward the
windows across the street, I saw no activity so I walked
around back and closed the side gate then let myself in
through my unlatched window into the guest room. Only
after I had the window fully open and a leg inside did it
occur to me that there could be an alarm system.

But no whistles, buzzes, or shrill electronics interrupted
the quiet of the house. And I remembered that the
landlord had simply unlocked the door and walked in, so
I felt better about that. I gave a quick perusal of every
drawer in the room and the closet, then moved on to the
master bedroom. I had to give credit for the quality of
the furnishings—this was no typical rental, and I wondered
how much the Day couple had been paying.

No matter. The bedroom drawers were all empty. In
the closet hung a couple of expensive dresses, size six. I
was surprised a woman would leave these behind. Maybe
they would fit me ...

*Quit it, Charlie. You don't go anywhere fancy enough to wear
them anyway.*

I moved the dresses aside, studying the floor and walls
for any hidden compartment. Nothing. Down the hall, I
went back into the study and gave it a thorough check.
Zilch there, too. And the living room yielded nothing.
In fact, it was almost pristine enough to suggest that the

couple had never spent any time there.

Next to the kitchen was a laundry room. I went so far as to peek inside both the washer and dryer, where I found a man's lone sock, black. A box of soap powder and packet of fabric softener sheets sat on a shelf, but nothing seemed to be concealed in either of those. A door out of the room led into the garage. And—no real surprise—the pink Cadillac was gone.

As there didn't appear to be any storage boxes, hidden cubbies, or toolboxes in the garage, I shut the door and went back. Kitchen and dining room were the only places I hadn't yet searched.

The kitchen was furnished with the basics, much more like a vacation rental than a long-term place. The espresso machine was a nice one, and I wondered whether it had come with the house or, like the dresses in the bedroom, had been left behind by the renters. I poked my way through cabinets and drawers, finding a set of decent dishes and serving pieces, flatware that was nice but nothing a renter would want to steal, very basic skillets and saucepans, a block of knives, and a tub of spatulas and whisks and such. One cupboard contained glassware, and tucked in beside a set of champagne flutes was a metal box. It caught my eye because it seemed somewhat utilitarian for its surroundings—here was beautiful crystal and a gray clunker about the size of a shoebox.

Gingerly, I edged the box past the delicate glasses and pulled it from the cupboard. Something inside rattled a little. Hm. I carried it to the countertop, a bright space filled with sunlight from the window above. The latch had a tiny combination lock, the kind where you roll the little wheels until the correct three digits line up. Not exactly

Fort Knox, but strong enough I would need a tool to get into it.

My heart rate picked up a little. Surely this was not standard rental furnishing, so it had to have been left behind by the Days. I couldn't wait to get into it. Unfortunately, I would have to—there were no reasonable tools in any of the kitchen drawers, and I was becoming uncomfortably aware of how long I'd already been inside the house.

I tucked the box under my arm and carried along my ruse of a file folder while I went back and relocked the guestroom window. Through the front windows I checked the street again (still no car at the next door neighbor's place—she must be having a great time with those grandkids).

Okay, deep breath, walk out the front door. I locked it with the little twist mechanism, then put on my act as though I'd just been chatting away with someone inside the house. Lots of smiles, a wave goodbye, holding the metal box to my chest with the file folder for cover … And I could only hope that anyone observing would think I'd just paid a visit and was innocently leaving.

I don't think my heartbeat returned to normal until I was safely locked inside my Jeep, unaccosted by a soul. I set the metal box on the floor of the passenger side and pulled away from the curb. Suddenly it felt like Christmas—what was in the box! I couldn't wait to get home and figure out how to break into the little sucker.

Chapter 36

Dottie's car sat in Gram's driveway when I pulled up to my house. The two ladies were just getting out, still wearing their dark dresses from the funeral. I realized they must have also gone to the reception afterward at the Stevens home. Gram motioned me over.

"As soon as I get out of these shoes I'll give you the rundown," she said, that conspirator look in her eye.

"And I'll make us all some lunch," Dottie said. "All they's servin' at that party was cookies and punch."

Since I was getting kind of hungry anyway, I carried the metal box into my house and stowed it in my t-shirt drawer, then Freckles and I walked over next door.

Dottie had added a bibbed apron over her good dress, substituting fuzzy house slippers for her dressy shoes. Gram came into the kitchen a couple minutes later, completely re-outfitted in a gingham housecoat and, I suspected, no bra. "I'm going for comfort," she announced.

I took the pitcher of iced tea from Dottie and poured three glasses, while she slathered mayo on whole wheat bread. A couple minutes later, we each had a ham sandwich in front of us, and a bag of barbecue flavored chips sat there, open for sharing.

"So, spill it," I said in Gram's favorite private eye manner. "What did we learn?"

"Well, the good news is that I don't seem to be a prime suspect for the stolen money anymore," Gram said.

"Weirdest thing, you ask me," Dottie added. "They ain't even askin' questions. Don't even seem all that worried."

Gram nodded. "It's true. I sort of got the feeling they're covering for Althea, the treasurer. She's a nice lady and they really don't have anyone else to take over the job if she quits it, so I think nobody wants to bring up how she should have caught these shortages."

I could see that. When people are volunteering for a job, they can walk away. "But the shop—that's not really Althea's responsibility, is it? Accounting for the cash in the business end of things was up to Carole, wasn't it?"

They both shrugged, sort of agreeing with me, sort of unsure.

"Did you tell Reverend Marshall how much we think is missing?"

"Not really. Didn't seem the time or place," Gram said. She picked up the second half of her sandwich. For a senior, the lady still has a great appetite.

"I might need to have a meeting with him myself," I said, musing as I helped myself to more chips. I looked up at Gram. "That is, if they want me to continue looking into this?"

"Oh, I think they do. Well, not really that they *want* you to, but no one objected."

Talk about feeling needed. Maybe I should just drop it all. If they weren't concerned about the losses, why was I? The police didn't seem to think Benny's death was suspicious; the church didn't seem to think the missing money was anything to worry about. Maybe I truly was overreacting.

Dottie read my expression, as she tends to do. "I say you stick with it. That bookkeeper lady, she rip off the store. That's money coulda gone to the poor."

"She's right," Gram said. "Once you tell Reverend Marshall how much we figured out is missing, I think he'll change his tune."

"You do got some proof it's that Carole, don't ya?"

"I think so." I hoped so. Which reminded me of the Christmas present waiting in my t-shirt drawer at home. I quickly finished my sandwich and excused myself, saying that the ladies ought to make time for a nap this afternoon.

I was rummaging through our household toolbox, thinking a good heavy wrench would work to smash the lock on the gray metal box, when Drake walked in.

"What's up?" He asked the question but one glance told him what I was trying to accomplish. He picked up the biggest, toughest screwdriver in the set, placed the tip in the narrow space between lid and box, and with one twist of the wrist he managed to pop it open.

"Thanks. You're my hero." Guys love it when you say that, too.

He gave me a kiss and walked back into the house where he took up residence at his desk. I carried the box to the dining table, finding a spot where the light was good, before I opened the lid and really took a good look inside.

It was filled with credit cards, passports, and drivers licenses. Holy cow!

Like a kid with a new set of Legos, I dug into the treasure and began assembling identities. There were four: one for the gray-haired man I thought I remembered from the one time I'd seen Carole's husband pick her up; three separate sets for the woman I'd seen driving the Caddy away from the post office. None of them used the surname Day.

I had to pace the room twice, ignoring Freckles' plea to play ball with her, before it occurred to me that, hmm ... if they were using the name Day now, they would have those documents with them. Everything in the box was backup. Or, were one of these personalities from the box the real ones, and Day was the fake?

And where was Carole? I went back and studied the faces of the females in the photos. The poses were unsmiling, serious. Sharper cheekbones, sculpted jawline, short hair in some, a bit longer in others, but none the color Carole wore hers. Of course, hair color was the easiest thing to change, nearly as quick as picking out a new outfit, so I couldn't judge by that.

Eyes and noses didn't change much—I studied those. But truthfully, I had to admit that I hadn't exactly been around Carole enough to memorize her features. I couldn't even tell you what color her eyes were. The woman in the various photos looked enough like Carole to be related ... but was it the same person? I couldn't say. I wished I had a photo of the thrift shop bookkeeper. It would be easier to compare with these.

I tossed the driver's licenses onto the table, frustrated.

Chapter 37

Was the traffic in Denver always this terrible, Rodney wondered as he steered for his life on I-25, hoping to get to their exit with themselves and the Cadillac intact. More than once he found himself cursing the old luxury car. Back in its day, a car hadn't been expected to maintain eighty miles an hour all day long. Well, a human wasn't meant to do that in Rodney's day either, and he realized how weary he felt.

Aside from the traffic and speed, the big car was like a dinosaur running with gazelles, as other cars zipped around and in front of him. He felt as though the pink monstrosity was the biggest, most obvious thing on the road (the easier to catch you with, my dear). But Pinkie was Cee-Cee's darling. She told him she had bought it, cash money, from the first successful job she pulled, several years before she met him. He knew that he dare not suggest they trade it for something more practical.

For now, the plan was to spend a couple of days in Denver, making the rounds of some post offices where they had Express mailed boxes of cash to themselves. It felt safer to have the cash with them now that they were out of New Mexico, but he'd begun to question that decision too. Maybe his nervous stomach would settle once they had put more miles behind them.

"Do we have more of those Tums?" he asked.

Cee-Cee reached into the glove compartment and pulled out a large bottle that was nearly empty. "Take these. We'll get more when we stop where there's a drugstore."

He chewed the tablets, wishing he had something to drink them down with, but that was another thing about the old car. Without built-in drink holders, he'd spilled more than one soda and his wife had made it a rule: no beverages in the car. He gritted his teeth and swallowed the dry tablets, along with the words that would have ruined the harmony with Cee-Cee.

He squinted at the green overhead signs, watching for the exit they needed. What should have been less than a six hour drive was coming up on eight hours. His stomach clenched again and his head was beginning to throb.

"This is it," Cee-Cee said, "one mile ahead. This exit takes us to the Cherry Creek post office, the first of our stops."

She looked over at him, noticing his pained expression. "We'll be there soon, honey. I can drive, if you'd like."

"No way to pull over at this moment." He knew his tone sounded abrupt, but did she not see what was going on all around them?

She retreated into her corner and let him negotiate the exit. At the red traffic light he asked her which way he should turn. The rest of the way, she answered in monosyllables. When he spotted the familiar US Postal Service sign ahead he turned in. It was five minutes to closing time.

Without a word, Cee-Cee got out of the car and race-walked to the front door. Rodney sank down in his seat and closed his eyes, resting his aching neck against the seat back, rubbing his stomach with both hands. An image came to him, one time when he and two of his former gang had narrowly escaped a dogged Pinkerton man in London. They'd packed up in the middle of the night and run through narrow alleys and wynds, their knapsacks and valises awkwardly flopping about and bumping their legs. They'd caught the night bus to the far end of the line, stolen a car from a parking lot, and driven halfway to Wales before stopping. And they'd laughed about it, treated it as a lark. For Cee-Cee's sake he needed to do that now, to rediscover the joy of the getaway rather than stressing over it.

He chewed the last two antacids from the bottle and looked up to see his beautiful wife returning, two very familiar looking boxes in her hands.

"Got 'em, no problem," she said, her face alight. She set the boxes into the back seat.

"About earlier …"

"I know. You're exhausted, honey. Let's go to the hotel I've picked out and have a nice dinner. You'll feel better in the morning. I'll drive."

He switched seats and took her up on the offer.

Chapter 38

The sets of identification sat in their neat little piles on my dining table, awaiting action on my part, so I started my search the way anyone does nowadays—Google.

The name on the man's driver's license was Robert O'Flannery, which unfortunately was common enough that the search returned quite a few matches. It didn't take long to eliminate the former US congressman, a car dealer in Las Vegas, and the CEO of Flannery Optimetrics, Inc. I was less certain about the bit-part actor whose IMDb profile showed an older man with gray hair in a style similar to what I remembered seeing. The face on the driver's license wasn't a great match, even though I reminded myself that actors have all sorts of ways to change their appearance and create alternate personalities. I left that search tab open so I could come back to it.

Two pages into the Google results I found a news story which included a Robert O'Flannery who had been arrested in New York on suspicion of robbing a bank. The article came from the historical archives of a newspaper which, I discovered, no longer existed. I read through the sixty-year-old story, fascinated with names like Billy 'The Buzz' Stoner, Mad Mike Mulligan, and 'Fingers' Latreque, who were all named as co-conspirators. Robert 'Robbie' O'Flannery had been the youngster of the group, charged with aiding and abetting the getaway of the others who had gotten into the bank's safe through a meticulously dug tunnel in a disused section of the subway line. The two men actually caught with the money in their possession did prison time, but young Robbie didn't seem to have suffered any consequences. The story made for fascinating reading, but I couldn't see how—other than the idea that once-a-crook-always-a-crook—this Robert O'Flannery could be the gray-haired man on the driver's license I'd found.

I started searching the various female identities and found a lot of the same thing—the names were common enough that I had to weed through a lot of useless chaff before finding possible matches. Twenty minutes into it, I had a big head-slap moment. All the identities used the same initials, the same as Carole Myerson. The same as C.M. Day, the registered owner of the Cadillac.

The realization did not exactly provide a way to get Carole arrested for stealing from Heavenly Treasures, but the pattern might provide the police with enough to build a case.

I quickly discovered that I got better results by tacking on the word 'arrest' after each of the names. Carla Matthews—nothing showed her on the wrong side of the law. Cathy Marks—nothing. Chris Manley—the same.

But Carolyn Malone's name appeared in a news article five years ago in Houston. A pawnshop owner had reported the theft of a large amount of cash and most of the high-end jewelry from his stock. Carolyn Malone, the day shift clerk had not shown up for work the next day. Suspicion immediately fell on Malone, but she had simply vanished. The address she'd provided proved to be a vacant lot; the phone number went to a Chinese restaurant. The only thing the pawn broker could remember that was distinctive about her was that she drove a pink Cadillac.

I read the article several times. It always came back to the pink car, but how had law enforcement missed such a distinctive vehicle? I was turning all the details over in my head when my phone rang.

"Charlie? It's Paul Marshall—from the church. I had a call from Elsa Higgins and she said you've been wanting to talk to me?"

My mind had to do an abrupt gear shift to catch up and remember what Gram and I had talked about at lunch.

"Yes. It's about the missing money from the thrift shop."

"I'm available at eight tonight, if you'd like to stop by the church. I host a men's prayer group until then, and I usually hang around a little longer in case any of them want to talk."

"Sure—I can be there."

For the first time in hours I actually looked out the window and noticed the sun was low in the sky. My internet searches were not exactly productive right now, or I just wasn't processing what I was reading. Anyway, it was time for some fresh air. I put on a light jacket and picked up the dog's leash, and Freckles came running.

"Shall I warm up some soup for dinner?" Drake called from his desk.

"Sounds great." I clipped on the leash and got dragged down the porch steps and across the front yard.

It was practically a sprint down to our little neighborhood park, but the exercise and fresh air did both me and the pup some good. She made the rounds of the park, sniffing out all the other visitors of the day, and I circled the perimeter at a brisk pace, clearing my head and thinking of the information I wanted to pass along to Marshall at our meeting.

Back at home, twenty minutes later, the aroma of soup filled the house, even though it was only leftovers that I had stuck in the freezer two weeks ago. While we ate our taco soup and tortilla chips at the kitchen table, Drake talked about the intricacies of calculating his flight fees for a job he was planning to bid on—something about stringing some power lines to a tiny remote community in northern Arizona. I have to admit that I probably only heard half of it and absorbed even less. My head was still into the countless facts and data I'd been trying to absorb for the past week.

I offered to do the dishes when we finished—hey, how difficult is it to put two bowls and two spoons into the dishwasher? He went back to his calculations, since his bid was due before midnight tonight. I tidied the kitchen and gathered the notes I'd made about the missing money at the thrift shop, based on the folders I'd so conveniently swiped from Carole Myerson's desk. And I still had a few minutes to waste before I needed to drive over to the church.

My laptop and the little metal box with all the identification documents still waited on our dining table, so I sat down and opened the lid on the computer. By default, up came a page of news headlines.

Theater Guild Meets Two Million Dollar Fundraising Goal would not normally have caught my attention, except the story from the *Albuquerque Journal* website included a familiar face. A smiling man was holding one of those giant oversized cardboard replicas of a check, and the woman receiving it was none other than the lady I'd seen driving away in the Caddy. She seemed to be fumbling with a wide-brimmed hat, but I recognized her short blonde haircut and the high cheekbones. She was identified as Cee-Cee Day, and the story went on to say that she and her husband Rodney Day would be matching the million dollars raised by the Theater Guild, for a total of two million, which would go to the refurbishment of the venue and upgrading the sound system.

So the owner of the car, C.M. Day was this Cee-Cee.

According to the background details, the Days were supposedly multimillionaire philanthropists who had recently moved to New Mexico from Arizona and were thrilled to be able to help such worthy causes … yada, yada, yada.

I was about to type in this additional search criteria but my gaze dropped to the clock in the lower corner of my screen and I realized I had only a few minutes to make my eight p.m. meeting. Freckles seemed horribly disappointed when I told her she couldn't come, but she'd get over it. Drake would, no doubt, be handing out treats before my car was hardly out of the driveway. I picked up my notes and headed out.

I'd attended church with Elsa a number of times as a child, so I knew exactly where I was going, but—full confession here—I'd not been back in years. With the passage of time and my own shifting perceptions, the place looked somewhat different. Trees in the neighborhood were larger, and what had once seemed like a vast parking lot really wasn't even close to what the local Walmart sported. Some things hadn't changed at all—the classic architecture of the white-pillared sanctuary, balanced by a smaller building on each side.

The dozen or so parked cars, and all the lights and activity were centered near the smallest of these, the one I recalled that was known as the fellowship hall. I parked among the others and watched until the men from the prayer group began to descend the steps. Meeting over.

Paul Marshall greeted me with a smile. "Right on time. Sometimes the guys get to talking after the lesson and we run a little long. Tonight everyone seemed eager to get going. I'm thinking that has more to do with the World Series than God's calling."

"Were you …?"

"Oh no. I like sports well enough, but basketball is more my thing. I'll catch the results on the news later." He gestured toward a table that held a ragged assortment of cookies and a nearly empty coffee carafe. "Come in, have something if you'd like."

When I declined the refreshments, he ushered me toward the circle of chairs the others had left in place.

"So, I'm afraid I don't have a clear picture of what's been going on with the finances at Heavenly Treasures. Althea is a dear, dear woman but she couldn't seem to explain it all. Remind me again. Something about one of the other volunteers noticing that a hundred dollars was missing?"

I perched on the edge of the metal folding chair with my notes on my lap. "That's how this began, yes. Elsa Higgins is like a grandmother to me. She took me in when I was orphaned at fifteen, and she raised me through what are probably the toughest years when dealing with a teenage girl."

He chuckled, apparently having heard that tale from many parents over the years.

"Anyway, she volunteers at the thrift shop and noticed that money was missing. A hundred dollar bill was especially remarkable because she knew exactly where she had put it. Elsa's ninety-three years old, and a lot of people might discount her memory or claim she's getting senile. Let me assure you, she isn't. So, when it looked like the blame for the missing money might fall on her, I offered to help figure out what happened to it."

He was nodding thoughtfully through all this, and I couldn't be certain how much was new information and how much was repetition. But he let me go on. I told everything I knew about the revenues from the shop dropping off in recent months, and how Elsa had noted all the cash transactions for several days and the discrepancies we found when we'd compared those with the cash shown on Carole's deposit slips.

"I knew the cash must be disappearing after it was taken from the register up front to the office. It pretty much had to be either the bookkeeper, Carole, or Benny Stevens. I was leaning toward Benny because, frankly, I discovered that his personal financial situation wasn't the greatest. Maybe he simply needed the money. But when I interviewed him—this was the day before he died—he seemed genuinely worried that he could be held responsible for the shop's dwindling revenues and that he could lose his job."

"But we're talking about a hundred dollars here or there, aren't we? Granted, if Benny needed money, I would have wanted to counsel him about that, see if we might help, but to take away his job over a thousand dollars or less …"

"I'm afraid it's a lot more than that." I pulled out a spreadsheet I'd created showing the figures I'd come up with. "Of course, these are only projections. Dealing with cash, there's no absolute proof."

When I handed him the page his eyes grew wide. "How did you come up with this?"

"I went back to the deposit slips I found in the file cabinet at the shop. Prior to six months ago, this was the average income …" I pointed to one of the columns. "Beginning in May, you'll notice it dropped just a little. This slight drop continued for three or four weeks, and then it began to plummet steadily. Compare the first week of this month, with what the shop was earning last spring. It's less than half."

Marshall had gone very still in his chair now.

"I'm sorry to say it, but I'd estimate there's more than a hundred thousand dollars missing right now. If the pattern continued, the loss to the shop within a year's time would easily be twice that much."

He swallowed hard. "I had no idea."

"I don't think anyone did. I know Althea does her best, but she can only report what she knows."

"Yes, yes. I don't see how any of the blame for this could fall to her."

"I'm not saying that at all, of course. Now that I've

had access to more of the records, I really believe it's the bookkeeper, Carole Myerson, who's behind it." How much to say, at this point about the Day couple and all the aliases? I decided to save that for later.

The preacher was becoming agitated, leaving his chair and pacing across the large room.

"How much does anyone know about Carole?" I asked. "I heard she's not a church member but was hired when she answered an ad or something?"

"Yes, I believe that's true. Hiring her was Benny's responsibility. The deacons and I had made the decision a few years ago to hire Benny to oversee the shop completely. He scheduled the volunteers and made the recommendation that we hire a bookkeeper as that added responsibility was too much for Althea."

"I understand."

"Surely—*surely*, Benny was not taking advantage of his position there." He seemed genuinely distressed at the thought, and I tried to reassure him.

"The more I've learned, the more I believe it was Carole who was embezzling the cash. Please don't think that I'm out to smear Benny's name or Althea's."

"So, what do we do?"

"What I need now is to find more proof, so complete access to the shop's records. I asked Althea if Benny kept any accounting records on his computer and she didn't seem to know. If it's all right with you, I'd need to access his computer, compare what might be on it with what's on the one Carole used."

"Of course. Please do."

"And, if I do locate enough to prove that a crime has been committed, I need to know whether you—well, the church—will press charges. Frankly, there's no point in putting together all the evidence if the criminal will not even be arrested. And the police don't seem inclined to get involved unless you do. Sorry, that's putting it bluntly."

"I understand." He paused near the stained glass windows on the far side of the room. "Yes, we must. As unpleasant as the thought is, we simply cannot accept that great a loss to our mission work. Let me give some thought to the hiring of a new manager. Losing Benny Stevens was very upsetting to the congregation, so I have to tread a bit carefully about replacing him. In the meantime, if you could document each day's receipts and get them to Althea?"

"Certainly. I'll go back to the shop tomorrow and start digging, and I will thoroughly go through the files I took from Carole's desk." I straightened my papers and stood up.

Marshall walked over to shake my hand and I assured him I would do my best. But as I went back to my car I wondered if my assumptions about the bookkeeper being the master criminal were true. There was still the possibility that some of the church members could get tangled up in the web as well.

Chapter 39

Rodney was not feeling better by morning. In fact, his gut was on fire and he'd not held his dinner down. Cee-Cee fussed over him, offering comfort food—which he couldn't even think about. She went down to the hotel gift shop where she picked up more antacids and a thermometer. His temperature was 102.

"We'll stay here a few days longer. No problem," she assured him.

But he could see the worry on her face. They'd meant to be a lot farther from Albuquerque before they relaxed. They wanted to be in Billings tonight, Missoula or even closer to their Oregon goal by tomorrow night. It wasn't going to happen, and Cee-Cee stressed when things didn't go according to plan.

"I'm going to run out to the two other post offices,"

she said, "and I need to start getting rid of those *certain items.*"

She was referring to the costume she'd devised for her Carole Myerson persona, the padded undergarments, larger clothing, and old-lady style blonde wig. Part of the reason for her success over the years was that she never left connections. The clothing could not have been left in Albuquerque, because you never knew who would find the wig or a recognizable shirt or dress. And you never knew how or when one of those items would make its way into the hands of the cops. She had an absurd vision of one of her Carole dresses getting donated to Heavenly Treasures and instantly being recognized by her coworkers.

"Where's my painting?" he rasped, his gut flaring at the thought of it in the trunk of the car downstairs in the parking garage.

"Right here, honey. Remember? We brought it up with us last night." She opened the armoire and showed him the tube containing the Picasso.

"I want it with me."

She carried it to the bed and he cuddled the tube against his side.

"I've put out the Do Not Disturb sign, and there's a glass of water right here on the nightstand. I should be back in an hour or so."

He closed his eyes and nodded. A moment later he heard the door open and close.

* * *

After months in Albuquerque, where nearly anything was no more than a twenty minute drive, she'd forgotten what it was like to drive in a huge city with all the connected suburbs. At the time she'd posted the boxes, it seemed wise to spread them out, have them arrive in various post offices.

From their downtown location, she'd retrieved the only packages she'd sent to Denver when they arrived in rush hour traffic yesterday. Now, she brought up the addresses of the other two on her phone and began to plan a route, lamenting the fact that one was in southeast Aurora and the other in Westminster, at complete opposite ends of the huge metroplex. She'd be lucky to get to the first of these in an hour's time.

No sense in disturbing Rodney's rest to tell him that. Odds were he would sleep all morning anyway. She set up the map to give verbal instructions and headed out of the underground parking garage.

Chapter 40

Being back in the office, seeing Benny Stevens' empty desk provided a sharp reminder that the financial crime wasn't the only item on my agenda. I still couldn't let go of the idea that a random bee didn't just *happen* to make its way into this room where it stung the one person who was highly allergic. As I searched for evidence of the missing money, I needed to be on the lookout for anything that seemed out of the ordinary in regard to the manager's death, as well.

I set my thermos of coffee on top of the metal file cabinet—I'd quickly learned that the coffee station for the volunteers was normally empty or down to the dregs—and stared around the room for a place to begin. Since I'd been rushing to go through Carole's desk the other night, I decided it could use a closer look, so that's where I started.

The main file drawer on the right was empty, of course. I'd taken everything to show to Althea. There was a smaller drawer with basic office junk—a small stapler, a box of paperclips, pair of scissors, generic mailing labels, four or five pens, and two mechanical pencils. The center drawer held postage stamps, more pens, a purse-sized pack of tissues, and a Chapstick. Hadn't there been a couple of other personal items in there before? I couldn't remember anything specific, just a general impression that the drawer had held more.

The left side of the desk had an open compartment where a stack of copy paper and a box of large envelopes were stored. It was likely where Carole would have set her purse during the work day. The power cord for the computer went through a small hole in the desk top and trailed down to a power strip on the floor, behind the envelopes. I didn't spot anything related to actual bookkeeping or finances. A small waste basket sat in front of the space, and I dumped its contents on the desk. Nothing of interest there. Even the wadded up notes consisted of a grocery list with all the items marked out and a reminder to "Call home after 1:00" which told me nothing. I smoothed out the two notes and set them aside. At the very least they could provide samples of Carole's handwriting, in case the police should find that relevant.

I stood up straight, nursing the crick in my neck. What next?

Reverend Marshall had given me permission to search Benny's desk and computer, in case he'd also kept copies of financial records. I felt fairly certain the police had already gone through the desk, but it couldn't hurt to look. And Benny, who'd been quite a bit younger than Carole, might have set up online access to the bank account. It would be one more way for me to cross-check and verify the information from the deposit slips.

I plopped myself onto his chair and looked around.

Here too, miscellaneous office supplies dominated the drawer space. Benny's included copies of the schedules and blank pages to be used for future months. I did come upon a small notebook, in which he'd noted his computer passwords. Not terribly secure, considering anyone who wanted to get into his computer (yes, like me) would find the information quite easily.

This computer was slightly more modern than the one at the other desk, but it still took an eternity to boot up. I poured myself some coffee and noticed that the buzz of sounds from the sales room was picking up. Customers had discovered Heavenly Treasures was open again. Benny's home screen wasn't password protected, so it was an easy enough matter to take a gander at what programs he used.

Frankly, there wasn't much—a word processor and spreadsheet, quick links to some solitaire games. I opened the browser and clicked to see his recent search history. It seemed he spent time on Facebook so I went there, where I discovered he'd mostly posted things about the thrift shop, little community service announcements about the shop's hours and occasionally about some exceptional item that had come in. Interesting.

There must be shoppers, beyond those who needed baby gear and common household items, who were on the lookout for antiques and pricier pieces. Seemed like a good service for the manager to provide, letting them know about unique offerings. His latest post showed a decorative pewter box with little claw feet and a miniature scene worked in metal on the top. I didn't remember seeing the piece in the shop, but since this was literally the land of ten-thousand things that wasn't surprising. There were other posts about fine china collections and one for an intricate hand-crocheted blanket purported to be more than fifty years old.

Fascinating as all that was, I had to remember that I was looking for banking transactions so I went back to the browsing history. Tops on the list were a couple of antiques appraisers, where it appeared Benny had searched out the values of items, some of them matching what he'd posted to the social media pages. By the names of some sites I couldn't tell what they would be, so I simply began clicking each one in turn.

By the time I reached the fifth or sixth web address on the list I was getting pretty quick about it. Click, take a glance, move on. Until I came to FindAMatch.com. The click revealed it to be a dating site. And a scroll down the page made it clear that this was a gay men's dating site.

Uh-oh. Benny, what were you doing here?

Back at the listing of his browsing history, I quickly saw that this was not one isolated visit. Benny Stevens had spent quite a lot of time at FindAMatch. This was research of an entirely different kind. I knew that many religious groups were becoming more accepting of gays, trans, and all the other versions of a person's sexual preferences. Maybe Benny's church was one of those.

But I didn't think any of the ones resembling mainstream religion condoned dating for married people with kids. I had to admit, it was pretty gutsy of Benny to use the computer here at the shop for his searches. Of course, it really wouldn't do to use the home computer for that either. I leaned back in the swivel chair to think about this.

The implications became staggering, the more I thought about it. This knowledge could be fuel for blackmail at the very least. Excommunication came to mind. And what about murder?

Could someone have intentionally put the bee in Benny's desk drawer and removed his EpiPen, the only means he had of saving his own life? The idea sent a sick feeling to the pit of my stomach.

Suddenly, my doubts about the man's death went from viewing it as a coincidence to knowing it was somehow connected with his deep secret. Who would have been most likely to take action—the wife, a lover, one of the church officials, maybe the Reverend Marshall himself? It could be anyone within the church, anyone at the shop, maybe even a neighbor or—who knows—his garage mechanic.

Okay, stop this. My mind could take the scenario in any direction, but I had to narrow down the suspects to someone with access to this office and this desk. Carole Myerson. She worked alongside the man for six months, so it was logical that she would have known about his allergy. And she could have easily glanced over the partition between their desks, wanting to ask a simple question perhaps, and spotted the forbidden images on his computer screen.

Maybe the stolen money wasn't at all the reason she'd disappeared. Not if she was a murderer.

Chapter 41

I reached for my coffee, which was now tepid, and movement caught my eye. Bonnie Stevens appeared at the edge of the cubicle divider, her preschooler kid attached to her leg.

"Hi, Charlie. Sorry to bother you." She didn't look good. Her face was haggard and I'd swear she had lost ten pounds since I last saw her. Her slacks had a couple of days' worth of wrinkles and there was some kind of food stain on her blouse. I had a hard time seeing her in this condition as a suspect but yet … grieving widow or guilt-ridden killer?

"I came by to get Benny's personal things out of your way. Reverend Marshall says he'll hire someone to take over the shop."

"Sure." I clicked to back away from the dating site and

made the computer go to a screensaver, this one of fish swimming around in a brilliantly colored aquarium.

Bonnie moved in, retrieving the framed family photo and a potted plant. "I gave him this. I always thought his workspace was too bland."

"Can I get you a box or something?" I edged past her and the shy child.

When I returned less than a minute later, she had a little stack on the desk—besides the photo and potted plant, there were some notepads imprinted with Benny's name, and a gold pen. She hastened to explain where each item came from, lest I think she was helping herself to property from the shop. As if most of the others weren't already doing that.

"Mommy, I like this," said the little boy, holding up a small metal box with claw feet.

"Oh, I don't think that's—" Bonnie took the box and handed it over to me.

"Thanks, yes, that definitely belongs to the shop."

I carried it out of sight before the kid could pitch a fit and guilt me into just giving it to him. It could wait safely in Carole's desk drawer until they were gone. If it had been important enough for Benny to post as an antique on their Facebook page, it definitely wasn't a child's toy.

"Are you doing all right, Bonnie? I mean, well, moneywise."

She nodded, placing the potted plant into the box I'd brought. "Our insurance man said he'd stay on top of the claim and get me some money as quickly as he could."

A million dollars, as I recalled.

"In fact, several from the church took up a little collection to see me through for a week or two, and I can't believe how generous everyone has been with food."

"Good. I imagine it's a challenge keeping teens fed."

For the first time, a little smile crossed her face.

She picked up the box of possessions and headed toward the door. "Thanks. For everything."

Other than bringing the container and standing aside while she picked up things, I couldn't think what I'd done. Well, I did close out the dating website before she or her kid could see it. But she had no way of knowing that.

I watched as Bonnie walked toward the front door, the various volunteers stopping to greet her and offer hugs along the way. As a wife who might have caught her husband cheating, she could certainly have motive to get rid of him but I certainly didn't see any suspicion or reservation on the faces of her friends. She was either innocent or she was the smoothest killer in history.

My thoughts went back to Carole. Motive: avoiding getting caught stealing. Means: as yet unknown. Opportunity: worked right there in the same room with the victim.

Once I saw Bonnie get into her minivan, I went back to Carole's desk and retrieved the small metal box. I should show it to Mariah Blinker and ask whether she knew anything about the decorative piece, where it came from, how much it might be worth. It seemed to be an item Benny had shown interest in, and posted on the website, just before he died.

But Mariah only shrugged. "I don't recall this piece at all. I do—did—often take items to Benny if I thought they could be extra valuable, but not this one."

"What about the other volunteers? Maybe someone in the donation intake area took it directly to him?"

She shrugged again. "No idea."

I went out back and asked. No one seemed to be familiar with the little box. Nancy Pomeroy opened the lid and looked inside. "Some kind of yellowish powder in it. Maybe the donor used it to store spices or something." Although when she took a sniff she didn't offer an opinion as to what spice that might be. She handed the box back.

In the shop, I held the box up and asked a few others, Dottie, Elsa, Eugene, Kiley. They all shook their heads.

"Charlie, Dottie and I are supposed to get off work in fifteen minutes," Elsa said. "Will you be ready to go by then, or should we find a little something extra to do?"

She looked a little tired and I was feeling stumped in my searches. "I'll be ready. Just come in the office when your replacement arrives."

I went back to Benny's desk and took one more look at his browser, typing in the word 'bank' to see if I could find a login to a banking site. But no, nothing came up. Apparently, Carole Myerson and Althea Benton were the only two involved with the banking, and they were both old-school enough to handle everything in writing rather than electronically.

Okay then, that was that. I put Benny's notebook with the passwords back in the center drawer, and that's when I noticed it. Yellowish residue inside the drawer. I knew immediately what it was—the medical investigator's report said there was bee pollen near Benny's hand, which was in the drawer when he died.

The decorative metal box was sitting right here, beside the computer screen, since I hadn't yet decided on a safe place to stow it away. I opened it. The yellow residue looked the same. I would need to get an expert to verify it, but I knew the answer was staring me in the face.

A bee got into the office because it had been carried here inside this box.

And I could only imagine how riled up a bee would feel after being shaken around inside a closed container. Mad enough to sting the first person who opened the box.

I could picture the scene. Benny, sitting here in this chair, opens the box he's planning to appraise. Bee flies out and nails him on the hand. He tries to shake it off at the same time he's reaching into the drawer for the medical device that will save his life. But the EpiPen isn't there. He's panicking, but his airway is closing and he doesn't have the strength to stand up or call for help.

Oh, God, what a horrible way to go.

Chapter 42

Cee-Cee was exhausted from the traffic, and she hadn't yet disposed of her old bits of disguise. She was sitting in the car in a parking lot, searching her phone for a place that would take used clothing donations. Ironic, she thought, since less than two days ago she'd been working at just such a shop. The post office branch she'd chosen, unknowingly, in Longmont wasn't in the best neighborhood, but she did find a Goodwill store a few blocks away.

She headed there now, fully aware that she had more than a hundred thousand dollars in the trunk and it wouldn't do to get separated from it or to drive into an area where a carjacking would be a possibility. It was a real pain, getting rid of the disguise in multiple places, but they had to keep their wits about them and stay off the radar. And they couldn't take the chance that Colorado law enforcement wouldn't get the word about what had been going on in neighboring New Mexico.

Rodney talked a lot about the good old days, and he was right. There was a time when there were no national and international criminal databases, no way for various agencies to effectively share information, but they had to face the fact that those much more carefree days were gone. One couldn't be too careful.

She sighed, pulling out into traffic again. What was it her mother used to say? Oh, what a tangled web we weave …

"Screw that," she said aloud to the empty car. "I'm not senile yet and I can figure this out."

Three more turns and she spotted the big Goodwill sign. One end of the building was devoted to accepting donations and she pulled up to the familiar blue bins. Of course, it would have been better to do this when no one was around to gawk at the pink car or at her, but there was no way she'd come back to this neighborhood after dark.

The black trash bag filled with size 12 clothing went into the bin and she was off.

It was another six blocks to the entrance ramp for the interstate, so she found a gas station where she topped off the tank and dropped her bulky padded undergarment into a greasy garbage dumpster at the back. It was strange, watching her alternate body so unceremoniously dumped. She'd sewn that getup herself. And if the day ever came when she needed another great disguise, she could do it again.

She held back at tossing in the old-woman style wig. Someone finding the body padding and the wig in the same place might put two and two together. She left it, like a plump, furry animal, to ride in the trunk. Right now, she just needed to get back downtown and check in on Rodney at the hotel.

A trickle of worry coursed down her spine. If he was truly sick and needed medical care, how would she handle that? She put the thought aside. Deal with it when and if it really happened.

What she found when she finally reached their room was only slightly reassuring. Her husband was still in bed, still in misery, although his fever had come down.

"What shall I do?" she asked. "Do we need to get a doctor?" It had occurred to her that this was a classy enough hotel, and they had plenty of money, a doctor could probably be summoned to the room.

He shook his head, one arm still around the tube containing his prized painting. "Must have been something I ate. I shall feel better in the morning."

He looked up from his pile of pillows. "You're tired, darling. Why don't you go down to the restaurant and have a decent meal."

"I can have some soup sent up for you."

"No. Not yet. I need to ride this out."

"I should just order room service. I feel bad, leaving you alone again."

"Really, love. The smell of food would do me in. I'd rather you went and enjoyed your own dinner."

She kissed him on the forehead and left the room after adding a tailored blazer to her jeans and businesslike shirt. Surely there was a restaurant, either on the premises or nearby, that wouldn't require she actually dress up for dinner.

The pub-style hotel bar proved perfect for her needs. She ordered a gin and tonic and settled into her small booth. She would relax for a few minutes and then order a seafood and pasta meal. As much as she loved Rodney, it was actually a bit of a relief to simply have dinner and a drink without his old-man grousing about either the menu or the service. Yes, things were more genteel in England. She got that. She just grew tired of hearing about it.

The first sip of her drink went down smoothly and she felt the pressures of the day easing out of her muscles. When the server noticed her glass was nearly empty, she smiled at the young man and said yes she would have another, and the pasta primavera as well.

She hadn't checked her email all day, but didn't expect much. She really had no friends other than Rodney—but she wasn't going to dwell on that—and she rarely subscribed to lists that would bombard her with messages. Only three. Her hairstylist, confirming her appointment for Thursday. She clicked the button to cancel it. One message from Phil Jackson, the good-looking doctor from Donner Hospital—delete. One from the chairman of the Theater Guild board, wondering when she would have the deposit for their architect. Hah—never. She deleted that one too.

Her second drink arrived, along with assurances that her dinner would be ready in just a few minutes. She gave the young man a smile and hoped his ingratiating give-me-a-bigger-tip manner wouldn't become too cloying.

While her mind was back in Albuquerque, she decided to see what was going on back there. Had anyone at Heavenly Treasures reported their suspicions about the money? Had anyone remarked that she had not attended Benny Stevens' funeral and had not shown up at work again, although she realized it was impossible for that sort of news to make the internet. She should have friended one or two of the volunteers to get in on the gossip.

She did a quick search on Albuquerque and Heavenly Treasures. The only thing that came up was the thrift shop's official website, showing the history, the shop hours, and talking about the mission work it supported. Yada, yada.

Albuquerque and Theater Guild was another story. A link appeared to the Channel 7 news page and the story about the quarter million dollar donation by Baxter & Company. And there was her picture, smiling and accepting that big cardboard check.

Crap.

They'd been so careful, and Rodney *had* brilliantly interrupted the video news crews. So where did this come from? Someone among the small crowd must have snapped it with their phone and the TV station probably even paid for it, since they had nothing better. She looked again. Her face was in profile, so not the best angle for someone to recognize her, still—it was not Carole, but Cee-Cee was the easier woman to recognize now.

Her meal arrived, but her appetite had gone. She poked around and picked out some of the shrimp and a few of the vegetables, but the pure enjoyment of the dinner alone was gone. She should tell Rodney about the photo online, but she really didn't want to.

Chapter 43

Bees were swarming all around me, landing on me. I couldn't feel their stings but the panicky feeling was there. I woke up with the sheet tangled around my legs, my face buried in my pillow. I lifted my head to see a brilliant sunrise showing at the bedroom window. Drake was gone, and I remembered he'd said he had an early start this morning.

I slipped my arms into my terry robe and wandered toward the kitchen, fuzzy headed but still feeling disturbed by the dream. Freckles brought me back to reality, wiggling and happy to see me, eager for her breakfast.

The coffee maker was on, my favorite morning blend all ready for me, along with cinnamon muffins my dear hubby had brought home from the bakery yesterday. Here was a guy with a demanding customer and a full day ahead, and he'd still thought to leave me some breakfast and a little love note. My heart warmed. We needed to find some time for a getaway, although autumn is one of the busiest seasons for him. I would put my mind to it and come up with something fun but with flexible timing.

Freckles dashed back inside and I noticed there were lights on next door already. Elsa and Dottie were on the work schedule again for Heavenly Treasures. Dottie would drive them, because as of last night I hadn't committed, although the dream about the bees meant Benny's death was still weighing heavily on my mind.

I poured and doctored my coffee with some cream. The first sip helped clear my head and I began thinking about my investigation. Reverend Marshall had entrusted the shop keys to Elsa, but he would soon have a new manager in place, so if I wanted access to the office—especially Benny's computer—I needed to move quickly. Much as I would love to hang out at home, snuggle my doggie and have more than one of those cinnamon muffins, I really should be at the thrift shop today.

I settled for a quick cuddle and a game of fetch with Freckles, ate two of the muffins, and checked for any emails or texts from my brother who probably wished I was spending time at our own office rather than this unpaid investigation I'd gotten myself into. He only had a couple of questions, which I answered quickly.

A steaming shower spray is a great place to think and plan, and I found myself reviewing what I'd learned yesterday and looking for the gaps that might lead me to answers. Of course one of those glaring gaps was the shocker revelation that Benny Stevens had been cruising around on gay dating sites. I should have found his password and looked at his account there.

An hour later, I was doing exactly that. FindAMatch looked like a pretty extensive website, but once I located Benny's password in his little notebook, I went straight to his account. He'd focused strictly on finding male matches, and his criteria for 'interesting' were of a similar type—dark hair, in their thirties, good looking but not necessarily male-model types. I tried to figure out a way to narrow down the pages of handsome faces and only show those Benny had actually selected to contact. There wasn't an easy way.

That seemed strange to me. Wouldn't a dating site want their members to quickly narrow down their choices? Or maybe that was the whole point—get people to spend as much time as possible browsing. If they paid for the service by the amount of time spent online, it would generate more revenues for the site provider. I have no idea how these things work.

Trying a different tactic, I started looking for data about Benny's history with the site—how long he'd been a member, how recently he had browsed for new matches, that kind of thing. It appeared he'd been very active earlier this summer, then there were no new searches for a stretch of time. Maybe he'd met Mr. Right?

But in the past couple of weeks there was more activity on the account and he'd marked several new faces. I was beginning to get the idea that maybe a person's dating history got erased after a certain amount of time. I could see that working—you meet the right person, or you don't, but you wouldn't want the new lover to get into your account and see everyone else you'd been interested in. Egos can be pretty fragile in a new relationship.

I could guess that maybe Benny had met someone and

started up with them four months ago. Then there was a breakup. After the split he began looking again. Like I said, I don't exactly know how these things work, and I don't have many friends who aren't either committed singles or happily married so there was no one I could readily think of to ask.

Then again, anyone looking at the Stevens family would assume Benny was, if not *happily* married, at least very committed to home and hearth, wife and kids.

I couldn't think what to do next, and the website was beginning to creep me out a little, delving into this. I've always figured that what goes on behind anyone's bedroom doors is an extremely private matter. I logged out of the site, but I did stick the little notebook of user names and passwords into my purse. The next person to take over this desk might not be quite so forgiving about the privacy stuff.

Again, I asked myself what I hoped to accomplish with this knowledge. Benny's secret life could be a motive for blackmail, certainly, but how was it a motive for murder? Um, other than Bonnie's being the humiliated wife who just happened to have a million dollar life insurance policy on her husband. The wife certainly knew about his allergy and where he kept the EpiPen.

The only flaw in that theory was that Bonnie hadn't been in the shop in the days leading up to her husband's death. When had she taken the EpiPen? How had she delivered the bee to his desk?

I drummed my fingers on the desk but was getting no answers. Maybe a candy bar would help. I left the office and headed toward the vending machines.

Elsa and Dottie had arrived. I gave each of them a

quick greeting. The other volunteers were beginning to look familiar to me, and all seemed busy in their normal areas of the shop. I put in my dollar and opted for a Twix—candy and cookie together, what's not to love?

I stopped by the counter on my way back to the office and offered half the Twix to Elsa. No argument from her; it's one of her favorites too.

"Has anyone talked about whether Carole is coming in?" I asked, even though I had every reason to believe she was gone for good.

"A couple people were saying they think she just quit. You know, after Benny died. She seemed a little nervous about the police asking questions."

My thoughts exactly. The pieces all fit—the pink Cadillac, the vacated house, the box with the various identities. And Carole Myerson had not returned to the shop since that day. I'd gotten so engrossed in trying to figure out whether Benny's death was intentional that I'd become sidetracked in my resolve to put together enough evidence to turn the money theft case over to the police.

There was one place I'd not thoroughly searched— Carole's browser history on the office computer. I hustled my little self back to the office and booted up her computer. I'd been so focused on the accounting entries and banking aspects that I hadn't done a general look-see. And now I found that in the days before everything fell apart here at the office, Carole had been one busy little lady.

Several travel sites showed searches for airline flights. She had selected itineraries for Phoenix and Houston. Some little memory came up—in the Day couple's past there had been connections with both of those places.

Scrolling a bit farther down the list of her recent

searches, I found travel itineraries also for Chicago and Cleveland. Was this for real? Who books trips to four different places, all spread out? It began to appear that sweet little Carole, who claimed not to know much about computers, was either masterminding something big, or she was planting so many seeds of evidence that it would be a colossal pain to sort it out and figure out what was real and which were red herrings.

The only thing I could think of to do was see if the couple had flown out of Albuquerque. From there, it would take law enforcement and search warrants to track down where they had actually gone. I grabbed my purse and headed out.

Chapter 44

You have no idea how many cars an airport parking lot holds until you've driven every inch of the place and looked at every vehicle. I started most logically with the long-term lot at the Albuquerque Sunport. A huge old pink Cadillac should stand out at a glance, but it didn't. Same with the hourly parking, multi-level garage. I paid for the hour it had taken me to search it all, then headed across the street where all the park-and-shuttle type places are.

Nobody seemed to have seen a pink Cadillac, even though a couple of the attendants were clearly car afficionados whose eyes lit up when I described the vehicle. One of them let me drive through their entire lot just to look around. I had to come back and report no success, and he seemed just as disappointed as I was.

So, okay, the whole airline reservation thing had been a

ruse and I'd just wasted most of a morning thinking they'd got on a plane. Well, as Ron says, a big part of investigative work is eliminating false clues so you can get on with the real ones.

This called for a Big Mac and fries, and I knew exactly where the closest ones could be found. I pulled through the drive-up, got my lunch, and headed home with it, nibbling fries the whole way. Gotta eat those babies while they're hot and crispy.

Freckles was thrilled to see me, and she helped with the last of my fries. I opened my laptop at the dining table and went back to where I'd been a couple days ago. The whole slew of different identities for a woman with the initials C.M. was still really bugging me, so I found a facial recognition app that let me scan the drivers license photos and compare them. Then I went to the news story I'd seen about the Theater Guild fundraiser, the one where this Cee-Cee Day was accepting a big donation check. They matched, all of them.

Problem was, I had pretty well figured out that much. What I needed was evidence that this same woman was Carole from the shop, and I couldn't quite put that together without a picture of Carole. At a glance they looked nothing alike, but that could be due to other types of disguise trickery.

I went back through the various stories I'd found when I searched these alternate identities coupled with terms such as 'arrest' or 'trial.' Only one included a photo of the suspect; it was a younger version of the slender woman I'd seen in the Cadillac, not the Carole I'd seen at work each day.

Frustrated, I picked up my phone, thinking I would ask Ron's advice. But instead of tapping on the phone icon, my eye caught the app for the nanny cam. Before Benny discovered it and snatched it away, it had been in the sales area of the shop for two days and then in the office for a little more than a brief moment.

I opened the app and went back through the video. In the sales area I had concentrated on aiming the camera so it looked down on the scene and photographed the handling of cash. I had lots of footage of the top of Elsa's head.

However, the wide angle did allow me to see anyone taking cash from the register and carrying it to the office. And I remembered Benny had been the one to pick up the money on the two days I filmed. After all, he'd been my main suspect at that time. Then I'd moved the camera into the office and set it up to view both of the desks, hoping to catch Benny stuffing a few bills into his own pockets before he put it on the bookkeeper's desk. I forwarded ahead to the video showing that view. And there was Carole slipping money into her top desk drawer. But the camera was behind her, so all I saw was the back of her fluffy blonde hair, her back, and the activity on her desk.

Did she stand up and move around in the office during the short time the camera had been in place? I began playing the video at a slower speed. And yes, there was the moment when she walked in, right after I'd set up the camera. Somehow, I had zoomed right past that.

She never looked directly at the camera, which would have been ideal for my purposes, but her face was mostly visible. I found one moment when the view was closest to ideal and captured that as a screenshot.

More telling was the fact, believing she was alone, she did a little adjustment to her clothing. A tug at the lower edge of her bra sort of shifted several things. In that fraction of a second, I could tell that her breasts, belly, and waistline all moved in unison. A real body doesn't do that—well, not unless one is jumping around in some kind of Zumba move.

Carole was wearing something under her clothing to pad her figure. And since that's not what women normally do—we all want to look slimmer, not pudgier—it became apparent she was wearing a costume.

The facial recognition software was finished with the screenshot of Carole's face, and I had asked it to compare with the best of the C.M. Day photos. A match!

Now I knew who our thief was, and there was likely a one-in-four chance that I had her real name. The police might not love those odds, but it was something.

I called detective Gary Broadman, the cop who had interviewed everyone after Benny's death. If he wasn't the one to report the money theft to, at least he could steer me in the right direction. I related how I'd spoken with Reverend Marshall and the church would be willing to press charges, and I gave the gist of the evidence I'd gathered. If I'd hoped for wild enthusiasm for him to investigate the case and catch the thief who'd taken, probably, a large amount of cash from the thrift shop's worthy cause, I didn't get it.

Broadman sounded distracted but he did agree to see me the next day if I could bring all my evidence down to the station.

I stacked the pieces of identification neatly back into the box in which I'd found them. My screenshots and facial recognition results got saved as images I could email to him. Then I dipped into the large banker's box of files I'd brought home after showing them to Althea Benton.

I needed to put them in an understandable sequence and match the dates with the days Elsa had documented the cash intake.

That mass of paper was spread over my dining table when I spotted Dottie's car pulling into the driveway next door. A glance at the clock and I saw it was late enough that the workday was over for the two ladies. Instead of going directly inside Elsa's, Dottie headed across my front lawn and rang the bell.

"Guess what I found," she said, eyes bright and faintly breathless with excitement.

She held out a small plastic bag with something inside. An EpiPen.

"What ... where did you find it?"

"In a waste basket at the shop. I notice nobody empty the trash for a few days, things pilin' up, so I went around to take care of that. This here pen thing in the big trash near the coffeepot."

Anyone could have put it there.

"I know you thinkin' of evidence so I put it in this bag, and I did it without touchin' the pen at all. And ... I got that girl Kiley to take a picture of it layin' there in the trash, and she already send it to you."

"Wow, Dottie, great thinking. I'll see that the police get it."

I told her I had an appointment the next day, although I didn't mention the detail that the topic was actually about the money, not about Benny's death. Since Broadman was convinced the bee sting was an accident, that whole subject needed more investigation and was probably best taken up with my old homicide detective buddy, Kent Taylor. But the pen was valuable evidence. I thanked Dottie once again, and she headed back to Elsa's.

Back at my table, I held the baggie up to the light and looked at the pen from different angles. A peek at my messages showed the photo of the pen in the midst of crumpled napkins, ripped sugar packets, and old coffee filters. Dottie must have partially emptied the large trash bin and then spotted this, buried under other things. There was no way Benny would have put it there.

So, who did?

Chapter 45

Cee-Cee gave the hotel room one final search, checking every drawer, every corner, under the bed. Using a hand towel, she wiped down the surfaces, faucets, and door handles. It was a life-long habit and she couldn't even say why she did it. A maid would be here within an hour or two; the removal of the linens and vacuuming of the carpet should take care of most traces they'd ever been here.

Still, when you spent your life moving from city to city, always a short jump ahead of the law, you learned to look out for yourself. She found a tube of her lipstick under the bathroom vanity and congratulated herself on being so thorough.

"Almost ready, honey?" She carried both of their toiletry cases from the bathroom and stuffed them into the suitcases.

Rodney was still putting on his socks. How long could a man take to get dressed in the morning? She stifled the thought. He'd been sick, and although he insisted he was feeling well enough to travel today, she could tell by watching the slowness of his movements that he wasn't top notch yet. The problem seemed to have been a stomach bug of some kind. Now she prayed she wouldn't catch it. They could not afford for both of them to be sick.

"I can call a bellman if you'd like," she suggested.

He shook his head. "I'll manage just fine, thanks."

His tone was terse and she wasn't sure if that was irritation—was she being overly solicitous—or was he subtly reminding her that they shouldn't do anything that would create a memory in an employee's mind. He enjoyed being a big tipper, but more than once a grateful waitress or pleased bellhop had remembered the handsome gray-haired man when the law came around asking questions.

He was right—they could manage on their own. She consolidated their possessions into the two suitcases, although Rodney insisted he could carry the tube that held his painting. Increasingly, he did not want the valued item out of his sight.

At last, he finished tying his shoe laces and stood. She kept a close eye as he slipped his suit coat on and adjusted his tie. Ever the gentleman, even on a long road trip in the car. She had dressed much more comfortably—jeans, a soft green sweater that brought out the dazzle in her eyes, and a lightweight blazer. Her hair was freshly washed and she'd spiked it upward at angles, making her look slightly different from the photo that had appeared on the Albuquerque news site yesterday.

They were heading north, and hopefully no one

in this neck of the woods took much interest in New Mexico news. But she knew they needed to be careful. Baxter & Company, the donor, had far-reaching business connections.

Rodney took the handle of his suitcase and stood aside so she could leave the room first. She shook her head, the towel still in hand. He stepped out into the hall and she pulled her bag out beside his. She slung her large purse over her shoulder, wiped both inner and outer door handles with the towel, and tossed it back into the room before letting the door ease closed on its own.

"We're off," she announced.

He was moving slowly still, but within a few minutes they were downstairs in the parking garage. Bags in the trunk, she helped Rodney and the Picasso settle into the passenger seat, and she climbed in behind the wheel.

They'd waited until the crush of morning traffic subsided and now they headed toward I-25 and the straightest route out of Denver. Billings, Montana by nightfall was her goal, but she didn't feel absolutely confident that Rodney's stamina would last the full eight hours. Nonetheless, they needed to put some miles behind them now. She hit the interstate and settled back, loving Pinkie's smooth ride. Her baby.

Just across the Wyoming border, on the outskirts of Cheyenne, she declared they needed a coffee break so she pulled into the lot of a small diner in hopes of meeting two goals: coffee and a dumpster out back where she might get rid of the last of her Carole costume, the wig.

Goal one, accomplished. Goal two ... she decided against it. The little restaurant had not yet emptied any garbage for the day, and a blonde wig in the bottom of an empty, filthy container could easily be spotted.

But a garage, where she paused to buy a roadmap for the sake of appearances, had exactly the right requirement for disposal of the wig. Their bin was half filled with greasy rags, empty oil cans, and what looked like the paper towel debris from the public restrooms. No one, surely, would go browsing through that mess. She picked up a nearby dead tree branch and used it to poke the wig deep into the nasty collection.

Rodney had settled back into his seat, eyes closed. He didn't complain, but she could tell he still didn't feel well. She turned the radio on, hoping for some soft music, but they weren't far north of Cheyenne when the old AM radio lost all signals.

With nothing but her thoughts to keep her company, she found herself dwelling on the wrong things. How long would it take for the Theater Guild to realize the money was never going to show up in their account? How long before that snoopy girl at the thrift shop figured out that Carole knew far more than she'd admitted about how the bee got into Benny's desk? And how long should they keep traveling as Rodney and Cee-Cee? Maybe when they reached Montana it would be the ideal time to switch to other names.

Chapter 46

I lucked into a decent parking spot in the city garage near the police station, and arrived for my meeting with Gary Broadman promptly at two o'clock, an expandable file tucked neatly under my arm. I'd spent the morning organizing all the shop's financial data as if I were about to give a presentation to a board of directors.

As he had yesterday on the phone, Broadman seemed distracted by a dozen other things, but when I asked that he do me the courtesy of at least listening to what I had, he did settle down and push his other files aside. I started with the figures in Elsa's notebook, explaining how and why we had collected that data.

When I compared her numbers with what was deposited in the bank on each of those days, he nodded. I showed him the short video clip that revealed Carole slipping cash into her desk drawer.

"Using the assumption that the bookkeeper had been helping herself to cash for weeks, if not months, the missing money could amount to several thousand a week. Tens of thousands in the months she had been working there." I pushed a page toward him where I had neatly laid out the totals I had conservatively estimated. I'd already researched the law on what constituted grand larceny, and this definitely fit.

This time he sat up straight and picked up the sheet to study the numbers.

"Who's going to press charges in the matter?" he asked.

Valid question. I told him about my conversation with Reverend Marshall. "He'll cooperate fully."

"Why isn't he here at this meeting?"

I should have foreseen that, but I came up with an answer. "He asked me to gather the information, put together the proof. I'm sure he would meet with you any time you like."

Broadman rubbed his jaw. "A case like this would go to major crimes. They've got forensic accountants and people in the division who really know this stuff. Afraid I can't tell you the name of anyone there, but I'll pass it along and I'm sure they'll be in touch." He gathered all my notes.

So that was it.

But I had saved my best card for last. I pulled out the metal box from the depths of my large bag, opening the lid to show him the collection of fake IDs.

"Where did you get these?"

Luckily, I had anticipated that question. "They were in a house abandoned by the suspects. I met the landlord there and he let me in."

"What do you make of them?" he asked, spreading out

the various passports and driver's licenses in the same way I had done.

"I did a little basic internet research, looking for old news stories and such. Some of the names returned no hits at all, but a couple had interesting histories. It seems that, as Carolyn Malone, she's left other cities under a cloud of suspicion for theft."

"We'll check it out." He gathered the evidence and glanced at his watch. I knew my time was finished here.

I walked out of the squad room feeling a little down. I'd done what I could to clear Elsa's name as far as the missing money went. I'd found far more than I would have imagined in the beginning, but now it looked as though I wouldn't have the satisfaction of catching the crook or knowing how the case turned out, unless someone decided to share that with me.

But I still had the other mystery, and even though it would mean letting go of my evidence in Benny's death too, I knew I had to turn it over to the police. I took the stairs down a floor and made my way to Kent Taylor's desk in the Homicide Division.

I wouldn't say that Taylor and I are friends, but I'd like to think there's been a growing respect from him as we've found ourselves chasing the same bad guys on more than one occasion. From being a young, smart-mouthed pain in his rear, I hope I'm now regarded as someone who really can work out the details of a crime and one who doesn't waste his time.

I'd like to believe all that, but the truth was that Taylor didn't exactly greet me with a smile and a hug when I walked in.

"Charlie."

"Kent, do you have a minute?"

"One. One minute."

I gave the shortest possible version of what had happened at the thrift shop—Benny's sudden death, the medical investigator's decision that it was an accidental death caused by a bee sting, and the fact that, legally, the matter was closed.

As I talked, he turned to his computer terminal and looked up the medical report. "Right. Accidental death, severe anaphylactic shock."

"I've come across some evidence that the sting might not have been accidental at all."

"This better be compelling."

I had to think fast.

Of course, I didn't have this case laid out nearly so neatly as the other, since I'd only come prepared to talk with Gary Broadman. But I pulled out my phone and showed the photo Kiley had sent me, the one of Benny's EpiPen in the trash.

"A person who knows he's in danger of suffering anaphylactic shock doesn't just misplace the medication that could save his life, and he most certainly wouldn't have thrown it in the trash."

While Taylor took a moment to look at the photo, I kept talking. "A dead bee was found in his desk drawer—in an office with a locked window and a closed door—and there was bee pollen both in the drawer and in a little box I later discovered in the office. I cannot believe all that is coincidental."

I knew from past experience that Kent Taylor hates the word 'coincidence' when he's investigating a crime. I had his attention now.

" You're saying a bee was purposely introduced into his office, and some killer knew this crazed insect would attack the *one* person who could be killed by it?"

So, okay, he was making it sound a little preposterous when he said it that way.

"When the bee is inside the desk drawer of the one person most likely to reach inside, yes, I think it's entirely possible."

He took a deep breath and let it out slowly.

"Charlie, I'm not saying I don't believe you. Maybe this scenario really could happen. But I need suspects, motives, something the district attorney won't laugh me out of the room when I present the case."

"I've been thinking about all that."

He held up one hand in a *halt* motion. "Okay, I can't stop you from thinking."

"But—"

"But, do you see this?" He pointed to an investigation file on his desk that was at least four inches thick. "If you've watched the news in the last three days, you know about this one. Brutal attack on a college coed, broad daylight, busy shopping center, and no one saw enough to lead us to her killer. The city's in a panic to catch this guy because his next victim could be anyone's wife or daughter or best friend."

I choked back a groan. I'd not listened to a newscast in more than a week.

"Right now, this takes precedence over everything else in my little world," Taylor said. "Until this killer is caught my squad is running 24/7. I have nothing more to give and, not to minimize anyone's trauma over your bee sting victim, but until my desk clears off a bit …"

"I know. I understand." I stood up and wished him luck with the coed case.

I walked out, knowing Taylor's desk would never be clear. His job consisted of the worst cases, the unending tragedies that befell people in this city almost daily. I wanted to be angry with him, but I couldn't. My energy was best directed elsewhere.

As I drove toward home, I realized that this was simply the reality. The police had to concentrate their efforts on catching the killer who might go out and murder some other unsuspecting person, the guy whose anger was unlimited.

Benny's death, tragic as it was, felt more personal—a vendetta, retaliation … revenge perhaps. Someone had taken very precise measures to get rid of him and to disguise their actions so the death would appear accidental. And they would have succeeded.

And that was exactly why I couldn't let it go. If I could gather enough evidence, present a strong case, maybe even get a confession, someone in authority would have to listen to me. It looked as if I had my work cut out for me, and I felt the surge of adrenaline that would carry me onward.

I arrived home a few minutes later to find Drake packing.

Chapter 47

There's a big wildfire at Yellowstone and they've called out all the Helitack aircraft and teams in the western states," he told me as he rummaged in the bottom of the closet for his boots. "Apparently it's now threatening some of the major tourist areas."

"What can I do to help?"

"I'd say you could come along, but you're not certified to actually be on the fire scene."

I was thinking more along the lines of making him some sandwiches for the trip.

"Do you have to leave right away?"

"As soon as the paperwork comes through. If that's this afternoon I'll get as far north as I can tonight, make the rest of the distance tomorrow."

I didn't want to distract him from his task. The Forest

Service requires a whole list of very specific items for every firefighter and there would be an inspection the moment he arrived, to make sure he had everything from the government approved boots to the right underwear. Intrusive, yes. But that's the way it is. I left him to concentrate on all that.

Freckles sensed the tension in all the hustle-bustle. I could see it in her expression and demeanor, wondering whether she'd be left behind or what would happen next. Dogs like their pack to be together and sticking with the daily routine. Already, she knew this was going to disrupt everything.

I gave her a long hug and said the magic 'cookie' word so she would follow me to the kitchen, where I made a couple of sandwiches for Drake, and she *happened* to catch a few bread crusts that dropped to the floor. In the other room I heard Drake's cell ring and then his voice, low and intense, talking business. I added another sandwich to the lunch pack, plus a couple of apples, some peanut butter crackers, and some protein bars.

Once he arrived at the fire scene he would be fed well. They always provided plenty of food for the hungry crews, but for a pilot those meals sometimes came many hours apart. I wanted him to have energy food he could grab during a fifteen minute refueling pause. I carried the small cooler into the living room and set it near the front door.

Drake was at the dining table with his sectional chart spread out, plotting the route he would take.

"I can make Durango by dark, and if I take off at first light in the morning, I'll be in West Yellowstone by one p.m. tomorrow."

"Got everything?"

He glanced toward the door. "Yeah. Most of the gear

is with the ship, out at the airport."

This was it then. I carried some of the items out to his truck, and we hugged. He cupped my face with his gentle hands and looked into my eyes. "Safe and sound," he said.

"Safe and sound."

I watched him drive away and swallowed the lump in my throat. We always did the ritual, and yet I always knew there could be one final time, the one where he wouldn't come back safe and sound. I turned and went back into the house, reminding myself that he would call when he could, hopefully once a day. We never knew how it would go. His part in the firefighting effort could last a few days or several weeks.

And in the meantime, all I could do to make the days pass was to keep busy.

Easier said than done, especially since I'd already done what I could toward my dual investigations. Gary Broadman had the financial data and would pass it along to Major Crimes where someone else would take it up with Reverend Marshall. Kent Taylor had promised to look into Benny's death, although there was little hope he would get around to it anytime soon. He hadn't expressly forbidden my continuing my investigation.

In fact, if I read his words in the broadest sense, hadn't he practically asked me to come back with a viable suspect? Sure, no cop was going to ask a civilian to do his job for him, but he really wouldn't mind if a simple case could be wrapped up in a simple manner, would he?

Simple case? I spread out the copies I'd kept of the various documents and photos. At this moment, I really wasn't seeing the simplicity in any of this.

I carried a sandwich and a glass of wine out to our

backyard gazebo and curled up in one of the chairs, thinking through everything I knew about Benny Stevens. His death had a spur-of-the-moment feel to it—as though someone's anger had flared and they tossed his EpiPen into the trash. But whoever killed him had also taken the time to capture a bee and bring it into the office. Maybe the unlucky insect had just happened to be buzzing around the outbuildings where the donations were collected, and *maybe* this person who was angry with Benny had been able to trap it in the little box …

I don't know. That seemed like too many maybes. Like Kent Taylor, I'd learned not to trust coincidences. I needed to figure out who was angry enough with Benny to go to those lengths to get rid of him. Benny had been in a mood, snapping at the volunteers, and not exactly Mr. Cheerful for a week or so before this happened.

So, what had set him off? I wondered if there was a way to track his movements in his final few days. I'd thought my time at Heavenly Treasures was done, but maybe I needed to go back and shake things up a little.

Chapter 48

The air was so smoky that traffic slowed to half the normal speed, and flashing signs cautioned motorists about low visibility and not to stop beside the roadway. Cee-Cee squinted into the gloom, looking for a sign that would say how many miles to Bozeman. Her head was pounding from concentrating so intensely, and Rodney had developed a cough.

She hoped if they could press on and get farther north, they would pass beyond the smoke, which the news was reporting was coming from a wildfire somewhere in Yellowstone. Already, the route she'd originally planned toward Oregon would have to be changed. She couldn't imagine another full day or two of driving in these conditions.

It was getting late in the afternoon and the light was rapidly dwindling when she began to see signs that they were nearing the city—billboards for local businesses, a junkyard, and a campground. She slowed the Cadillac even further and followed another car's taillights down the exit ramp.

This didn't seem like the type of city to have luxury hotels, but all the standard chains were represented and Cee-Cee didn't feel they had the option of being picky. She pulled in at the first three-star place she spotted.

"Sorry, all booked. Everyone's trying to get off the road," the clerk said when she walked in. "I just haven't had time to put up the sign yet."

Cee-Cee thanked the young woman and went back out to the car. The next three places had lit-up No Vacancy signs and she was beginning to feel a touch of worry. It was getting darker by the minute and neither she nor Rodney had any business driving in less than optimal conditions. Finally, she got a positive response and pulled out enough cash to pay.

If this room was three stars, it barely made the cut, but beggars couldn't be choosers. She got Rodney settled in the room, where he immediately kicked off his shoes and crawled under the covers with his Picasso snugged up against him. Cee-Cee went back out to the Caddy for the rest of their belongings. This wasn't a neighborhood where she felt safe leaving the boxes of cash—or really, anything—in the car overnight, especially since she'd not been able to get a parking spot within view of their room.

It took several trips back and forth before she had both suitcases and all the Express Mail boxes safely in the room. Rodney was lying on his back with an arm over his face, blocking the overhead light from his eyes.

"Honey, did you put the metal box into your suitcase?" she asked.

He peered out from beneath his arm. "What, the strongbox?"

"I can't find it anywhere in the car. I shined a flashlight around under the seats and everything."

"It's in the hidden compartment in the trunk. Where I had the tube, where we always put it."

"No, it's not there."

He went into a coughing fit, rolled toward the edge of the bed, and nearly fell off. "Has to be. It's where we always put it."

She helped him up and brought him a plastic cup of water from the bathroom. "No, honey. I tell you."

He was still coughing but waved away the water.

"Do you want to go out there and check? I'm telling you, I can't find it."

"Stay—in the room—with everything else," he managed while putting on his shoes.

He was back in five minutes, his face pale and drawn. "It's not there. You must not have packed it."

"Me? The box was always yours to watch over, yours to pack when we traveled."

His face grew red and the coughing began again. Truthfully, neither of them had specific tasks. She apologized for snapping at him. It had been a stressful couple of days.

Still, this was a disaster with even worse implications than if the cash had gone missing. If those documents fell into the wrong hands ...

Rodney sank down to sit on the edge of the bed once his cough subsided. "What are we going to do?"

Cee-Cee paced the length of the room and back, five times. "I'll phone the landlord, tell him where to find the box and ask that he mail it to us."

"What if he opens it and looks closely at the documents?"

Right. Bad idea. They couldn't risk him, or anyone, mentioning the multiple identities.

"If he doesn't find the box, who else might be likely to find it? The next renter who goes poking around in the kitchen cabinets?"

She parted the curtains and stared out into the dark, chewing at her lower lip. She couldn't even begin to fathom what someone would do with the information if they found it.

"Should we turn back? With luck we could get to the house and retrieve the box before it's found," he said.

She thought of the long miles behind them, and for a moment she was tempted anyway. But then she remembered the empty drawer at her desk in the thrift shop, the questions over Benny Stevens' death, the camera he'd discovered in the office. If that evidence was now in the hands of the police …

"No. We can't go back. The problem is, I'm not sure we can go forward either." She felt as though a dark cloud had descended over their carefree plans.

Rodney picked up a small tent-shaped card with an ad for pizza delivery. "I feel like I should eat something. Maybe if I get my strength back, I'll begin to think more clearly."

"Pizza? Really? After the upset stomach you've had. I'll go out and pick up something, maybe a nice meat and potatoes kind of meal."

"I actually feel like having a good dinner, somewhere we sit down and have a waiter bring the food," he said.

"We shouldn't leave the room, both of us at once." She stared pointedly at the tube containing the painting and then at the boxes of cash.

"Fine. I'll go do it myself." He stood abruptly and picked up the plastic room key from the desk where she'd left it. "See you soon."

"Rodney ... let's don't bicker over this."

But he was gone.

Chapter 49

Neither of them slept. Their alternate identities, those documents they had spent years acquiring and safeguarding, could now be in the hands of nearly anyone. Cee-Cee was right—they couldn't risk going back and walking straight into a trap. It would be no more than a few days before the board members figured out all that money they'd raised never did end up in their account. Someone would come to the house looking for them.

No, just like Houston, Phoenix, and a number of other cities, Albuquerque was now in their past. They would not go there again, ever.

"I've been thinking about Oregon," Rodney whispered in the dark.

"Me too."

"I don't know that it's such a good idea anymore."

"I agree. There's too much cooperation between police departments these days."

He'd had the same thought. "What about Canada? We have our real passports and we're close enough to the border. Maybe we take the back roads and use one of the smaller border crossings."

"We don't want to stand out. Maybe a more crowded entry point, where they process hundreds of cars a day is better."

He was silent for a couple minutes. "You do know the thing that makes us stand out, darling."

She nodded in the dark and he could hear her sniffle.

"We have to get rid of Pinkie. And we have to do it in a way so that no one connects our faces and the car."

"I know." Her voice was thick, barely a whisper.

He stretched his arm upward and she rolled toward him to fit up against his chest. He held her for a few minutes before the urgency of their situation and thoughts of the hundred little details made him restless.

"Up with you then," he said, trying to put a cheerful note on it.

She groaned.

"I know. Neither of is rested, but we need to get moving. We'll repack all our belongings. Put the packets of cash in the bottom of each suitcase and cover it with items of clothing. Leave out some clothes if you need to, but be sure to keep enough to conceal the money."

Once she was out of bed, Cee-Cee began to move quickly and quietly. It was two a.m. and they couldn't call attention to themselves by waking the other guests. Rodney used his pocket knife to open the Express Mail boxes and she dumped the contents of her bag on the bed.

Stacked tightly, she fitted the money bundles from two of the boxes in her bag, the other two and the Picasso in Rodney's. She wrapped shirts and blouses around the cash, making it more difficult to detect. They were crossing an international border, and anything they carried could be subject to inspection. Cee-Cee's final touch, whenever they traveled internationally, was to pack their underwear on top of everything else. She'd learned along the way that customs officials often shied away from handling a lady's lacy underthings.

As she worked with the bags, Rodney flattened the cardboard boxes and removed the labels. Too bad they didn't have a shredder with them, but he did his best to cut everything with their names on it into very small pieces. Those would be scattered over such a wide area no one could ever piece them together again. The boxes would be left off at the first chance he spotted a recycling bin for them, where they would blend in with the discards of everyone else.

The bedside clock ticked over to 2:59 and the two of them stood near the door, surveying the room. They'd rechecked the bathroom twice, and neither had put anything into the dresser drawers. As everywhere, Cee-Cee now made one final pass with a hand towel, wiping off fingerprints.

The two large suitcases weighed more than when they'd arrived, but they hefted them into the trunk of the Cadillac. Two shopping bags of clothing would be discarded somewhere, along with the flat boxes.

Cee-Cee was staring fondly at the old car.

"We don't have to make the switch just yet," Rodney said. He'd already decided Bozeman was a small enough town that the car would have drawn attention when they drove in. They should get a bit farther down the road. He handed Cee-Cee the keys. To all appearances they were just two seniors, taking a nice vacation to Canada, with not a care in the world.

The air still smelled of smoke from the Yellowstone fire but at this hour of the morning it was cool enough that the visibility was better. Still, they wanted to get away from the smoke and north of the interstate highway before traffic picked up and the smoke thickened again.

Cee-Cee headed west then took the first highway north, driving more slowly than usual. Rodney hoped it was her way of spending more time with her beloved Pinkie, but he feared she was feeling poorly and might have caught the stomach bug that had laid him low.

A thread of worry ran through him. They were not in the clear yet, not by any means.

Chapter 50

I'm not good at sleeping alone anymore, but Drake gets enough out-of-town work that I've learned to cope. Of course, this time it didn't help that I was still mentally juggling two investigations and trying to decide what to do next. After the tenth time of reminding myself that the police and the church had what they needed to press charges against Carole Myerson, I was able to put that one aside. But it bothered me that the longer Benny's death went unsolved the greater the chance a killer would get away with the crime.

Around four a.m. I finally got out of bed and went to make myself some hot chocolate. The only way I was going to catch the killer was to plant a seed, some kind of a time bomb that would make the person react. I simply had too many suspects to go about questioning and re-questioning each of them, in hopes that their story would change.

It might be different at a police station where the intimidation factor was high, but I had to admit it—they simply weren't afraid of me. So, what could I do?

With mug in hand, I picked up my phone and retreated to a corner of the sofa. Going through my photos, I studied the pictures I'd taken of the antique box used for transporting the bee. Everyone at the shop had seen it already, so it wasn't likely to bring a reaction. I could stand up and make an announcement about Benny's time on the gay dating website. Made loudly enough, that seemed sure to grab someone's attention. It would also have the unfortunate effect of trashing the dead guy's reputation, something his family didn't really deserve.

I puzzled over the dilemma until I began to get sleepy— how would I get the killer to react?

Dawn was showing around the windows, so I dragged myself out of my half-doze and decided I'd better get a shower and start the day. A bit later, I had let Freckles out the back door when Elsa spotted me.

"There's a mandatory meeting of all the volunteers at the shop this morning," she called out.

I walked over to her back porch.

"Reverend Marshall wants everyone there to hear the announcement about the new shop manager. He called last night but I guess he doesn't have your number, since you aren't really officially on the list," she said. "Everyone is to show up a half hour before the regular time."

"I'll be there." Now I needed inspiration—fast.

* * *

We all gathered in the open area between the buildings, the spot where donors brought pickup loads of items and backed up to the big garage doors to drop them off. It was the only spot uncluttered enough that thirty people could fit. Paul Marshall wasn't tall enough to be seen through the crowd, until someone brought out a sturdy coffee table of solid oak.

He stepped up and called for attention. "I know this seems a bit formal, but I have a couple of announcements. Firstly, for those who weren't at Sunday's service,"—was he looking at me?— "Mrs. Bonnie Stevens wishes to convey her thanks to everyone who has been so supportive since Benny's death. She sent all your casserole dishes and serving bowls with me, and you can pick your items up from my car, as soon as we're finished here. And may I add my personal thanks to our church family for taking such good care of the Stevenses in their time of grief."

I had positioned myself near the front where I could appear to be paying rapt attention to the pastor's words but could also watch the reactions of everyone else. At this point, most were merely nodding politely—we were only doing what anyone would do.

"And now, on to business. The shop needs a manager, and there are big shoes to fill as Benny did such a wonderful job of keeping the schedule working smoothly, and making certain that our shop fulfilled its purpose—the support of our mission work."

Laying it on a little thick there, Rev? After all, Benny had allowed embezzlement to go on right under his nose, and he had been breaking his marriage vows by cruising around dating websites. But I kept my expression neutral and watched the crowd.

A couple of people shuffled their feet and several gazes dropped to the ground. I made mental notes.

"The deacons and I have interviewed several managerial prospects, and we're in agreement that someone who has already put in time as a volunteer will have the best background for the job and will make the transition easiest for all. So, without further ado, I'm happy to announce that our new manager is ... Nancy Pomeroy!"

Only a fool wouldn't have guessed the choice. Nancy had been standing at Marshall's side, waiting for this very moment. She smiled and gave a little wave when light applause broke out. He offered to relinquish his spot on the makeshift dais, but she declined.

"All I want to say is that the office door will always be open. Come to me with any concerns at all. Thanks."

Since the entire meeting hadn't taken even half of the allotted time, everyone in the crowd milled around, and I saw the perfect chance for the bombshell.

I nudged Dottie, and she launched into our little prearranged drama. "Murder! Serious? The cops?" Her voice carried well enough that more than a dozen people easily heard.

"Yeah, there's a video showing the killer as they delivered a little box to Benny's desk." I dropped my voice, because if there's one thing that will grab people's attention more than a shout, it's a whisper.

Two people stepped nearer, the better to catch every nuance.

"You know there was also some money missing," I continued, "so they asked me to set up a little hidden camera to find out what was going on. Who knew it would also show that a bee was purposely let loose at Benny's desk. I was shocked when I saw it, and I'll tell you, the police are super interested. I'm taking the video to them today."

If that didn't get the killer to follow me, I don't know what would. Only problem was, it's a lie. As much as I'd stared at every frame of the video, in a supreme touch of irony, Benny himself had spotted the camera and grabbed it away before the box was brought in.

No matter. It's not what you actually know, it's what they think you know. All I needed was a reaction. Someone would come after that camera as soon as the rumor spread far enough.

I let Dottie and Elsa go to their jobs, and I stepped over to congratulate Nancy.

"I did a little cleaning in the office the other day," I said, maybe a little too loudly, "but I haven't yet had time to clear Benny's personal browser history from the computer at your desk. I should do that so you can start fresh."

She didn't seem to care, which I took as an invitation to go ahead.

The bait had been dangled. The trap was set. Now I just needed to stay vigilant and wait for the killer to show up.

Chapter 51

Whispers passed among the workers, and each group I passed turned and got really busy as I walked by. I shifted my eyes left and right, watching for the one person who would be sending deadly vibes my way. I didn't spot any, but the day was young.

I went into the office and left the door standing open as I took a seat behind Benny's desk. While the computer booted up, I set up the nanny cam to face the desk and my phone to record conversation. All I had to do was tap one button the moment someone walked into the room.

As a precaution, I'd tucked my pistol into my purse this morning at home. Now I set it beside my right leg, tucked into the crevice between the chair seat and the arm. I'm licensed to carry it, but I knew it would be a last-second resort. With a camera on me, I would only pull the gun if my life was imminently in danger and there was no choice.

Out in the sales area, I could tell the store had opened for business. Voices blended and I heard Elsa speaking to a customer. I fully intended to do what I'd told Nancy, to clear Benny's browser history. I looked again at the list of sites he'd recently visited and came back to that dating site, FindAMatch.

I hadn't logged out of Benny's account and it came up without need for a password this time. A red banner appeared now across the top with words in white: "Are you sure?"

Hm. Sure of what?

The next smaller print said "You've previously selected this person for a date. Are you sure you want to delete their profile from your matches?"

I clicked No and watched the banner curl up and go away. The face behind the banner was one I recognized. I was just beginning to process the surprise when I sensed motion and looked up.

"Eugene! What can I do for you?" I picked up a pen and tried my best to look nonchalant while my heart was beating a zillion times a second.

"I think you know, Charlie." His eyes were wild, his movements nervous and jerky.

I sneaked my left hand over to tap the record button on my phone.

"You've put it together about Benny and me, haven't you? How we found each other and fell in love."

Afraid my face couldn't hide my response to that. After all, I'd only spotted Eugene's photo about thirty seconds ago.

"He was about to delete your profile from his contacts. What happened?"

"He broke my heart—that's what happened."

"So, you were dating."

"Benny got nervous after a few dates, afraid his wife would figure it out. And she probably would have. Bonnie looks like this sweet little churchy housewife, but she's pretty sharp."

"*Did* Bonnie figure it out?" All at once, she might be back on my suspect list.

Eugene gave a laugh that was more like a quick bark. "Ha! Not exactly."

He paced to the other end of the room, realizing our voices might carry, and closed the office door. I really hoped the little hidden camera was catching all this but I had no way of knowing.

"It was Benny's idea to break it off with me. And he did it in the worst—" his voice cracked. He swallowed and started over. "The worst way possible, in a public place, a *restaurant*. I was devastated."

"Benny was really grumpy around the office last week. Was that when it happened?"

Eugene hung his head, nodding. "I threw a fit. When he told me. I just—just—threw my drink in his face and stormed out."

Ooh. That had to be rough, for both of them.

"And then he just couldn't come around. I tried to make up. Tried to win him back … That was the day he chewed me out here in the store, in front of other people."

Which, I sensed, was the last straw. A picture came into my head and everything clicked into place. Eugene's mother's house down in the valley. She had an orchard—apples—and there were bee hives.

Tears had begun to run down Eugene's face. "I was

just so angry over the humiliation; all I could think of was payback."

I sat very, very still. This could go any direction.

"I just caught a couple of the bees in a little box Mom had sitting around the house. Brought them here ..." His eyes still held that wild, unpredictable look. "I swear, I didn't want him to die. I'd seen his EpiPen and he said he was allergic to bee venom, but I had no idea it was that severe. I thought he'd only swell up a little bit and then he'd be sorry for breaking up, especially when I rushed in with the pen in my hand and saved the day. Then he'd love me again."

"So ... *you* took the pen from his desk?"

He nodded, his face a red and miserable mess now. "I put it in my pocket. I was right out in the next room, so when the shaken up bees were let loose I'd know it and I could get right to him. I thought there would be plenty of time. *I didn't want him to die ...*"

One of the bees must have flown away. The other did the dirty deed.

"Oh, Eugene. I'm so sorry that your romance didn't turn out as you wanted. But you can't play around with this kind of thing."

I was referring to all of it—messing around with a married man, underestimating the severity of the sting, removing the medical device that Benny had been reaching for in his final moments.

Eugene dropped to the floor, sobbing, while I turned off the recording and the camera. I called the police. It didn't feel like much of a victory, but I had a confession.

Chapter 52

Once the police had taken Eugene into custody, I felt at loose ends. One case solved, the other in the hands of the police and Reverend Marshall. I left the thrift shop and spent the afternoon at my desk at RJP Investigations, mainly so I wouldn't wander the house aimlessly, popping brownie bites and Milky Ways.

I found myself checking the news obsessively, mainly because Drake was away and in a dangerous place. In some ways I began to wish I'd gone along with him. I still could. I went online and checked flights. Then I talked myself out of it. He'd be airborne all day and would be exhausted at night.

We talked a few minutes that evening and the next. The Forest Service had ordered way more aircraft than needed, and he worried they were just getting in each other's way.

But until he was released from the job, he could only do his best to help and at least the pay was good. I went to bed early and read a Ben Pecos mystery, loved it, started and devoured another one.

Three days into the routine, I was practically clawing the walls. I needed to be busy, but even Ron and Victoria had other plans when I called. I don't handle boredom well, and the TV was now on nearly all day. And so it was that I caught a familiar name.

"Police are saying the couple, who apparently came to Albuquerque only six or seven months ago, managed to gain the trust of the board of directors at the Theater Guild. That trust was, sadly, misplaced. The couple, identified as Rodney and Carole Day, attended a number of gala fundraisers and became deeply involved in the raising of money for refurbishment of the theater's venue."

My ears perked up and I stared at the screen as the male co-anchor took over.

"In a scheme where the supposedly wealthy couple would match incoming donations up to a million dollars, they have now apparently absconded with all the donation money. Theater Guild board members have filed a complaint with the police, but have been unavailable for comment to Channel 7. Police say the couple have been known to use various aliases. An all points bulletin has been issued for the Day's vehicle, and we understand it was spotted two days ago, north of Denver. More on this breaking story as we have it."

Wow. This made the tens of thousands taken from the thrift shop look like peanuts. I pictured what I'd seen in the Day's rental house. The classy lifestyle and the formal clothing left behind—it made sense that Carole and Rodney were setting themselves up to fit into that social set. I shook my head, still having a hard time picturing frumpy Carole from Heavenly Treasures being able to transform herself into the tall, slender woman in a beaded gown. But it was increasingly obvious now that was exactly what she'd done.

Then it hit me—did the police realize this was the same woman involved in the case I'd turned over to them? Had they yet made the connection between the glamour couple and the thrift shop thefts? I called the number from the bottom of the news screen and was connected to a Sergeant Rodriguez in Major Crimes.

He hadn't a clue who I was, and only vaguely recollected having received a box of evidence from Detective Gary Broadman. I felt frustration well up inside me.

"The Days are driving a pink Cadillac," I said. "I know it's the same couple."

"The color and make of the car weren't announced on the news," he said.

"I know. The news said only that there's an APB out on it, and they've already left New Mexico. I've seen that car, I tell you, and it was being driven by this couple."

Rodriguez took my name and number and basically left it with a don't call us, we'll call you attitude.

Well, this man doesn't know me. I immediately called Gary Broadman and repeated my conviction that these two crimes were committed by the same couple. At least this cop was sympathetic.

"None of this is in my hands, Charlie, but hold on a minute."

Before I could respond he'd put me on hold, but at least it wasn't the brush-off—yet. When he came back, he assured me he'd passed along the information to someone in Major Crimes.

"I don't know if it will make much difference. So far, it seems the runaway Cadillac has only been tracked by local and state law enforcement in each jurisdiction. At some point, the FBI will most likely be called in, but there are channels and I'm out of the loop."

"So, the car has been spotted in multiple places? You said 'each jurisdiction' ..."

"Colorado and Wyoming, and there was one in Billings, Montana, who swore he had seen it. This is part of the reason we don't put the vehicle description out over the news. Everybody and their dog will start seeing pink Cadillacs everywhere, and it will become too many to follow up on."

"I understand. These reports have come from law enforcement?"

"Right."

He thanked me for the tip and I thanked him for listening to me, but he was unwilling or unable to share much more about the progress of the chase. I got the impression that APD's involvement was minimal at this point and if state cops in other places could pinpoint the couple's location, the FBI *might* step in for an arrest.

I thought back to the articles I'd read. Under various aliases, the Days had been suspected in a bunch of financial crimes all over the country. They'd even been questioned a few times. But they always managed to slip away, to avoid conviction. Now, more than a million dollars was involved and they were about to pull their same old tricks and get away with it.

Call it righteous indignation or plain old outrage, but something welled up inside me. I could not let this happen.

I was pondering my next step when my phone rang and I saw it was Drake.

"Hey, guess what. I've been released from the fire job. I can head south this afternoon."

Click went an idea in my head. "Can you hang around another day or so? I might just want to join you."

Bless my dear husband, he didn't ask for details. I told him I'd see what I could put together and would call him back.

Detective Broadman had mentioned Billings, Montana, so that's where I started. Billings isn't a small town, but it's not a huge city either. I only had to wait on hold through two transfers before I got an officer on the line who said he'd spotted the 1959 Eldorado. I gave him the bare minimum of reasons for my interest in the couple driving the vehicle.

"I stared for a minute because my granny used to have one like it, a blue one," he said.

"Do you think the car is still somewhere in Billings?"

"Doubt it. This was yesterday, early in the day—before we heard anything about the APB—and it was headed out of town then."

"Which direction?"

"West on I-90. Toward Bozeman."

I thanked him and we exchanged names and numbers. Told him I'd appreciate a call if anyone else reported seeing the car.

Call it an instinct or a hunch. I had an idea there was a slim chance we could catch the thieves if we acted quickly. I called Drake back and outlined my plan. An hour later I'd dropped off Freckles with Elsa and I was on my way to the airport.

Chapter 53

By the time I reached the ticket counter at the airport, I'd had two calls from my contact in the Billings police department.

"They're heading north," he reported the first time. "The car was spotted at a gas station in Helena. That pretty much rules out their heading directly for Idaho, Washington, or Oregon."

"I'm heading that way. Where should I fly into?"

"They keep heading the same way, Great Falls would be your best bet."

"Keep me posted."

The ticket agent was waiting. I bought my ticket for the next flight out and barely had time to make it to the gate. I took my seat and texted Drake my arrival details.

He was waiting in the passenger greeting area when

I came rolling out with my carry-on bag, and we shared some heartfelt hugs and kisses, appropriate to the days and nights we'd been apart.

"Our ship is in the general aviation section," he said, taking the handle of my bag. "We can get a ride out front, then you let me know where we're going next."

I texted the officer in Billings, the one I was starting to think of as a buddy. Any more pink Caddy sightings?

Great Falls, four hours ago. Nothing since.

Drake flagged down a cab. I pondered what the news about the Cadillac meant. It was getting dark, so the couple were possibly settling in to spend the night here. I texted back to my friend and asked if he could get the local police here to do drive-throughs of the hotel and motel parking lots. I had no idea if that was a simple request or a huge job, but he responded right back: Sure!

The ride to the general aviation area of the international airport was a quick one, and I spotted our familiar JetRanger tied down outside a large hangar.

"So, what's next?" Drake asked as he unloaded my bag.

I wasn't sure.

"Dinner? I get the feeling you haven't eaten anything all day," he said.

"Not true. I had a nutritious bag of pretzels on the plane."

"We're getting you some real food." He got the cabbie's attention again and asked where was the nearest steakhouse.

I supposed it wouldn't hurt to slow down and eat something. We had half the area's cops looking out for the pink car, and we had the quickest means of transportation waiting to catch up with them once we found it. For once,

I wouldn't mind showing off a little, landing the helicopter in a motel parking lot to prevent the Days from driving away, if that's what it took.

I was halfway through my ribeye when my phone began pinging with text messages.

No luck on the car at the motels but

But *what*?

Next message: Sorry. A sharp officer spotted one on the lot at a used car place.

What? Same car?

Not sure. They're checking it out.

I couldn't swallow another bite, so Drake insisted on having the rest of my meal boxed up to go.

Five minutes later, another message. Must be the right car, NM plates.

Where? Address please.

The information came through a minute later, along with the name of the officer on the scene, Harry Strum. I looked up the address and found that it was closer to the car lot than going back to the airport, so we called our taxi guy back and he promised to come right away. We were probably going to wish we'd rented a car, what with all these taxi charges.

Harry Strum's police cruiser sat crosswise at the entry to A-1 Rides: Used Cars With Style.

"I called the car lot owner," Strum said after we'd introduced ourselves. "He says he's got no pink Cadillac on the lot. He's coming right down."

Hm. If the lot had no record of the car, what was it doing here?

"This that vehicle that's got the multi-state APB out on it? Guess there were a lot of sightings of it," Strum said, looking a bit proud that he was the one who'd spotted it.

The owner of the business arrived just then, pulling in behind Strum's cruiser in a late-model Mercedes. He introduced himself as Rex Chance, and he seemed genuinely surprised to see the Caddy sitting in the second row.

"Never saw it before in my life," he said. "I swear, this car was not here when I closed the office at six o'clock."

That was only an hour ago, so it made sense the Days were still in the area. I had an idea.

"Can you check the whole lot and tell me what's missing?"

"Huh?"

"If they abandoned their car here, it makes sense that they took another one in its place. If you can tell us the make and model of the missing one, it's that much quicker we can catch them."

But there wasn't an empty spot on the lot, and the area around the office and garages didn't seem to be missing anything either.

"Darndest thing," Rex Chance said. "This baby's pristine, gotta be worth over two hundred grand. Why would somebody leave it?"

The figure stunned me, but I knew exactly why they'd left it behind. The beloved car had become a liability and their only hope for escape was to be in something far less ostentatious. I looked up and down the street, which was still fairly busy after hours. In the few blocks I could see, there were three more car lots. I knew what they'd done.

"Can we get these other lots checked, too?" I asked Officer Strum. "They've taken a car from one of them. I'm certain of it."

He hemmed and hawed for a moment until Chance offered to help. "I know the competition. I'll give 'em a call."

It took another hour and a half, during which I paced and chafed at the delay, but eventually we learned that a red Jeep Wagoneer with vintage woodgrain side paneling was missing from Joe's Best Deals, a lot two blocks west on the same street. Bless them, Rodney and Carole couldn't resist driving a distinctive vehicle.

"I suppose it would be too much to ask all of your officers to make another run through the motel parking lots …"

Strum didn't look hopeful, but he put the call in to his chief. The answer came back. No way. There'd been a big bar fight on the south end of town and a traffic pileup on I-15. Pretty much everyone was needed.

Drake and I talked it over. "In the morning we can take off and watch from the air," he said. "No one will think twice about a helicopter—all the news stations usually have one to report traffic situations."

Strum cleared his throat. "Tomorrow's supposed to be my day off, but … Well, I'd love to see how this thing plays out."

"It'd be smart to have law enforcement along," Drake pointed out to me. "You can't arrest these people yourself."

And so the plan was set. We'd meet at daylight. Strum graciously took us out to the hangar to get some overnight things. He then dropped us at the nearest of the airport hotels.

Chapter 54

I didn't think I'd sleep at all, anticipating tomorrow's showdown, but exhaustion set in and must have told my body otherwise. We'd set alarms for four a.m. and I was out cold until the sound brought me back to life. A quick shower, tucking everything back into my carry-on bag, and a slug of coffee from the little machine in the room—I was ready as the sky began to lighten up a bit after six.

Officer Strum must have been even more excited than we were. He was waiting in the lobby when we appeared, and we teased him about whether he'd slept there. He didn't actually deny it, but he was in civilian clothes today—Levi's, a plaid shirt, sheepskin jacket, and felt Stetson. He carried his service pistol and badge.

We arrived at the hangar, where Drake proceeded with his regular pre-flight inspection. Strum and I chatted and helped ourselves to a couple of the FBO's donuts.

"Good thing we have your helicopter," he said. "There are several roads leading out of Great Falls, going all directions. Our chief here is a cooperative guy, but I couldn't see him stationing officers at every possible intersection where this vehicle might attempt their getaway. He'd want any of us ready to take a traffic call or stop a speeder ..."

"Perfectly understandable. It's not really your problem, the fact that this couple stole a bunch of money in New Mexico." I paused. "Or do I have to say they *allegedly* stole it."

He chuckled. "I know it's PC and it's what we have to officially say, but I trust you when you say you've got all the evidence to prove it."

I held out both hands, fingers spread. "That's up to the Albuquerque PD. But if we can help get these people extradited, it could well be the end of a very long crime spree."

Drake gave the go-ahead and we climbed aboard. Ten minutes later we were circling the city, with emphasis on the area Strum pointed out, where I-15 and Highways 89 and 87 converged near each other.

At first, the vehicles below looked like nothing more than a mass of crawling shapes, like ants milling about the central hub of an anthill, but soon I began to pick out details and as the light got better, I was able to see colors more distinctly. The Jeep we were looking for was actually a maroon shade, and boxy vehicles in that color were not too common.

Drake spotted it first. "Look, there on the interstate, our three o'clock," he said, pointing over his right shoulder. He turned the aircraft so we were facing the same direction as the strip of highway. "I need to stay above and behind them so they don't notice us."

"Can we verify it's the right vehicle?" I asked. It would be pretty embarrassing to corner this one, only to find out there were dozens of these older Jeeps on the road.

"Binoculars," Drake said, "under the back seat."

Strum reached around and found them, taking them from the case, and aiming them in the right direction.

"Don't stare through the lenses too long," Drake cautioned. "You'll get queasy."

The officer took his advice, looking ahead and then away. "What's the tag number that car lot guy gave us?"

I read it off from the note I'd made.

"It's them." He looked away from the binoculars. "And that town ahead—that's Shelby, and the only thing farther out is Sweet Grass. They're heading for the Canadian border."

Drake let loose with a curse. "That can't happen."

I gulped and turned to face the officer in the back seat. "He's right. We can't simply fly across an international border. There are procedures and forms and everything."

Drake adjusted his flight speed. "Strum, I need you to call out the reinforcements. Tell the state police and any local departments where we are and what we're chasing. Let them know the suspects are now an international flight risk."

Drake backed away slightly. Without backup, we had to be careful how we dealt with this. The highway was a busy one and, unlike in the movies, a helicopter doesn't necessarily have great odds of forcing a speeding vehicle. We might intimidate them into stopping, but if they were armed they could do a lot of damage to us.

"At this point I'd suggest we let them get through the

town," Strum said. "There's an intersection and we'll know whether they'll make a turn. After that, it's a straight shot to the border. It'd be the place to set up roadblocks if we need to."

His phone vibrated and he picked it up. "Yeah? Okay, good." When he set the phone back down he leaned toward Drake. "Border Patrol and State Police have been alerted. We'll have all the backup we need."

We watched ahead as the Jeep sped on through Shelby and stayed the course northbound. From our vantage point we could see the border station ahead.

"Okay, folks, it's time," Drake said, his eyes on the traffic and our target.

He gave the throttle an extra burst and brought our altitude down to a hundred feet, just above powerline height. "I hope those officers show up. We're running out of territory real soon."

I looked ahead and behind but didn't see a law enforcement vehicle in sight.

Chapter 55

We were practically on top of the Jeep, Drake matching the helicopter's speed to theirs, when the occupants became aware of us. The Jeep swerved slightly then righted its course. I had one moment's flash of a thought that if we had misjudged the whole situation and this car wasn't the Day's getaway vehicle, we would have some real explaining to do.

"You got a bullhorn in here?" Strum asked.

"Better. A good PA system." Drake's hands were busy maintaining control but he tilted his head toward the microphone mounted to the cockpit instrument panel. I lifted the mic and stretched the cord out to hand it over to Strum.

He keyed the button. "You, in the Jeep Wagoneer, pull over and stop your vehicle."

The Jeep sped up.

"City, state, and federal law enforcement have you in sight. Stop the vehicle now."

I thought he sounded full of authority, but these folks were either incredibly brave or really, really stupid.

Drake eased the helicopter to the right side of the Jeep and brought her down to sixty feet. There was no way the car's occupants weren't aware of who was following and how close we were. A peek over my shoulder revealed a string of cruisers coming up behind with lights flashing. All the other traffic had slowed way down or pulled off the road.

Ahead, the border crossing was no more than a couple miles away. I don't know if this pair thought they could drive straight through the border crossing and somehow get away. They weren't Butch and Sundance, and things don't work that way anymore.

"Can we get in front of them?" Strum asked, his voice high with tension.

"We can do that." Drake sped up a little.

Now directly over the highway, he matched the Jeep's speed and turned the aircraft so we were at a forty-five degree angle to the vehicle, staring straight into their windshield. It was definitely Rodney and Carole. She was at the wheel and looked ready to brazen her way through.

Rodney reached across and gripped the steering wheel, shouting something at his wife. For an incredibly long second, I thought she would resist, but then the Jeep slowed. It shimmied when she hit the brakes and then it swerved to a stop in the center of the highway.

The helicopter hovered in front of the now-sideways Jeep until the state police cars caught up, then Drake landed on the road, thirty feet away. Strum and I unbuckled and hopped out. I had no idea whether the fugitive pair were armed, but they had no real options when six uniformed officers took a stance with guns aimed at them.

They emerged from the Jeep with their hands in the air. The cops holstered their pistols.

Rodney Day defaulted to what was apparently his old modus operandi, pouring on the charm, trying to wheedle the officers into believing it was all a simple misunderstanding, that they had no idea they'd been driving a little too fast.

"That's not going to cut it," I said. "We've tracked you all the way from Albuquerque."

The woman looked at me as one of the state cops took her wrists and cuffed them. "Charlie Parker. I knew you were trouble."

Her perfect posture and elegant bearing were gone. Aside from the short, stylish haircut, I could now see Carole Myerson in the woman whose face sagged and shoulders slumped as the officer recited her rights. She looked much older than her sixty-five years now. Gone was the elegant woman driving a classic pink Cadillac.

Rodney straightened his jacket and tugged his tie into place. Gentlemanly, even when his world was coming to an end, he wanted to look his best for his mugshot photo, I supposed.

Strum led the way to the back of the Jeep, slipping on latex gloves he'd pulled from a back pocket. When he unzipped each of the suitcases and lifted the layers of clothing, there were bundles of cash—lots of it.

"What's this?" he asked, pulling a long metal tube from among Rodney's possessions.

The suspects were now being led to Montana State

Police vehicles, but Rodney was keeping an eye on our actions.

"My Picasso!" he cried out.

But by the time Strum had pulled the end cap off the tube and slipped the painting out, Mr. Day had nothing to say about it from his seat in the back of a cruiser.

Chapter 56

A few weeks have passed since all that drama unfolded, and I've been happy enough to settle back into my normal days and wait for the holiday season, which will be here before we know it.

Eugene Towner's confession, in the hands of a sharp attorney, might have been thrown out and he could have pleaded for sympathy with a jury. He would have had mine. The poor man was a broken soul, and I felt terrible as I handed over the camera and the recording to Kent Taylor. But Eugene didn't go that route. His mother sort of pitched a fit, but he felt the weight of his actions and stood before the judge, ready to accept whatever was imposed.

The judge seemed like a fair man, one who believed that even though Benny's death, in itself, had been accidental, the premeditation that went into Eugene's carrying the bee into the office and removing the EpiPen warranted a punishment. So, the ex-deacon who'd fallen for a married man was found guilty of involuntary manslaughter and sentenced to five years.

Elsa, Dottie, and I had attended the hearing and we watched Eugene walk out, cuffed and accompanied by a bailiff, his head hung low and tears running down his face. His mother looked shellshocked, and I felt sorry for her. Bonnie Stevens still seemed stunned by everything that had happened.

The church celebrated a much better victory in the case of the missing money. There was a quick extradition of Rodney and Carole Day from Montana. The couple refused to confess to anything, including how a Picasso missing from a New York art gallery for more than twenty-five years ended up in their possession. So, there will be a trial, most likely a lengthy one. I've already been informed that I will have to testify and explain how I came up with the figures for the money taken from the thrift shop. The footage from my little hidden camera will play a major part in the prosecution, so it seems that was money well spent. Even if it takes a while, it looks like the church will get its money back. Elsa is everyone's hero right now. She was awarded Volunteer of the Month at the shop, and Reverend Marshall made a big deal of her ethical and quick-witted actions. We're all very proud.

In preparation for my own court testimony, the forensic accounting team in the district attorney's office have already let me know that they easily tracked the transfers of money from the Theater Guild's fundraiser accounts that Carole did with her smartphone. She might have been sharp, but she wasn't *that* sharp.

When I asked how the attorneys envisioned the couple

would present a defense, they suggested that most likely the two will show up in court, dressed down and making the jury believe they're just two helpless old folks who couldn't have possibly masterminded anything so elaborate.

I could well believe it, having seen the amazing transformation Carole had done, from elegant socialite to frumpy office worker. Unfortunately, as the cops interviewed dozens of people who were part of the theater crowd, no photos seemed to exist of Carole or Rodney Day. The pair were like ghosts when it came to facing a camera lens, so proving their chameleon-like abilities to a jury could prove tricky. I imagined that was exactly why they'd been suspected so often in the past but never convicted.

Yes, I'd say the law has its work cut out for it with that case.

Meanwhile, Drake and I have settled into our home routine. We're getting together with Ron and Victoria tonight, for dinner and to hear all about Jason's experience at a wilderness survival camp his class went to. It sounds like my teenage nephew is coming around and we're all hoping and praying he'll stay on the right side of the law. He'll be home at Thanksgiving, in just a few weeks. I think we'll all have much to be thankful for this year.

Thank you for taking the time to read *Money Can Be Murder*. If you enjoyed it, please consider telling your friends or posting a short review. Word of mouth is an author's best friend and is much appreciated.

Thank you,

Connie Shelton

There's more coming for Charlie and family!

In the meantime, if you've missed any...

Turn the page to get the list of all my books.

Books by Connie Shelton

The Charlie Parker Series
Deadly Gamble
Vacations Can Be Murder
Partnerships Can Be Murder
Small Towns Can Be Murder
Memories Can Be Murder
Honeymoons Can Be Murder
Reunions Can Be Murder
Competition Can Be Murder
Balloons Can Be Murder
Obsessions Can Be Murder
Gossip Can Be Murder
Stardom Can Be Murder
Phantoms Can Be Murder
Buried Secrets Can Be Murder
Legends Can Be Murder
Weddings Can Be Murder
Alibis Can Be Murder
Escapes Can Be Murder
Old Bones Can Be Murder
Sweethearts Can Be Murder
Money Can Be Murder
Holidays Can Be Murder - a Christmas novella

The Heist Ladies Series
Diamonds Aren't Forever
The Trophy Wife Exchange
Movie Mogul Mama
Homeless in Heaven
Show Me the Money

The Samantha Sweet Series
Sweet Masterpiece
Sweet's Sweets
Sweet Holidays
Sweet Hearts
Bitter Sweet
Sweets Galore
Sweets Begorra
Sweet Payback
Sweet Somethings
Sweets Forgotten
Spooky Sweet
Sticky Sweet
Sweet Magic
Deadly Sweet Dreams
The Ghost of Christmas Sweet
Spellbound Sweets – a Halloween novella
The Woodcarver's Secret – the series prequel

Children's Books
Daisy and Maisie and the Great Lizard Hunt
Daisy and Maisie and the Lost Kitten

Sign up for Connie Shelton's free mystery newsletter at
www.connieshelton.com
and receive advance information about new books, along
with a chance at prizes, discounts,
and other mystery news!

Contact by email: connie@connieshelton.com
Follow Connie Shelton on Twitter, Pinterest and
Facebook